PENGUIN BOOKS

THE HIKE

Drew Magary is a correspondent ⎯⎯⎯⎯⎯⎯⎯⎯⎯⎯⎯⎯⎯⎯ _in_. He is the author of the memoir ⎯⎯⎯⎯⎯⎯⎯⎯⎯⎯⎯⎯ ovel _The Postmortal_. His writing ha ⎯⎯⎯⎯⎯⎯⎯⎯⎯⎯⎯ _The Atlantic, Bon Appétit, The Huffin⎯⎯⎯⎯⎯⎯⎯⎯⎯⎯ use, Playboy, Rolling Stone_, and on ⎯⎯⎯⎯⎯⎯⎯⎯⎯⎯⎯⎯oo!, ESPN, and more. He's been featured on _Good Morning America_ and has been interviewed by the AV Club, the _New York Observer, USA Today, U.S. News & World Report_, and many others. He lives in Maryland with his wife and three kids, and is a _Chopped_ champion.

Praise for _The Hike_

"Drew Magary's new novel, _The Hike_, follows Ben, a dad trying to get home after wandering into a parallel universe on a business trip. . . . Buy it for all your friends—everyone loves a good dad odyssey." —_GQ_

"_The Hike_ just works. It's like early, good Chuck Palahniuk leeched of all bitterness and class warfare—back when Chuck was still weird and tired and furious. It's like a story you tell yourself on a long drive alone in the dark. It's fun and fast and bizarre, familiar yet completely _other_. But the real kicker? Magary underhands a twist in at the end that hits you like a sharp jab at the bell. You'll see stars, I promise, but I don't want to come within a million miles of spoiling it for you. It's just that good." —NPR.org

"A page-turner . . . A successful work of contemporary fantasy. It displays a writer in command of his voice and experimenting with more traditional forms of narrative, while being inventive, funny, and, by the end of the work, quietly profound and touching." —_BoingBoing_

"It's kind of a more cynical version of _The Phantom Tollbooth_ mixed with a game of Dungeons & Dragons from _Community_ creator Dan Harmon's podcast _Harmontown_." —_Wired_ (This Summer's 14 Must-Read Books)

"At once heartfelt, nerve-wracking, and soul-searching, *The Hike* is an emotional punch to the gut draped in the trappings of fantasy and psychological horror. It's a beautifully written novel with thoughtful characters, crunchy descriptions, and crisp action. I loved every single ounce of this book. I'm already looking forward to rereading it and I only finished it a few days ago. Easily a contender for a slot in my top five favorite books of 2016."
—Tor.com

"Often hilarious, as you would expect any book by Magary to be, but like *The Postmortal* there is a real darkness and thoughtfulness to Ben's journey that will keep you engrossed." — i09.com's Summer Reading Guide

"A gonzo fantasy adventure with a simple premise: a guy gets lost in the woods. Yet with Magary, getting lost means being chased by dog-faced murderers, crashing into an iceberg, almost getting eaten by a giant, and being forced to build a castle for the undead. In short, things get weird."
—*Men's Journal*

"*The Hike* does for casual hiking what *Jaws* did for swimming in the ocean. . . . An existential, metaphysical journey into what would happen if you ended up in an alternate universe that challenged everything you thought you knew about yourself."
—GeekDad.com

"A fun and funny book."
—PopMatters.com

"*The Hike* reads like a mix of *The Odyssey* and *The Phantom Tollbooth*, with the same humor Magary uses on *Deadspin*. . . . Along the way, Magary's hero hunts for an enigmatic mastermind, encounters man-eating giants and monsters, and teams up with a talking crab. What starts out as a saga of suburban ennui quickly turns into a gripping tale of survival."
—*Washington City Paper*

"Among the strangest books I have ever had the pleasure of reading . . . True to its nature, the story stays unpredictable and weird right up to the climax. Magary's book is a love letter to fans of gaming, fantasy, and adventure, but above all, to open-minded readers who can relax and hang on for the ride."
—*BookPage*

"A road novel, a psychedelic *Pilgrim's Progress* for the twenty-first century, Cormac McCarthy after three scotches . . . I loved every single page of it. . . . [This book] is very good. Tell your friends."

—*The Free Lance-Star*

"Magary's second novel (after *The Postmortal*) features elements reminiscent of Homer's *Odyssey*, Stephen King's Dark Tower series, Lewis Carroll's *Alice in Wonderland*, and the PC game *King's Quest*. Mostly it is a reminder of not only how easy it is to get lost but also how difficult it can be to find one's way back. Fast-paced and immensely entertaining, this is highly recommended for sf fans and adventurous literary readers."

—*Library Journal* (starred review)

"In this literary odyssey, Magary combines fascinating dream imagery, assorted video game tropes, and a story structure that's deliberately predictable (with nods to many other tales of wandering through strange lands before returning home) but still surprising." —*Publishers Weekly*

"Creepy . . . Magary isn't shy about getting weird fast. . . . [He] even nails the ending with a *Twilight Zone* twist that would have Rod Serling nodding with approval. An eerie odyssey that would be right at home in the pages of the pulpy Warren comics." —*Kirkus Reviews*

"*The Hike* is Cormac McCarthy's *Alice in Wonderland*—gritty and terrifying but with deliriously surreal twists and turns. There's not a chapter that doesn't shock and surprise, and underneath it all is the levity and wit I've come to expect of Drew Magary's writing."

—Jeffrey Cranor, *New York Times* bestselling cowriter of *Welcome to Night Vale*

"*The Hike* is so much fun, has so much pure velocity, that I didn't realize until it was too late—what I thought was a drumbeat of excitement was actually the novel's secret, powerful heart. Magary's new book is a metaphysical thrill ride that will stay with me."

—Charles Yu, author of *How to Live Safely in a Science Fictional Universe*

**Also by Drew Magary**

*Someone Could Get Hurt: A Memoir of*
*Twenty-first-Century Parenthood*

*The Postmortal: A Novel*

*Men with Balls: The Professional*
*Athlete's Hand book*

# THE
# HIKE

## DREW MAGARY

PENGUIN BOOKS

PENGUIN BOOKS

An imprint of Penguin Random House LLC

375 Hudson Street

New York, New York 10014

penguin.com

First published in the United States of America by Viking Penguin,

an imprint of Penguin Random House LLC, 2016

Published in Penguin Books 2017

ISBN 9780399563850 (hardcover)

ISBN 9780399563874 (paperback)

ISBN 9780399563867 (ebook)

Printed in the United States of America

1  3  5  7  9  10  8  6  4  2

Set in Warnock Pro

Designed by Alissa Rose Theodor

FOR MY WIFE

I.

CHAPTER ONE

# THE PATH

There were deer all over the road. He drove past a street crew in orange vests carrying a dead one off to the side of the highway, gripping the animal by its dainty hooves and moving it like they were carrying a small table upside down. After that, he saw more and more of the deer: some whole, some ripped in half, some just pieces of raw meat. Some were consigned to the shoulder, and he wondered if they had been dragged there or if the big, hulking trucks had plowed into them and chewed them up and spat them out in random pieces off to the side. There were a lot of trucks on this highway, all of them faceless. They didn't seem to be driven by people at all. They were just *there*, seemingly operated by some grand master switchboard, programmed to never stop. And they were legion. They had paved the asphalt with all that deer blood under him.

His only companion in the car was the disembodied female GPS voice coming from his phone. She kept silent for fifty miles as he looked out his window at the last gasps of fall in the distant hills—pretty red and yellow swaths of foliage surrounded by sad patches of gray, like an unfinished oil painting. Eventually, the GPS, with an inhuman calm, led him off the highway, down a ramp and to the right, then up a hill and to the left. Then she commanded:

*In five hundred feet, turn right.*

She was ordering him to turn directly into a cliff face, which he disobeyed. He stared down at his phone after passing up the proposed turn into oblivion: *Rerouting, rerouting, rerouting...*

"Come on."

Eventually, the GPS stopped screwing with him, and led him up the steeply sloped driveway of a small mountain resort. It was a wedding mill. He could tell. There was an entire villa of wedding party bungalows, along with designated "Smile Spots" where a pushy photographer could hold a dozen groomsmen hostage for forty-five minutes without access to a cocktail. He drove up the private road, past a bridal salon and an open courtyard for summer ceremonies, all the way to the surprisingly dumpy main inn at the end of the loop. It was a Tuesday. *Not even cheapskates get married on a Tuesday.* His was one of only three cars in the driveway. He got out and left a message for his vendor:

*Hey, it's Ben. I'm here. See you at seven.*

He walked through the main entrance and was greeted by an old, shabby lobby. Yellowed wallpaper. A table of frosted, maple leaf-shaped cookies wrapped up in little bags that cost five bucks each. Coffee urns that had been drained hours ago. Off to the left, Ben spied a wooden bar with swivel stools, but no bartender present. A small girl in a billowy cupcake nightgown danced around the cookie table in her bare feet as her mother screamed at her.

"Will you get dressed? This floor isn't clean!"

She shooed her daughter up the stairs as Ben walked over to the reception area. No one was at the desk, but he could see a sad little office open behind it. He let out a meek "Hello?," the kind of "Hello?" you use when you creep downstairs at night to see if a robber has broken in. A short old lady shuffled out of the office and took his credit card and ID.

She looked at him funny. He was used to that. He had a long scar that ran down from his eye to the corner of his mouth. Whenever people looked at him, they saw the scar and assumed he was a mean person, even though he wasn't. Or, at least, he wasn't in the beginning.

"What time does the bar close?" he asked the clerk.

"The bar?"

"Yes, the bar. The one over there."

"I think the bar closes around nine." His little business dinner would probably end well after that. Drinking at the hotel would take more planning than drinking at a hotel usually requires.

"It's very pretty around here. Is there a path where I can go hiking?" he asked her.

"A path?" *Yeah, lady. A fucking path.*

"Yeah, like a trail, you know?"

"No, I don't think we have any paths around here."

"Really?"

"No."

Ben couldn't believe that. *You're in the middle of a gorgeous mountain region that has long been settled by humans, and you don't think anyone has blazed a trail back there?* He was gonna walk anyway. He'd find something.

She checked him in and gave him a room key. An actual key. Not a key card.

"Ma'am, can you tell me where the elevator is?" he asked her.

"We don't have one."

"Oh. Well, thank you anyway."

Ben grabbed his rollerboard and trudged awkwardly up the staircase with it. There was no porter to help. The hallway upstairs was alarmingly narrow. He would've had to turn sideways to let another man pass by. He came to room 19, turned the key, and was greeted by a musty, red-painted room. Nothing about the joint felt comfortable. It was like staying at a hated aunt's house.

He called his wife. The kids were screaming in the background when she picked up. They were always screaming in the background.

"Hey."

"You make it?" she asked.

"I did."

"How's the hotel?"

"Little shaky, to be honest. Not wild about the idea of staying an entire night here."

"Oof. Don't put your suitcase on the bed. Bedbugs."

"I'll have you know that I put it on the table. It never touched the bedspread."

"Good boy."

"It's pretty here, though. You could have come. Oma could have looked after the kids."

"Please. They're too much for her. They're too much for *me*."

"Yeah, that's true. How are things there?"

"I had to kill a huge cricket in the basement. Second-biggest one I've ever seen."

"Oh, Jesus."

"Yeah, so enjoy the time to yourself, you lucky bastard."

"It's a work trip. It's not that fun."

"Sure, it isn't."

"It's not. Don't give me shit for it."

"So what are you gonna do with all that free . . . FLORA, I AM ON THE PHONE. . . . FLORA, JUST ASK HIM FOR IT. . . . Christ. I gotta go."

"No worries. Love you." With three children, they never properly finished any conversation.

He threw on his workout clothes and walked back downstairs, passing through the empty lobby into a small fitness center and then out a pair of glass doors to the outside. He had his phone and room key on him, but nothing else. No watch or wallet. Behind the main inn was an open gravel driveway and a flimsy shed for the groundskeepers' equipment: ATVs and lawn mowers and piles of mulch and whatnot. Past that, he could see a flattened road that led into the countryside. Looked like a path to him. Maybe it was for authorized personnel only, but no one was around to stop him. He cruised past the shed and found the trail widening in front of him. After three minutes, he came across a birdhouse and a trail posting that read "0.1 Miles." He felt the urge to uproot the sign out of the ground and bring it back to the lobby. *Look at this, you crazy lady. Look at the marked path that's right behind your hotel.*

Ben kept on walking. The path ran atop an esker, with the ground sloping down on either side, like moving along one continuous peak. Down below he could see a valley that was blanketed by massive estates: acres of pristine grass that required hours upon hours of care every day to maintain. He saw big houses plopped down in the center of those green fields, each one fit for a retired president. They probably had kitchens with marble islands and everything. You could have your friends over to one of these houses and serve them fine cheeses and drink good red wine and make merry from middle age until death. It would be a nice little rut to find yourself stuck in. He wanted to jump off the mountainside and fly down to one of them.

The rest of the path beckoned. He felt the urge to jog but a history of knee injuries made that dicey. His right knee was a gnarled root of scar tissue and grafted ligaments, and he would rub it like a talisman whenever he exercised, even when it didn't hurt. So he gave the knee a reassuring pat and walked faster. He passed a second marker, and then a third, and then a fourth, which was encircled by birdhouses. They really were houses, too—with shingled roofs and stepped gables and little doors and windows for a family of sparrows to peek out of. Maybe they had kitchen islands as well. Maybe *everyone* got a cool house around here.

And then he came to the half-mile marker and found a circle of benches built from tree-trunk sections that had been sawed in half and bolted to big flat discs taken from sections of another tree. There was a stone pit in the center and a scattering of ashes. From any seat, you had a nice vantage point of the surrounding Poconos. You could smoke pot here. You could play guitar here. You could split a flask of whiskey here and then go have sex behind a tree. It was *that* kind of spot. A good spot. Back near his home in Maryland, there weren't many spots like this. Things were cramped and congested and busy, every last bit of real estate claimed. There were no more secret passageways.

The path circled around the sitting area and led right back to the inn. This was the end of the trail . . . *except.* Except there were ATV tire tracks leading away from the circle and down into the hard forest below. He took out his phone (he could never go very long without checking it) and noted the time: 3:12 P.M. There was no point being stuck back in Bed-and-Breakfast Land, suffocated by all that quaintness that only people over sixty yearn for. He had time. He had all the time in the world. And the GPS could always lead him back, even if that meant the occasional hiccup. When he was getting ready this morning, he accidentally pressed the walking prompt for directions instead of the driving prompt. The prompt told him he would need eight days to walk to the hotel. He laughed when he saw that.

He pocketed the phone and followed the tracks.

CHAPTER TWO

# THE GATE

The signposts were gone now, but the path remained fairly consistent. Ben walked along parallel tracks of pressed-down leaves as the woods spread out behind him. The trail descended and he had to walk in a zigzag to keep his footing on the loose, unsettled rocks. Going back up the mountain would be a real pain in the ass, but again, he had time. Maybe the path went in a circle. Maybe there was a more gradual, friendly slope back up the mountain so he wouldn't have to double back. He could keep moving forward but still end up home.

He kept expecting to see another walker come crossing by, or a jogger, or a hotel attendant on break time, but there was no one. He was alone, for the first time in a very long time. There was that little itch to check his phone, but he quashed it the best he could and tried to enjoy the moment like a responsible adult . . . to take in the majesty of the forest. Oh, the majesty! The leaves flittering and the sound of distant tractors from across the mountain and the royal blue sky above. Yes yes, this was all worth soaking in for the sake of personal betterment.

And then he came to a fork. The ATV tracks split in two here. To the right, he could see them bend down toward a main road. Through the dwindling leaves, Ben caught the occasional glint of a passing car. If he went that way, he would eventually hit that road and have to turn around because there were no sidewalks to be had. That was a country road. You were either driving on it, or you were the dead deer lying next to it.

So he followed the tracks to the left and stayed perched along a ridge, walking along as the country road option disappeared behind him. He would remember the split if he had to go back. It was unmistakable. There was no other spot where the path turned vertical like it did right there, so he walked on with a great deal of confidence. He saw the country McMansions below come back into view and now he was moving back closer toward the inn, if not exactly on the same level. He was good. This was all fine. The path split again and this time, he took out his phone and opened up the Notes app and jotted down the markings so he wouldn't forget them: "Two trees with split trunks at junction." He thought about calling home a second time to talk to the kids (on the phone, they were adorably unintelligible), but he saw the top left corner of the screen offer nothing but "Searching . . ." The only way to bring the phone back to life was to move on.

Soon, he could see a gate in the distance: one of those old iron-bar gates that you have to get out of your car to unchain. It was hanging open now, with a big NO TRESPASSING sign posted next to it, and past that was an old white pickup in front of a two-story aluminum shed.

Then Ben heard a whirring sound, like the motor of a leaf blower or a hedge trimmer . . . the kind of motor you can make squeal just by squeezing a trigger. It got louder and louder as he approached, but he couldn't see any people and he couldn't tell where the noise was coming from. Suddenly, he felt more vulnerable than he had five seconds earlier.

As he got closer to the gate, Ben slowed down, without even realizing it at first. One moment he was walking briskly, the next he was stepping around quietly, like a drunken teenager trying not to wake his parents up. *Maybe I should turn back around.* Seemed like a good idea. This was probably the end of the trail anyway. He could go back up the mountain and get back to the hotel and shower and get dressed and maybe lie there for a moment before his meeting. The hotel didn't seem so bad anymore. It probably had hot water. Ben wasn't exactly a marathoner. Every step forward was now going to be an extra step back, and it was wearing on him and his corroded knee joint. There was nothing more out here for him to see.

And then he saw the man: a big, hulking man wearing a denim shirt and cheap jeans, dragging a body out of the shed. The corpse was small and clad in a little cupcake nightgown. Her feet were gone. Her hair was bloody and tangled. Her hands were limp and Ben could see the chipped blue nail polish on her fingernails. The legs were just a couple of stumps dragging along the ground. He saw the red, like the butchered deer parts on the side of the road. *Saw it.* Then the man turned to him and their eyes met and *fuck.*

The man's face wasn't visible. It was covered by the skinned-off face of a black Rottweiler, ears included.

Before Ben could process anything, he was running. He couldn't feel his body moving at all. Sight and sound took over his brain: the sight of the path cutting through the forest, the sound of the killer dropping the corpse to the ground, and his footsteps kicking into high gear: first lumbering, and then jogging, and now booming behind Ben in big thumps, like a giant stepping across acres of grassland at a time. Soon, he could hear the killer panting, and laughing in a low demonic register. He was closing in.

*Don't slow down. Don't slow down even for a second.*

Ben cried "HELP!" again and again but all he could hear was the growing laughter of the man behind him. His face grew deep red. He felt like he was about to start bleeding out of his eyes. He considered taking out his phone but that would only slow his progress, and his goal at the moment was to not get caught. The path stretched out ahead, but he could barely see it now because his mind was presenting him with a slideshow of terrors: the dog-faced murderer closing in, the future sight of his own mangled body, his wife getting the call and screaming out in horror and dropping her phone to the ground in shock. He had to look back. He couldn't resist it any longer.

The killer was twenty yards away, a healthy distance and yet not comforting to Ben at all. The man was twice Ben's size and had a big butcher knife in his hands. Even from this distance Ben could see that the edge of the blade looked cleaner and newer than the rest of the knife, ground down by a fresh sharpening, now gleaming and ready to hack through bone and skin and tendons and whatever else got in its way. The man would catch him, and then Ben would see the man's sickly green eyes and feel his awful dog breath and watch the knife plunge into his body and that final moment would linger into his afterlife and well beyond.

Now Ben wasn't bothering to form the word "HELP" when he screamed. He was screaming purely . . . all random, soft, extended vowels spewing out like vomit. He had no control over it. He could hear the maniac still laughing behind him. And then he heard him say what sounded like. . . .

*"I've been waiting for this since the day you were born."*

He spotted bizarrely arranged piles of sticks off to the side as he blitzed down the path, structures he had never seen before. Maybe this killer, this *dogface*, had been waiting for Ben the whole time. Trapped him. Maybe he would be gutted and lashed to those sticks and left for a faceless dog to chew on. Ben turned to look again. The distance between them had grown to thirty yards and he was praying he would be able to get back to his signpost and turn up the mountain and leave that man in the dust for good, then make it to the hotel and call the cops and get in his car and go home and never ever ever come back here. *Thanks for everything, Pennsylvania, but fuck you eternally.*

Just when Ben was getting his hopes up about escaping, another man leapt into the trail ten yards in front of him. Also in a dog mask. He had a knife, too. Through the holes in the dog's skinned-off mouth, Ben could make out the second man's lips and teeth. He was also laughing and smiling and clearly deranged. Ben screamed again in holy fright. He was throwing his screams, as if they were a last-ditch weapon for him to hurl at the madmen.

*Run right at him.* That was Ben's first thought. Ben played football when he was a kid. Fullback. Not a great player, but not an embarrassing one either. Whenever they were facing a team that had a really good defensive lineman, his coach always used the same strategy: *Run right at the guy. Don't let him chase you. Don't try to fool him. Just bowl the fucker over and take him by surprise.* There was a killer in front of and behind Ben now, with the treacherous mountain slopes on either side of the path, waiting to trip him up and render him easy prey. There was only one real option: the football option.

So he kept running. He imagined having a football in the crook of his arm and then he barreled forward, screaming for war.

The second dogface didn't expect that. By the time he was rearing back with the knife, Ben was already knocking him down. Stiff-armed him flush on the chin and dropped him like it was nothing, like he'd been waiting all these years to play one final, perfect down. If he had diagrammed it and practiced it for a week, he couldn't have executed it better.

He was running so fast now that his muscles felt like they were exploding, sending random bits of stray tissue to other parts of his body where those bits didn't belong. He looked back and the first dog-face was hunched over the second dogface thirty yards away, then forty, then fifty, and then out of view entirely. Soon, he didn't hear them at all. He was extending his lead. He was gonna make it back to the hotel. He was gonna live.

But when he scoured for the two split-trunk trees marking his way up the mountain, he couldn't find them. The trail bent to the right instead of the left, as he had originally anticipated, and now he was seeing bigger maple trees and other things he hadn't recognized on the way in: odd rock formations, uneven slopes, patches of thick mud. A family of deer began sprinting alongside him, their bodies melting into the trees and then reappearing again. He looked down the mountain and saw no signs of a road, or of any McMansions at all. They were all gone. Everything . . . everyone . . . was gone.

# CHAPTER THREE

# THE MOUNTAINTOP

Ben took his phone out in midsprint for the time (4:02 P.M.) and a clear signal, but there were no bars. It was still "Searching..." The longer it searched, the more quickly the battery would drain. He became frantic—all hard breaths and shaking limbs—running faster down the trail, searching for another glimpse of road or chrome or man-made structures, but nothing materialized ... nothing he could recognize from the previous hour. Keeping one eye on the path, he opened the Maps app on the off chance that the phone would finally pick up a tower signal, but it only showed a single blue, pulsing dot, with the world waiting to be filled in around it.

"HELP! ANYONE?! HELP!"

Nothing. He fumbled the phone to the ground, he was shaking so hard.

"Shit."

He picked the phone up and kept running. The adrenaline had worn off a bit since he had eluded the two dogfaces, and now the terror was sinking in well after the fact, taking up full residence in his mind. He didn't feel as if he had outrun them at all. They still felt present—part of the atmosphere—along with the dead girl and her mutilated legs, the exposed bits of her veins and bones and flesh coloring the leaves below like a pair of paintbrushes. *That poor girl's mother.* The images and sounds became clearer to him and hardened into firm memories as he continued to run. *I've been waiting for this since the day you were born.* In his mind, he could see their hideous Rottweiler faces mouthing the words. God, how he *hated* Rottweilers. He scanned the mountain above for any tiered birdhouses or log benches, but nothing came into view. The path shot forward with no discernible end in sight.

But how far could he really be from the hotel? He wasn't some crazy distance runner, and he hadn't been out *that* long. If he went to the top of the mountain and doubled back, he'd happen upon the hotel again, right? It would be back in the same direction of the dogfaces, but surely he would discover something eventually (although that would be true if he continued in *any* direction, since he was just seventy-five miles outside of New York City). He looked down at the phone and still the blue dot pulsed, and pulsed. He tried his wife again, but the call cut out.

*This is a dream. This is not a physically possible situation, which means all I have to do is wake up.* If he just gave his brain a light tap within the dream, he would stir, and eventually float back up to the surface of his consciousness. He woke up from nightmares like this on occasion. So he screamed out, "AHHHHHH!!!" as loud as he could. Seemed like a real scream. Seemed like it was really him doing the screaming. Here. In real life. Not a dream. Shit.

At a loss, Ben spied a narrow tributary of the path that branched off up the mountain. Maybe the killers would rush by it without noticing. He turned and began to climb hastily, desperate to maintain separation between himself and the dogfaces. It was not a graceful climb—lots of slipping on leaves and awkwardly jumping around fat branches and thorny weeds—but still he managed. He came to a lull between two peaks, mountains rising up on either side, the path turning to the right. He could make out a small peak behind him where the hotel *should* have been. But there was no esker anymore. The topography was completely different. Now he was both terrified *and* pissed off.

Back home, he liked watching survival shows, and now he remembered one of the key tips: If you're lost, search out the highest point possible, so you can get a layout of the ground below. Made perfect sense. He followed the path to the right and up toward the small peak, pushing through the choked corridor of tangled sticks and mossy rocks and low-hanging conifers that refused to offer him soft needles to brush against. It was much harder labor than he was accustomed to, and he was rapidly succumbing to fatigue. His knee was throbbing now, and he was getting a nasty case of Museum Feet. There were little burrs all over his pants. Flecks of mud peppered his shoes and ankles until he had one smooth layer of filth covering everything below his knees. But he kept going because he knew that if he stopped moving, the dogfaces would find him and cut him up.

The sun was going down as he reached the top. This mountain was still well below the tree line, with spruces and lichen-coated pines blocking his view in every direction, all impossible to climb. He tried to get a decent view down below, but the light was fading and he couldn't make out any houses or hotels. No roads. No lights. No smoke rising up from chimneys. He took out the phone and it was still "Searching . . ." The battery was now in the red. It would die within an hour if he kept it on, but he couldn't fathom turning it off just when he needed it the most, when he needed the fucking thing to *work*. He tried his wife again and there was nothing on the other end.

"Come on. . . . *Come on*, you fucker."

He kept expecting to hear the laughter of the dogfaces return, but for now, he couldn't hear a thing: not a bird or a squirrel or a tree sway-ing in the wind. There was only him and his dying tether to the rest of the world.

There was a compass in the Utilities folder of the phone's operat-ing system, one of the few things that didn't require a stupid signal to function. Facing back down the hill, toward the murder scene, was west. West was bad. East seemed better. He would head east until he found something. There was a rock nearby to rest on, so he opened up the Notes app and jotted down "craggy rock" for a signpost. Then he pressed hard on the power-down button on top of the phone, swiped across the screen to turn it all the way off, and watched as the screen gave way to a spinning white wheel in the center of a black void, spin-ning into nowhere until it finally died, too.

Ben put the phone back into his pocket, sat down on the rock for a moment, and cried into his T-shirt.

CHAPTER FOUR

# THE FIRE

He walked briskly back down the mountain, along the tight, barely blazed trail to the east. Even though he saw no evidence of anything useful in that direction, he was still operating under the reasonable notion that he was close to salvation. *How lost could I be? I'm in America.* Acting like a castaway in the middle of resort-area Pennsylvania was a ludicrous idea. He was tired and frightened, but also embarrassed for himself. *What kind of idiot dies because he got lost outside a fucking hotel?*

The mountain seemed to slope down forever. At one point, he had to lie belly-down on top of a large boulder and slowly lower himself to the ground below. Darkness was wrapping around the mountain, but he could still make out most everything in his immediate vicinity, namely trees. One tall, shedding tree after the next. It was a street fair of trees. He kept up a brisk pace down the mountain but was failing to stave off the cold. It was here now, freezing up the sweat in his shirt fibers and sending waves of chilled air up his shorts. And this was just the start. It was gonna get colder. It was comical how easily the cold could get to him. Put him in a climate-controlled house with ample light and heat, and he could pretend to be a hardy man. But a couple of hours in thirty-degree weather and he was basically as helpless as a kitten. It would take nothing to kill him. The weather could do it. The dogfaces could do it. An infected mosquito could do it. He probably wouldn't even last this night if he didn't find safe haven.

He pressed on, unwilling to give up and freeze his ass off trying to sleep on a mountaintop, with the dogfaces ready to pick him off at any second. Then, suddenly, the ground leveled out under Ben's feet and the path opened up wide as a promenade. There were no tire treads of any kind. The space between the trees was flat and clear and continued straight to the east. This was a path that clearly led *somewhere:* preferably somewhere with a warm shower and a hot bowl of soup and a phone charger and a kind police officer who was good at taking notes.

He broke into a delirious, hopefully final run. He figured that one last push would be enough to get him there. But soon the horizon sealed off the sun for good, and whatever it was Ben was hoping to find—a gas station, a road, a diner—refused to show itself. His second wind began to fade. He couldn't make out much in the way of signposts or memorable path markings, and his energy was flipping back over to despair and the horrifying realization that he was becoming *more* lost.

Hours passed as he straggled forward, the moon his only companion. He was on the verge of breaking down in tears once more when he finally saw the path open up to a campground on the right. It was a clearing, with a dead fire pit in the center and a circle of folding golf chairs around it: the kind with nylon armrests and little mesh cup holders for your beer. There was also a small red tent over to the side. *People.* Real, living people with human faces might be in that tent. He was saved.

"HELP! HELLO?! HELP ME, PLEASE! DEAR GOD, HELP!"

Ben reached the campground and stood in front of the small pup tent. It could hold two people. Definitely no more than that.

"Hello?"

No answer. *You can't knock on a tent.* He stepped cautiously toward the opening and unzipped the entrance from the ground up. He peeled back the flap and all he saw inside was a blue backpack, a shrink-wrapped case of bottled water, and a small, fleecy red blanket. That was it.

"Anyone there?" There was clearly no one inside, but he asked anyway out of sheer hope. Then he dove for the water. Thirsty, yes. He was thirsty. And hungry. God, he was so hungry and thirsty now. Once the thought occurred to him, it became his only thought. His stomach hadn't been this empty in ages. He had forgotten what *real* hunger felt like: irritating, miserable, lovesick for food. He could eat a barn.

Inside the backpack he found a bag of potato rolls, two packages of hot dogs, and several pouches of gas station beef jerky. Good enough. He ate every last potato roll in the bag and guzzled down three of the little water bottles. Hunger and thirst had now been addressed.

Next: warmth. Running in those flimsy shorts in the bitter cold had deadened his poor legs. The front pocket of the backpack had a small BIC lighter inside, which was a profound little miracle. The fire pit was nothing more than a circle of flat ashes, but there were plenty of dry leaves and sticks to be had around the clearing. He could build a fire, although building a fire meant submitting to the idea of staying there. All night. He would be giving up, putting himself in danger, and officially making himself the world's dumbest lost person. But his body was dead, the backpack offered him no flashlight, and the woods surrounding him presented absolutely no other forms of life. There was no decision to be made, really. He felt around his pockets and realized his hotel room key was gone. It must have fallen out when he was running away. He'd never be able to go back for it.

"Oh, no."

He grabbed leaves by the handful, taking care to avoid the moist, matted-down ones under the top layer of brush. He crinkled and crunched the leaves before dropping them into the center of the pit. After he had a nice pile of tinder built up, he went for the sticks, laying a dozen flat and then arranging more of them in a cone on top of that. Ben's old man liked to build fires almost as much as he liked getting shitfaced, and he would let Ben help with the chore when he was a little kid. This was back before the divorce, when his parents were still living together in Minnesota, before the old man snapped and drifted away from Ben and his mom down a lazy river of ten-dollar vodka. He and his dad would drag in bundles of logs from the cord pile outside their house, then take old newspaper sheets and roll them up, tie them into Nantucket knots, and put them on the hearth. Then they would stack the logs on top, crisscrossed. Then his old man would light the thing and Ben would stare at it, grabbing for the poker anytime the fire died down—always stoking it, always mindful of it, always wanting it to stay alive and vigorous.

At the campsite now, he flicked the lighter a few times to get a flame, but the striker wheel chafed his thumb tip and he sucked on it to soothe the pain. One last try and the leaves finally took, spreading the flames out and sending an elegant plume of smoke up above the trees.

*Maybe someone will see the smoke and come rescue me*, he thought. *Or come kill me.*

It was night, and even if any Good Samaritan saw the smoke, it wasn't like they would come running. This was America. No one was lost in America. If they saw the smoke, they would say, "Looks like someone's having a fire!" and then go have a burger. Resigned, he took off his shoes and peeled off his filthy socks and put his clammy, puffy white feet close to the fire to reanimate them. It felt good to make fists with his toes. The time had come for him to collapse in a heap. He could have slept upside down, he was so tired. Temporarily free of the dogfaces, his basic needs—food, warmth, rest—were crashing down on him in waves. Sleep was gonna be miserable, but he needed to recover some strength to get up and start running again. The tent was in decent shape, even if it offered little protection from the weather. Not that big a step down from the hotel room. But he couldn't sleep in it. It would be too easy to spot. He would have to use the tent as a decoy. He let the fire die to keep the dogfaces from spotting him, and then he found a downed tree ten yards behind the tent and cowered behind it, covering himself with the little blanket and topping the blanket with brush to keep it camouflaged. Every sound coming from the woods sent a fresh surge of tremors through his body.

He turned on his phone. It was now 12:03 A.M. There were a few family photos and videos on the phone. Not many: It didn't have enough space for him to keep the old ones for very long (he would download them onto his computer back home for safekeeping). But some were better than none. He wanted to conserve battery power, but he had to see Teresa and the children one more time, in case something came for him in the middle of the night and never let him see them again.

He opened the photo gallery and saw a picture of the kids dressed up for Halloween: nine-year-old Flora in a vampire costume; six-year-old Rudy in a puppy outfit; and three-year-old Peter, holding a trick-or-treat bag but not wearing a costume, because you can only keep a costume on a three-year-old for so long. And then he saw his wife, crouching down beside the children, the only one disciplined enough to smile for the camera. There were a few more pictures in the album, but that was all he had now. Just thumbnails.

He opened up the Videos app and, with the volume at its lowest setting, watched Rudy swinging from a tree while wearing only one shoe, screaming his head off. "I'M SWINGING WITHOUT A SHOE!" The boy said it over and over and laughed every time. Ben wasn't much of a videographer. Before smartphones, he never bothered to buy a video camera, because he didn't want to be one of *those* dads, always trailing behind his kids with a camcorder like a complete dipshit. But now all phones came with a camera built in and, man, did those kids like to watch videos of themselves. So he took a few videos and kept them in his archive. It was such a weird thing: all those hours and weeks and years he spent with them . . . Now he could boil down their lives to these random little capsules of their existence. He missed them all so terribly. It was like he had been gone for months.

When he stopped the video because he couldn't take missing them any longer, he saw one bar in the top left corner of the screen.

*A signal.*

He called his wife right away and she picked up.

"Ben?"

"Teresa!" he whispered. "Teresa, I'm lost! I love you! Please send . . ."

The call cut out. Worse yet, the single bar disappeared and the "Searching . . ." returned.

"No. Nonononononono. NO!"

He leapt up from behind the log and held the phone aloft, scouring for the signal. If it was there before, it would be there again. *Where is it? Where is the fucking signal?* He wished he could see all the radio waves and gamma waves and X-rays wafting around in the air so he could hunt the signal down and scream every last profanity at it. *Fuck you, you fucking piss shit stupid cunt signal.* He circled the extinguished fire pit and waved the phone around, making sure it covered every patch of air around him, but it was no use. After five minutes of twenty-first-century desperation, the phone gave out. The screen went black and the wheel began to spin.

"No! Fuck you, NO!"

He booted it back up a few more times as he paced, only to watch it die again and again. Eventually, all he got was a graphic of an empty battery and a little plug icon. It was dead. *He* was dead. He went back behind the log and pounded at the ground until exhaustion bested him and he passed out.

It wasn't long before he woke up again. Still night. Without the phone, he had no clue what time it was, but he could feel a fire blazing nearby. Someone had built it. Lit it. And then . . .

Someone was playing a guitar. Next to the fire. They were right there. He could hear the strumming. *What if it's the dogfaces? What if they've found me and are just toying with me now?* They would cut his face off. They would cut off his feet and drag him to their little spot in the woods and do whatever it was they did with footless corpses. He would be ground up, defiled, maybe eaten. There was no way of escaping them this time. Not in the shape he was in.

Then he heard a woman giggling. A *woman*. It was a woman playing the music.

He popped up from behind the log and saw a blond girl sitting cross-legged on a blanket by the fire with an old acoustic guitar on her lap. She wore a blue fleece and black workout pants and snug hiking boots, and around her were a bunch of empty beer cans and wine bottles. Her face was red with cheerful drunkenness.

Ben ran to her. "You have to help me!"

"Are you all right?" she asked.

"No! No, someone has . . ." but he forgot what to say. He remembered this girl now. This was Annie Derrickson. From college. She hadn't aged a day. Literally. She was still twenty-two years old. She still had the faded blond hair and the pointy nose, and the smooth, mottled, creamy white skin that Ben wanted to glide across.

"Annie?"

"Ben? Why are you here?"

*I was here for a business dinner and then I got lost in the woods and two men chased after me with knives and I really want to go home and see my family please help.* That was what he was prepared to say, but his mind was being wiped clean. He tried to snatch hold of the memories before they were gone, but it was no use. *Business dinner? There's no business dinner. Lost? You're not lost. Your wife and kids? You don't have a wife and kids. Job? You don't have a job. Men with knives chasing you? No one's chasing you. Don't be silly.*

Ben looked down at his knee. The scars from his ACL surgeries? Gone. His skin felt softer and smoother. There was no longer a wedding ring on his hand. *But why would you have a wedding ring on your hand? You're twenty-one years old. You're not tired. You're not lost. This isn't a crisis. This is exactly where you want to be, Ben. Isn't it? Alone, with* her?

"Do you want a beer?" she asked.

"Yeah. Yeah, definitely."

She stopped playing the guitar and reached over for a lukewarm can of cheap beer. Ben drank it all in one gulp. Any beer was good beer.

"Why are you here?" he asked her, stifling a burp.

"For the party."

"What party?"

"The party!"

"Where are we?"

She gestured to the trees. "In the woods, dummy!"

"But . . ."

"My favorite part of the party is when the party is over. When I don't feel obligated to have a good time, and I can just sit and chill with whoever's left to chill with, you know?"

He nodded like a simpleton. "Totally."

*The last time you saw her, she was a senior, wasn't she? One class ahead of you. Remember how nice she was to you? Nicer than girls usually were. She had that boyfriend, remember? Dave. Dave was all right, except for the fact that he had her and you didn't. And then, her final week at school, she ditched that boyfriend. Remember that one night? She was out at a party, now single and available. You stood near her that night as the stereo blared out through the frat house living room, and she scooped your hand up in hers. You never expected her to make a move. You never expected something that good to ever happen, did you, Ben? And you never expected to be so shitfaced at that exact moment. You could barely stand. So nothing happened. When you woke up the next morning, you had to go back home while she stayed on campus for graduation. That wasn't long ago. You remember her hand, don't you? Why don't you take her hand now? Why don't you get a taste of what a second chance feels like, kid?*

He took her hand. She gave him a playful squeeze to let him know she liked it. She was wearing a friendship bracelet and the frayed ends tickled his wrist.

"Did I fuck up with you?" he asked her.

"What do you mean?"

"You took my hand that one night, and I didn't do anything with it. I think I fucked that up."

"Oh, I've fucked up worse. I was in a bar once, and I saw this cute guy, so I went to drag him out to the dance floor without realizing that his leg was in a cast. I dragged him ten feet before letting him go."

"No, you didn't."

"Honest to God."

"Where are you living now? Do you have a job or something?"

"No, I'm just hanging out."

"That's cool." *"That's cool"? That's all you can think to say, you idiot? Stop talking before you fuck up again.*

Ben felt so hot next to her and the fire, but it was that wonderful, toasty kind of body heat that never gets uncomfortable. It was like sinking into a feather bed that only gets softer and warmer and more pleasurable to lie on.

"How did we get here?" he asked her.

"The path."

A brief silence. All he could think to say was, "I wish I hadn't fucked up with you." *So typical. Guys always get too serious too quickly, and they never realize it until it's too late.*

But it was all right tonight. Annie wasn't scared off. "You didn't fuck up anything," she told him. "Sometimes the moment gets away from you, and that's it. Doesn't mean I ran away from you. Doesn't mean I don't *like* you, Ben."

She laid the guitar on the ground next to her and smiled at him. She looked stunning in the firelight. He leaned in and kissed her and holy shit, was she a good kisser. Soft and warm as sex. He never wanted to stop. She threw her fleecy arms around his neck and they reclined to the forest floor, his hands feeling everywhere around her. He wanted every inch of his skin to touch every inch of *her* skin.

"Let's go in the tent," she whispered. And she got up and led him to the flap. The best part of having sex with a girl was when they led you to the sex. Ben wanted to be led forever, to some bedroom a million miles away. It was all young joy.

———

He woke up a few hours later in the tent. Annie was gone. It was only him, barely covered by the pathetic square red blanket he had found. He looked quickly at his knee and saw the scars. Thirty-eight years old. Teresa. The kids. The dogfaces. They were all there. They were back. It was a dream, and yet it didn't feel that way at all. He very much remembered Annie leading him into that tent and doing everything to him he ever wanted her to do. He remembered his hands were gripping her soft hips and she was rocking back and forth on top of him, naked and sunny and giggling. He was there for that. It made him want to throw up.

He got dressed and opened the flap. The fire had died. Beyond the pit he saw the guitar and the empty beer cans and wine bottles. Those were all still there.

*What the fuck?*

He was still lost, and now maybe a philanderer on top of it. Bile gurgled in his stomach. He put the jerky and hot dogs and the water bottles and the blanket into the backpack, which still seemed quite light, and he ran out of the tent to pick up the beer cans and feel them, to make sure they were real, tangible objects. On top of the guitar was a little envelope with his name written in polite script across the front. He quickly opened it and found a small stationery card inside, with the same script handwriting:

*Stay on the path, or you will die.*

Off to the side, he saw two black lumps resting under the trees. There were flies buzzing around them. He only needed to take a couple of steps before realizing what he was looking at: two dead, black Rottweilers, their faces skinned clean off.

CHAPTER FIVE

# COURTSHIRE

The flies had eaten out the dogs' eyes and all Ben could see was a layer of white subcutaneous fat slicking their skulls. He was definitely gonna throw up now. *Yep, time to barf.* He turned away from the dogs and let out all of the previous night's potato roll supper.

*Maybe if I smash a rock against my head . . . if I just bash the crazy out of my skull, I'll wake up somewhere, strapped to a gurney, and everything will be terrible but at least it will make sense.* Instead, he wrapped himself in the blanket, put his filthy socks and shoes back on, threw the backpack over his shoulder, and ran away from the campground as fast as he could.

And he screamed. Or tried to. His voice had dried to a croak.

"Help! ANYONE! Teresa? Kids?" He took out some jerky and chewed it on the run before seeing a house on the path in the distance. It looked real. It had a stick-style exterior, with jolly puffs of white smoke piping out of the chimney. *A house!* He ran so fast he barely had time to chew. Outside the cottage was a little wood fence that enclosed a lush green lawn and a garden with rows of little flowers (in November?) and gooseberry bushes and vines ripe with fresh tomatoes.

Maybe it was a trap. Maybe there was a witch living there. No matter. Ben made it to the thick oak front door and pounded as hard as he could, not caring if he scared off whoever was inside.

The door swung open and there stood a short old woman with bobbed hair, wearing a long, thick skirt and a white blouse with a red shawl over it. Wooden clogs peeked out from under her frock. She looked familiar to Ben, although he couldn't put a name to the face.

"Please ma'am, I need help!" Ben pleaded.

"Who are you, my dear?" she asked. She had a British accent.

"My name's Ben and I'm lost and two people have tried to kill me and they're still out there. I need to use your phone."

"Phone?"

"Yes, your cell phone. Or a landline if you have one."

"Landline?"

*Oh shit, I've run all the way to Amish country.* "A phone! Do you have a phone? Do you know someone nearby who has a phone? Does anyone live near here? Is there a town nearby?"

"Oh, the town is miles down the path."

"And what town is that?"

"Courtshire."

"What is Courtshire?"

She was puzzled by the question. "It's . . . It's Courtshire! The town!"

"Am I still in Pennsylvania?"

"Pennsylvania?"

He may as well have been speaking Japanese. Every answer of hers seemed to make things *less* clear.

"Is there someone in the town who can help me? A policeman? A doctor?"

"You can find help there, yes. I don't like the idea of murderers and thieves running loose. I can help you get to Courtshire."

"My goodness, thank you. Thank you so much. Do you have a car?"

"A car?"

"Okay, a horse or something."

"Oh, ho ho! No, I'm afraid I'm much too poor to afford a horse, but I can help you get to Courtshire still. But first, I'll need you to weed my garden."

"What."

"I've grown old and weak and you look like a fine, stout young man. Pull the weeds in the front of the cottage and I'll get you on your way to Courtshire."

"I don't think you understand. I am in grave danger. *You* are in grave danger. We have to leave for Courtshire."

"Now? Oh, I'm not going anywhere."

He grabbed her. "You have to come with me!"

"Take your hands off me, young man."

He stepped back. "I'm sorry. I'm not a violent person, but these men killed a little girl. It wasn't that far away from here. They killed two dogs as well. I can show you the bodies."

"You can go where you like, but I feel safest here, in my home. Not out there in the forest. If you want me to help you get where you need to go, you'll pull my weeds."

She stuck her hand out to consummate the deal. *Has the universe lost its fucking mind?* But there were no other offers to consider. He shook on it.

"The weeds are small but pesky," she warned him. "Finish by noon and I'll be sure to feed you before you go on your way."

She shut the door and now Ben was confronted with a morning's worth of tedious labor. Between the rows of tomatoes were little arachnid weeds that sprouted out instead of up. He knelt down and his right knee—the bad one—flared up from the impact. After taking a moment to wince, he thrust his hand into the soil, which was surprisingly warm for this time of year. He figured the weeds would come up easily, but when he went to pull, they stayed firmly rooted. He grabbed at the base of the shoot, but all that did was rip away the shoot, leaving him with a tiny stump to yank out of the ground. The only way to get the weed out was to grab the whole hunk of soil around it and pull. The first weed came loose and the thin, tensile roots stretched down one foot, then two, then five, then ten. It was like reeling in a fishing line. The roots seemed to have no end. By the time he was finished with the first weed, there was a coil of root sitting in the dirt, long as a garden hose. Down the row, there were hundreds more to pull. More punishment.

After an hour, he had cast off the blanket and sweat was running in torrents down his face. What he would have given for fresh clothes. A bright red tomato hanging down in front of him beckoned. He plucked it and ate it like a peach, the seeds and juices dribbling down his chin. Best tomato he'd ever eaten. The oak door swung open.

"NO EATING FROM THE GARDEN!"

"All right! All right!"

"Can I make you some tea, dear?"

"Can you make it iced?"

"Iced? Where would I get ice?"

"Regular tea is fine, then."

The sun ticktocked over the forest as he toiled, nervously scanning for dogfaces every few minutes from the demon garden. They were still out there. Maybe they were still hunting him.

At last, he yanked out the final nasty little shit weed and piled all of them in a compost heap outside the fence. The garden was lovely now, and the cottage door swung open once again. The old woman stood next to Ben, her hands clasped over her tummy. She looked delighted.

"This is magnificent. It looks better than it has in years!" She took his arm. "Come inside. I have some things for you."

She led him inside the cottage. It was just a single room, with a wood stove over in the corner and a bed of hay on the other side. In the center was a heavy wooden table laid out with fresh pies and jams and piping hot loaves of crusty bread and big hunks of hard cheese that looked like cliff faces. In the center of the table was a trivet, on top of which rested a bubbling pot of beef stew. The old woman went over to the table and poured him a cup of hot tea.

"Come eat."

He sat down and began eating everything immediately. His appetite had no attention span of any kind: a little bit of stew, then a roll, then a slice of pie, then more stew, then a hunk of cheese and a sip of tea. Even if the food was all poisoned and the old lady was just waiting to skin his face off, it was all very real and very tasty. Within five minutes, he was full and bursting.

"How was it?"

"Excellent. Thank you, ma'am." He stared at her for longer than was comfortable. "Do I know you?" he asked.

"Well, you do now!"

"No, but I mean from before. Have we ever met?"

"Oh, I doubt that. Now, I didn't forget my promise to you." She took a small leather pouch out of her apron pocket and slid it toward him. He peered inside and saw three hard brown seeds. "You're a good, hardworking lad, and you've done well today," she said. "Those seeds will get you to Courtshire."

He pulsed with anger. "How is that?"

"The first one you throw down on the ground will become an iron tower. The second, a wolf. And the third, a wall of flame."

"Are you kidding me? I just worked in your stupid yard for five hours."

"Take the seeds. But please note: They'll only grow at the exact moment you need them."

Ben had to restrain himself from throttling her. He pressed down on his fury like a spring and wedged it into the corner of his psyche as best he could. He prayed that his unhinged mind was giving him a series of clues: a way out of his own lunacy.

He grabbed the seeds, silently fuming at the old crone.

"You won't reach Courtshire until nightfall," she said. "Take some of my food. I don't have clothes for a boy your size, but I can feed you well enough." She filled up a bunch of porcelain jars with stew and jam, then grabbed the backpack from off his shoulder and stuffed them in, along with some loaves of bread and pieces of cheese. She also snuck in the cheese knife, in case he needed something sharp. Again, everything fit. When she gave the backpack back to him, it felt as light as when it had been nearly empty.

"Are you really not coming with me?" he asked.

"I told you I would help get you to Courtshire, and I have. I'm certain of it."

"Where am I? Just tell me, please. What's happening to me?"

She said nothing and instead beckoned him over to the door and pushed it open. The path was waiting for him.

"Tell me your name, at least," he begged her.

"It's Mrs. Blackwell."

"Where is Mr. Blackwell?"

"Gone," she said, looking darkly out to the road. "He left the path." That was all she would say.

"That's pretty messed up."

"Never leave the path," she told him.

"I've been told that before."

"You were told correctly."

"Who are you, really? Do I know you?"

She said nothing. He stepped out the door and through the garden, back out onto the leafy path, and watched Mrs. Blackwell close the door behind her.

# CHAPTER SIX

# THE YELLOW LIGHT

**N**ight fell and the cold was inside Ben again. It was making his fingertips buzz. He felt like he could transmit it to others now. He hugged himself and shivered as he trudged down the path, which never seemed to turn or bend. Just a straight shot into nothing. The path was a hole, and the farther he walked, the farther he was falling, making it impossible to ever climb out. He tried to warm up by thinking about Teresa and the children, but all of that was rendered bittersweet by his tryst with Annie, which he knew he would never be able to explain in a believable manner.

The dogfaces were gone, but he still felt the menace on him, like a lingering scent. Menace was underrated. When he was on a business trip once, another traveler accosted him in an airport. Accused Ben of cutting in front of him in line, which was a lie. They nearly came to blows before Ben backed down.

When he boarded the plane, the man was sitting directly across the aisle from him. Stared at Ben the whole flight. Leered at him, like he was an appetizer. He felt menaced for four hours. When the plane landed, the man followed right behind Ben up the Jetway, through the terminal, and all the way to the parking garage. It was 1 A.M. At 1 A.M. a parking garage feels like a crime scene in waiting. Ben walked briskly to his car and the man stayed behind him in his tight black shirt and angry glasses. They were alone now, and Ben couldn't take it any longer.

"What the fuck do you want from me?"

The man popped Ben in the face with a sharp right jab. His scar split open.

"Remember that," the man said, and he walked away. Just that one punch was all the man needed to put the menace inside Ben and leave it there. Anytime he parked his car after that, and anytime he went to an airport, he could feel it. Menace could do that to you. Menace could own you.

The sun set behind the trees and the cold took over his mind, holding it hostage, wiping out all thoughts of tent sex and the old lady's horrid garden. *God, it's cold. Where is the town? Where is the fucking town?*

To the right, off in the distance, he spotted a soft light in the air. It was yellow and artificial, like a parking lot light. It looked like modern civilization, not whatever Mennonite wizard land he had apparently stumbled upon. He picked up his pace, pumping his arms to keep warm, hoping the path would bring him to the light.

But the stupid path just kept going straight, and he could see the light pulling up alongside him and then falling behind, like the moon when you're driving at night. Ahead, there was only darkness.

*Never leave the path.* That was what the note said. That was what Mrs. Blackwell also said. That was the warning. But here, in this yellow light, was a point he could aim for. It killed him to just let it go. *Why would you listen to that old lady? She was talking to you about magic seeds, for shit's sake. That town she was going on about probably doesn't even exist.* The light was all he had. He stepped off the path and began walking to it, taking out one of the loaves of bread and breaking it into big crumbs, leaving a trail of pieces behind him that he could follow back to the path if he needed to. And he made rock piles every ten yards or so.

The brush had mostly disappeared from the forest floor. No gnarled roots. No surprise rocks to trip over. Everything remained flat and eminently passable. The light was farther away than it first appeared, like when you're swimming far out in the ocean and it takes forever to reach a shore that appears to be close by. Still, he trudged on.

*Teresa must be hysterical by now.*

The light wasn't getting any closer, and Ben was beginning to get the feeling that Mrs. Blackwell knew what she was talking about. There was a heavy stir off to the side. Here came the dread: full and horrible.

Another step and he saw their outlines in front of him: two men, with the silhouettes of their heads in the moonlight flanked by short, floppy dog ears. The yellow light was nothing more than bait. He turned and sprinted back along the path of bread hunks.

"GET THE FUCK AWAY FROM ME!"

He could hear them stampeding after him, their laughter growing. They sounded as if they had been born in a pit. In the shifting moonlight, Ben could barely make out the cubes of bread he had left for himself along the ground, but he kept his focus down on his feet and never looked back. He saw the rock piles and breathed a sigh of relief that, at last, some things in this world had managed to stay in place.

*"We're going to rip your face off and show it to you before we kill you."*

Ben began screaming nonsense again. By the time he was back on the path, his vocal cords were raw and stinging with cold, as if he had swallowed a box of tacks. The path kept straight, as always, and the men followed close behind. Ben almost *wanted* them to catch him.

*May as well get it over with.* The path was coming to an end up ahead. The wide canal between the trees was about to give way to a wall of pure forest. There was no town. There was no one to save him. Once he reached the end of the path, this would all be academic.

Except . . . Well now, he had that bag of seeds.

Ben slipped the backpack off one shoulder and dug into the front pocket for the little leather pouch. *The first one you throw down on the ground will become an iron tower. The second, a wolf. And the third, a wall of flame.* Which seed did what? They weren't marked "WOLF" or anything. Did the order matter?

He grabbed one hard seed out of the pouch and threw it up ahead. Three steps later, he smacked hard into the wooden door of an iron spire that stretched a hundred feet up into the air, standing sentry over the woods.

"Holy . . ."

Ben could hear the dogfaces closing in, so he threw the tower door open and closed it behind him. There were lit torches encircling the atrium, and a series of locks lining the front door from top to bottom: hinges and bolts and chains and knobs. He locked every last one of them as the dogfaces reached the door and began pounding on it. The fevered percussions rung in his skull and sickened him. They sounded like they were going to eat their way through the door, so he backed away, until he tripped over a small stone stair. To the right, there was a *second* door that led . . . Well, he was through trying to figure out what led where. Behind him, the stairs wound up and up and up. He would have the high ground on the dogfaces, but also be trapped up at the top if they managed to knock the door down.

The pounding wouldn't stop. The killers seemed to get stronger as the minutes passed on. Ben saw a knife go full through the heavy door, the blade twisting and bending, the dogfaces trying to weaken the oak. They would not stop. They would not simply go away. He was their quarry. They were created for killing him.

He climbed the stairs three at a time, pausing to rest at one point because he had already physically pushed himself well past any point in his lifetime in which he had previously pushed himself. He was running and climbing himself to death. After a few minutes, he finally made it to the top and felt like an out-of-shape tourist. The top of the stairwell gave way to an observation deck that surveyed the entirety of the forest surrounding him in every direction, nothing but trees and gently rolling hills. No yellow lights. No roads. No towns. He peeked over the stone guard wall and saw the two dogfaces standing still, looking up at him.

"What do you want?!" he asked them from above. They said nothing. "I didn't do anything! I wanna go home to my family! That's all!"

*"We're going to kill you."*

"Maybe we could talk about this."

*"We're going to kill you."*

He ducked back behind the wall and reached into the pouch, his hands shaking. Then he dropped one of the seeds and watched it plummet, bounding off the side of the tower and landing hard on the cold ground.

Two red wolf eyes stared up at Ben instantly.

The wolf set upon the killers and began to tear them apart, taking its time to hunt both of them down and burrow through their guts. The dogfaces howled in agony as Ben sunk back down behind the guard wall and covered his ears. He couldn't stand the sound. His body sagged and now he was lying on the floor of the observation deck, sobbing with grief as the wolf ripped and tore away at the monsters below.

When the screams finally subsided, he looked back over and the wolf was staring up at *him*. Still very hungry. It began pawing at the door, and then attacking it, aiming to finish what the dogfaces started. *I wish the* door *had been made out of iron. Big design flaw.* The wolf gnashed and wailed. Like the dogfaces, it had some mystical power that would prevent it from ever tiring.

"Wolf!"

The wolf stopped, looked at him, and then went back to clawing.

"Can you talk, wolf?" It was a reasonable question at this point. But no, the wolf couldn't talk. It could only kick ass on that door with maximum aggression. Ben ran back down the spiral staircase and eyed the front door. *And the third, a wall of flame.* Ben took out the third seed and slammed it down in front of the door. But nothing happened. The seed stayed a seed.

He picked the seed back up and turned to the second door. *This* one was iron. The wolf wouldn't get past that. Of course, who knew what would be on the other side of that door: another wolf, another dogface, the Land of Oz.

Ben turned the mighty knob of the iron door, peeked into the thick darkness, took one step in, and promptly fell down a very deep hole.

# CHAPTER SEVEN

# THE BEACH

He fell asleep while falling. Passed out from terror, really. He screamed and cried out in midair for Teresa and the kids, and then he blacked out. No dreams.

When Ben woke up, he was on a beach. One side of his face was buried in the cool sand, little grains of it stuck to the corner of his mouth. He had left a small pearl of drool down on the sand that looked like a tiny jellyfish. The waves were crashing in twenty yards away and the sky had a very thin cover of sheet clouds, the kind that would anger you if you wanted a full day of hot sunbathing. Behind him, the sun shone opaque through the sheer cloud cover. A series of rolling, grassy dunes provided cover for a single row of houses.

*Houses.*

He got up and beheld them. In front of him, two long lines in the sand ran parallel along the beach, as far as he could see, never turning into any of the houses. *The path? The path. Screw the path. Those are real houses.*

The dune grass was sharp and lashed against his ankles as he sprinted toward the house closest to his landing spot. It was a blue house with white shutters, and it stood up on stilts for protection from high tides. Ben waved his arms and stared into the windows.

"Hello! Hello! Can anyone help?"

As he drew closer to the house, he saw a worn-out dirt road behind it that stretched along the row of neighboring units. On the other side of that road was the sea. There was no land to be found past the expanse. He was on a massive sandbar. There were no telephone poles outside the house. No visible power lines. No cars. No bikes. No wagons. No vehicles of any kind. And no people. He was getting used to disappointment. He went up the loose plank stairs to the front door of the blue house (which faced away from the first expanse of ocean he had encountered) and began rapping furiously on the door.

No one answered. He dared to turn the knob and the door came open with ease. Inside was a spartan summer home designed to be lived in for only ten weeks a year. There was a little kitchen with ancient appliances, but no cookware of any kind. The kitchen opened to a living room with a pair of cute old lounge chairs and a cracked pleather sofa. Ben scoured the walls for outlets and phone jacks but saw nothing. Upstairs, he found three bedrooms with empty drawers and bare mattresses. He ran into a bathroom and turned on the faucet but no water came out.

"Hello?"

The closets were empty. Pacing from window to window, he could see that the neighboring houses didn't seem to be harboring any traces of life either. He booted up his phone on the off chance that it would power up for just a moment and give him a signal. If you left the phone off for a while, sometimes the battery was resurrected just long enough for you to get angry at it again. But this time, it couldn't even make it past the greeting logo. He pocketed it once more. His whole life was just taking his phone out and putting it back in again.

Up and down the sand spit, each house offered him the same kind of nothing: no people, no communications equipment, no food in the fridge, no water. It was a ghost resort. A trap, like the yellow light in the forest. Every sign of life was just a piece of bait to draw him away from the path.

And now the sea began to swell up. The whitecaps rippled and churned and, from the front porch of a three-story red Victorian, he saw a massive wall of water forming on the horizon: a wave higher than any building he had ever set foot inside of. Seagulls flew away from the wave with supreme urgency, but the water enveloped them as it drew closer to the coastline, their caws snuffed out by the coming catastrophe.

He ran down the porch steps through the bristling dune grass until he came to the parallel lines in the sand that had probably been drawn for him by some cruel God. The tsunami was arriving, ready to claim the sandbar. Ben reached into the seed pouch and took out the final hard nut. He threw it at the wet sand just as the wave was gathering up the front of the ocean and preparing to throw it all back on top of him.

The fire immediately blazed up and down the coastline, reaching past the cloud sheet and into the stratosphere: a wall of fire with no limit to its height or width. Ben got down and the hot sand began baking him like a buried clam. He could hear the fire snuffing out the wave, steam loudly hissing all above him.

And then the wall died down and the ocean returned to its resting state, gently lapping at the edge of the beach. Wisps of steam rose up and broke apart in the air—ghosts of the tsunami—as thin and frail as the little clouds above him. That was his final warning. No more seeds to save him. No more leaving the path. He sat up in the sand and wrapped his arms around his knees and started to cry again. The hysteria had ebbed and flowed, and now it was walloping him again. He began saying *I miss you* over and over, in his hushed and croaky voice, hoping all the *I miss you*s would be carried like a signal through the atmosphere back home.

"I miss you all so much. Someone . . . someone please help me."

But there was no response. Then Ben rose to his feet and shouted up at the sky.

"WHAT DO YOU WANT FROM ME?! WHAT IS THIS SHIT?"

That was all he could muster up the energy to say. He was reduced to a random jumble of profanity and loud questions. There was nothing on this beach, nothing in these houses, no one to talk to. The stillness all around him made it obvious.

Up ahead, he saw a slight deviation in the parallel lines, so he walked toward it. Again, everything looked much closer than it actually was. All this grand visibility was making his feet ache. The padding between his skin and bones had worn down to nothing. He was a pillow someone had ripped open and emptied of feathers.

As he neared the veer in the path, he saw a faded billboard next to one of the ghost houses:

COURTSHIRE ESTATES! NEW CONDOS STARTING AT JUST $350,000!

This was Courtshire. Courtshire had nothing.

*Stupid old lady.*

His shoes were growing intolerable: wet and sweaty and stinking from all that running and fleeing and magic seed throwing. These sneakers weren't accustomed to Ben being quite this active, and now they were falling apart like a lemon rolling off the used car lot. He kicked the shoes off and stripped away his socks, now flattened and brown (how did the *bottoms* of the socks get so dirty while contained within a pair of sneakers?). Then he mashed his feet into the sand and dug around. A piece of dead dune grass pricked his toe like a syringe. *Stupid grass. Stupid path. Stupid goddamn everything.*

After a mile-long drag, the path finally took a left, leading to yet another ghost beach house, this one a story taller than the rest. *Maybe this one has new shoes.* Ben dropped his shoes and socks in the sand, then made the turn and ran barefoot up the sandy front-porch steps. The parallel lines in the beach spread wide like an open mouth and faded away, giving him permission, at last, to safely explore an entire property. The house was unlocked. The people who had fled Courtshire—if any people had *ever* lived here—must have been in a hurry.

Another empty living room and kitchen. The faucets: dead. The closets: barren. He searched around for supplies and clean socks and shoes, but it was no use. Near a picture window looking out onto the surf was a small end table with a big glass vase on it. The vase was empty. Ben grabbed it and hurled it through the window. If he couldn't talk to anyone, he would express himself in other, more violent ways. He ripped the cabinet doors off and smashed them on the floor. There were pipes snaking up from the bathroom toilet and he tore those out of the wall. Anything that could be broken, he broke. Who was gonna see? Who was gonna care? He broke it all. Then Ben went upstairs and tore the bedposts off their frames, the wood splintering and the loud cracks soothing his terrified soul. When it was all over and the place was trashed, he sat down, ate some bread from his pack, and passed out on the hardwood floor.

Twenty minutes later, he let his eyelids split a quarter open and noticed a staircase going up to the third floor. This was the only house in the row that had an extra level, and the path had led him here. Of course, this had all been a massive cosmic troll job. Ben fully expected to walk up those stairs and find a giant papier-mâché middle finger waiting for him.

He took his time getting up, still sore to the bone. Buildings have been constructed with more haste. These were the only unfinished stairs in the house. The rest of the place had scrolls of dull tan carpet going up to the second floor and down to the basement, the carpet you see in any new suburban McMansion that's been thrown up by a contractor in under three months. But this upper staircase was just a bunch of old planks. There was a flimsy door at the top and Ben could sense a presence behind it. There was a thing there. There was something the path was trying to get him to discover.

*I need a weapon.*

Bereft of the powers to summon a wolf (more of those seeds would have been nice), he rooted through the backpack and found Mrs. Blackwell's cheese knife. It wasn't much, as weapons went. A bazooka would have been handier. The knife was about eight inches long, with a teak handle and a curved fork at the end. It probably wasn't even all that great at cutting through a cheese block, much less a psychotic murderer. Hopefully, the only thing Ben would confront behind that door was an angry wheel of Brie.

The door beckoned. There was no alternative. No other place the path led. It would take him to the attic, and then give him further instructions. Any deviation from that would result in death. Besides, he had to know what was behind the door now, regardless of how terrible it was. It goaded him on: a scab you know you shouldn't be picking at.

One step closer to the staircase and Ben could feel the door pulsing above him, the bolts just barely keeping it from flying open. And with his first step on the rickety planks, he heard something.

He heard the scratching.

CHAPTER EIGHT

# THE ATTIC

"Hello?" He was getting tired of shouting out "HELLO" to no one.

The scratching continued.

"I have a knife!" he cried. "But I'm not here to hurt anyone. Is it okay to come up?"

The scratching grew fevered. It sounded like a bunch of kids were gouging the door with forks.

And then it stopped. *Did I cause that?* Ben thought. No. No, he didn't. Whatever was behind that door stopped scratching because it felt like it, and not because of the white guy holding a cocktail knife. At home, Ben could cut an intimidating presence. You can say a lot with silence and a scar. His kids called him Scary Dad whenever he got mad, and he would use that to his advantage when he needed them to listen. *You guys don't want Scary Dad, right? So please put on your shoes.* He could turn into Scary Dad all too easily, and hated himself for it. But Scary Dad worked. Scary Dad could get them to fall in line. But that was with small children. It would not be as easy to make whatever was behind that door quake in fright.

The scratching came back, and then it went silent again, and then it came back, and then it returned, off and on. *It's the wolf. It didn't get me at the tower, and now it's here.* Perfectly logical conclusion. He listened for growling, but there was only the scratching and scraping.

He waited for a random gap in his mounting terror: that lull that sometimes occurs in your brain whenever you psych yourself out for something, like jumping into a cold pool. He found it, took a deep breath, and walked raggedly up the staircase, as if he were dragging along an unwilling participant. Then he seized the knob and turned it before he could change his mind. He pushed the door open.

He wished that he hadn't.

Inside the attic was a cave cricket. He knew the species well from the basement of his Maryland home, with their sickly, mottled brown shells, and their creepy extended hind legs, and their probing antennae, and their curved, larval backs. They didn't bite. They weren't poisonous. They just *jumped*. Constantly and chaotically, without rhyme or reason. Before you hit them, they would leap in great bounds out of the way: past you, behind you, over you. It was like they could teleport. They would come jumping through the heat ducts and terrify the whole family. He and Teresa would suck them up with a vacuum, but you had to get them on the first try, otherwise they knew you were coming for them, and they would never stop hopping. They made *him* jump. One time, a cave cricket came at him and he jumped so high he bashed his head on the ceiling. It hurt for a week.

This cave cricket in front of Ben in the attic was over six feet tall.

It was in the back of the attic, facing sideways. Behind it was some kind of control console that Ben couldn't make out, because there was a very large cricket in front of it. Ben wanted to die. He turned and reached for the door but that was an enormous mistake, because the cricket got spooked and jumped up, landing on him and knocking him to the floor.

"Oh my fucking God."

He could feel its slimy underbelly rubbing against him. Then it jumped again and smashed him in the head with one of its hind legs. Ben started screaming, yelling out nonsense and cursing as loudly as possible to scare it, and to make himself feel as if his voice were a separate companion in the room, there to aid him.

The cricket jumped again and landed on him. Its round black eyes loomed over him. They were unreadable. Maybe it wanted to kill him. Eat him. Gut him and lay eggs inside him.

He stabbed the pathetic cheese knife upward at the cricket and the blade bounced off its exoskeleton, breaking off at the handle. It was drooling on him now, secreting some kind of noxious syrup that coated him and was gradually immobilizing him. Ben was flailing and screaming and the cricket leapt around some more, battering his midsection and knocking him over one, two, three more times.

Ben reached into his sack and yanked out the loaf of bread, throwing it to the back of the room. The cricket seized on it hungrily and Ben felt little choice but to mount the distracted insect, with the bare cheese blade still wrapped in his right hand. He was clenching it so tightly that it cut through his palm, but he couldn't feel it digging in. The cricket leapt again and smashed Ben against the ceiling. He grasped at its antennae like they were reins and brought the blade down into its hulking black eyeball, slicing across the lens.

White ooze gushed out of the eyeball. The cricket's jumping became more furious. It was like a stuck bull now. Ben fell off and dropped the knife in the process. He could discern a pattern to it now. Four jumps: one forward, one sideways, a short one back, and then sideways again. He could time it. He dodged the cricket's leaps and found himself facing its blinded eye. With one swift motion, he plunged his fist into the eye socket and buried his arm shoulder deep in the cricket's head, punching through its brain. The cricket finally came to rest in the center of the room and collapsed, the white fluid seeping down Ben's side and soaking him entirely. Hysterical, he fled down the stairs and ran out to the front deck, so he wouldn't have to look at the thing again.

He sprinted from the deck, fell to the sand, and screamed until he was wheezing.

CHAPTER NINE

# THE CONTROLS

Once Ben could scream no more, he began to talk. He couldn't hold it back any longer. Teresa was gone but he spoke to her through his tears as if he were speaking to God. "Teresa, please help me. . . . I love you so much. I just wanna be home. Please Teresa. Please God, help me find my way home." The sides of his mouth turned down like levers and his jaw quivered uncontrollably as he opened his mouth and wailed, giving him the face of a Greek tragedy mask.

His hand was bleeding and began to throb. He grabbed a bit of cheesecloth from inside the backpack and wrapped it around the wound. The cloth turned red in an instant.

He was gonna have to go back up to the attic. Whatever was behind that cricket was his "prize" for besting it. Better go claim it. But he didn't want to go back. The idea of seeing the thing again paralyzed him . . . seeing its innards spilled out on the floor, watching it come back to life because why wouldn't it at this point? Why should anything make sense now? Why *wouldn't* it reanimate and pounce on him and gobble him right up? *Throw the dogfaces in there while you're at it, God. Be that much of a prick.*

He remembered burying his knife into the monster's eye and threw up into the sand nearby, covering up the pile of vomit. Then he lay back down and hyperventilated. When his youngest son, Peter, was a year old, the pediatrician said the little boy's head was too large. The doctor took out the charts for weight and height and head size—those baseline curves that they always used to tell if your boy was bigger than other children (*Well done, boy!*) or smaller than other children (*Good thing he won't be fat!*). As the doctor drew the growth curve of young Peter's head for Ben and Teresa, his pen left the paper. Peter had broken the percentiles. The doctor explained that there may be water building up in Peter's brain. They were going to do a scan on his head and if they found anything, a neurosurgeon would have to drain the water by cutting it open and breaking apart the plates of his skull.

Ben took Peter to the hospital and watched the neurosurgeon sedate him and feed him into the ghastly MRI machine, which looked like a container used on an alien spaceship to store kidnapped human specimens. The results took two weeks to get back to Ben and Teresa. They were negative. No surgery needed. Soon his body would catch up to his head and everything would be in correct proportion. The nurse on the other end of the phone delivered the news as if she were ordering a pizza.

*This nightmare . . . This is what that surgery would have been like for Peter. This is what it's like to have your skull taken apart and rearranged. . . .*

"Hey."

Someone on the beach was talking to him. Sounded like an older man.

"Hey, you," the voice said.

"Hello?"

"Here. I'm over here, shithead."

Ben propped himself up on his elbows and came face-to-face with a small blue crab. It was up on its hind legs in the center of the path. There were no human beings behind it. Ben looked left and right to get a full panorama of the sandbar. The crab was the only living thing he saw.

"Are you . . . the crab talking to me?" he asked it.

"Yeah, amigo. I'm the crab."

"Why are you talking?"

"I don't know. Why are *you* talking?"

Ben stood up and kicked sand at the crab.

"Hey, stop that."

"Leave me alone," Ben said. "Whatever my mind is doing to me, STOP IT."

"You should go back up in that attic and see what's what."

"What do you mean?"

"Why should I tell you anything else? You kicked that sand at me."

Now the crab dug down out of sight. Ben ran to the spot and started digging furiously.

"Get back here," he said to it.

"Piss off!"

Ben felt a hard pinch on his fingertip and yanked his hand out of the sand, yowling in pain. He stomped on the spot where the crab had dug in.

"I'm gonna . . . I'm gonna fucking crush you!"

"That's not gonna work," said the muffled crab voice. "Stop doing that. You're being stupid."

"I hate you!"

"Don't dig down here again. You'll be needing that hand to work the controls."

"Controls of what?"

No reply.

"CONTROLS OF WHAT?!"

No reply.

"GOD DAMMIT!"

Ben sucked on his fingertip and whirled around to face the beach house. The cricket was in his head again—twitching, jerking, regaining its strength, becoming hungry. Menace on top of menace.

"I can't go," he said to the crab. "I can't go back in there alone." He turned to the spot in the sand. Now that Ben had heard another voice—a benign voice, though not exactly friendly—he couldn't bear to let it go. "Will you come with me?"

No reply.

"Please?"

"Why do you need me?" the crab asked.

"I need someone. Anyone, even if it's a hallucination. I'm sorry I got pissed at you, all right? I can't be alone one second longer or I'll go mad. I know I've *already* gone mad, but I'll swim out into the ocean and never come back if I have to be alone another moment."

The little crab popped back out of the sand.

"You won't fuck with me if I go?" it asked Ben.

"I promise."

"'Cause I can take that whole finger off, you know. I'm just that strong and you're just that clumsy."

"Deal."

They walked toward the house together, side by side.

"What's your name?" Ben asked.

"I'm a crab. I don't have a name."

"Well, where did you come from?"

"Idaho. Where do you think I came from? The fucking sea."

"Do you have any friends?"

"No."

"How old are you?"

"I don't know."

"Where are we?"

"Beats the shit outta me."

"I'm gonna give you a name."

"Don't give me a name," said the crab. "I've done just fine so far without one."

"Frank."

"I don't want to be fuckin' Frank. I'm a crab. Don't go naming me or I'll clip a toe off."

"Fine."

"If you call me Frank, I'm gonna call you Shithead."

"Okay, I got it. Understood. Crab it is."

Ben stopped at the sliding doors that opened to the deck of the cricket house.

"How do you know what's up there?" he asked Crab.

"I took a look around once."

"Have you ever seen people on this beach?"

"No. Apart from you."

"How did you know I'd been in the house?"

"Because I saw you go in and then come screaming out like a fuckin' horse on fire. It didn't require any ace detective work."

"If you saw what I saw, you'd be screaming, too."

"What's *your* name, buddy?" Crab asked.

"Ben."

"That's only a little bit better than Shithead."

"I take it back. You can go back to the ocean now."

"I'm just messing with you."

"Yeah, well, you picked the wrong time to be messing with me."

"All right, all right, I can ease up. So are we going in that house? Or are we just gonna stand here?"

"We're going. I just need a moment." He turned to Crab. "Can you send someone a message for me if I don't make it out of this house alive?"

"No."

"Why not?"

"I'm not your courier, dickhead. I'm just walking up here to see if you spaz out again."

Ben didn't bother trying to move this particular bit of conversation forward. He walked into the house and over the broken furniture and went back up the flight of stairs, pausing at the bottom of the third-floor staircase. The door to the attic was still hanging wide open. Nothing up there made a sound.

"I don't suppose you'd wanna look up there for me before I go," he said to Crab.

"Eh, I got nothin' better to do."

Crab skittered along the wooden toe-kick lining the staircase and zipped into the attic. He came back down seconds later.

"There's a big fucking cricket in there."

"Is it dead?"

"Looked like it."

"Did it move?"

"No."

Ben stood still. He could smell the cricket's guts from the bottom of the staircase: a belly full of old digested fungal mat bits, putrefying and oozing into the floorboards . . . a rotten thing spreading its rot all over.

"You gonna go up there?" Crab asked.

"I'm working up to it."

"You sure take your time working up to everything. Won't be any easier to walk up there five minutes from now."

"No, I guess it won't."

Ben started up the stairs and the massive bug's carcass came back into view. The eyes leaked jellied whiteness. It made Ben want to tear his skin off. He would never be able to ascend or descend a staircase again without anticipating a cave cricket the size of a horse being there, ready to pounce. If he ever made it back home, he would have to move his family to a ranch-style house. His current house had three floors. Too many floors. *No more attics or basements. Burn all the attics and basements.*

Behind the cricket, he saw the control panel. It looked brand new. It was polished chrome, with a red lever and two large black knobs. Alongside each knob was an empty black square. Through the plate glass window past the controls, Ben could see the ocean in full. Directly in front of this particular house, he could now see a silhouette in the water, the black outline of something substantial. But the silhouette didn't move at all. It wasn't a fish. Something was anchored to that spot on the ocean floor.

"Do you know what's out there?" he asked Crab. Crab shimmied up to the windowsill.

"Looks big, whatever it is."

Ben yanked on the lever but it wouldn't give. He felt the knob on the right, letting his fingertips slide over the smooth matte finish. The sides of each knob had reeded edges, and he could see a tiny number etched into each notch: from zero to ninety-nine. The console looked like a piece of very expensive stereo equipment, like some crazy engineer from Denmark had perfected the craft of knob twirling and forged this as his masterpiece.

Ben gave the left knob a turn and felt it click. The black square next to the dial turned red. He turned it another click and the square turned green. Then yellow. Then white. Then purple. Then pink. Then back to black. He turned the other knob and the same colors appeared.

He tried the lever again but it wouldn't budge.

"There's some combination here that'll make the lever work," he said to Crab.

"So what is it?"

"I have no idea. Usually, with puzzles like this, there's some other element. There's a clue to solving it. We just have to find the clue." He pressed his hand to the ceiling, looking for a soft spot—some kind of secret compartment. But the room was bare. He raced downstairs and searched through the ransacked kitchen and living area for hints, but all he could find were loose coat hangers and musty throw pillows. He tore open the pillows, little cubes of gray foam bursting out and tumbling all over. He tore off the wallpaper and searched for holes in the crawl space. He ran outside the house, making sure that he wasn't overstepping the property line and angering the path. Then he searched the house's undercarriage, feeling eagerly along the timbers and around the pipes. Still, the clue eluded him. He went back inside and broke things that were already broken.

He came back up to the attic, at a loss.

"I can't find anything," he said to Crab. "I looked everywhere."

"No, you didn't."

"What do you mean, I didn't?"

Crab extended a pincer out at the cricket.

Ben understood perfectly. Now that he thought about it, he remembered reaching through the cricket's eye and feeling something in there, but he had assumed it was just a body part.

"You wouldn't want to go in there for me . . . ," he hinted to Crab.

"Shit, no."

Ben went back to the dials and feverishly began attempting every possible combination of colors and numbers, but it was pointless. The colors and numbers lined up differently after successive full spins, rendering the permutations endless.

He turned back to the monster insect. Its hind legs were reared up, and its thin antennae extended out in all directions, as if it wanted to touch everything.

Ben reached into the eye with his bad hand. He threw up on the floor as he dug deeper inside the monster's innards, feeling around for the object he chanced upon the first time around. Finally, after far longer than he had expected or hoped, he seized a small hard disc and yanked it from the cricket's eye. It was covered in smeared, yellowing pus. He dragged the disc along the attic floor to clean it off, picking up bits of dust and sand along the way. Finally, he was able to make out a red side to the disc and a white side. The red side said 61. The white side said 12. He turned to the controllers and spun the knobs to line up the combination: Red 61 on the left, White 12 on the right.

He yanked the lever and it flipped back effortlessly. Out the window, he saw a churning in the ocean where the giant silhouette was. The water roiled and bubbled, and up from the shallows a 70-foot-long hovercraft emerged, with a clean white body made of reinforced fiberglass and a thick rubber skirt splaying out from the bottom. The hovercraft faced out toward the ocean, and Ben could see its massive, twin-propeller airfoil tower up at the rear. It looked as if it could blast away the entirety of the sea. The hovercraft was tethered to a cleat in a dock slip that was shaped like a giant tuning fork, and Ben watched as the path in the sand reformed and created two distinct parallel lines leading to the dock.

"Oh, *that's* what that was," Crab said.

# CHAPTER TEN

# THE CRAFT

B en's hand was still bleeding from the fight with the cricket. He was all out of cheesecloth, so he wandered down to the beach—staying within the path—and washed his sliced palm in the surf. It wasn't an easy task; the incoming waves kept kicking up loose sand that spilled into the cut. He found himself having to endlessly rinse everything off. Crab waited ten feet behind him.

The hovercraft was enormous, a mansion on the sea. Ben had never ridden in one before. Given recent events, he didn't expect anyone to be inside the thing.

"Are you coming with me?" he asked Crab.

"That boat looks fancy as hell. I'd get on that."

"Okay."

"I need water and food, though. If you don't feed me, I'll just pitch over the side and you can go eat shit."

"I'm sure we can figure out something. Do you know who's doing this?"

"Doing what?"

Ben gestured all around. "This. Is this God?"

"Who's God?" Crab asked.

"Are *you* God?"

"You call me God, I call you Shithead. Same deal as calling me Frank."

Ben searched for the beginning of a proper explanation. "Do you know what humans are?"

"Yes. I'm looking at one right now. Not a very impressive one."

"Okay, well, humans have families. Male humans and female humans get together and have human babies and all that."

"Sounds like a riot."

"I'm trying to make this as clear as I can. I'm not trying to wow you."

"Go on."

"I have a family. We live in a place called Maryland."

"I know Maryland. I got family there."

"Great. Yesterday I took a trip, away from Maryland, and I got lost. You with me so far?"

"Yeah."

"And then I ended up here, and I don't know where I am. I don't know which way Maryland is. I don't know what town this is. I don't know what ocean that is out there. I don't even know if I'm still on Earth, or if I ate some kind of bad mushroom or something. I don't know anything. But this path opened up and anytime I leave it, something tries to kill me. And so here I am. I have to have keep following this path. I have to *hope* that it will guide me back home somehow, when it's this same path that keeps leading me farther and farther away from it. And I don't know who's doing this to me. So I'm very frightened, Crab. I feel like my family has died, or maybe *I* died. I didn't even get to say good-bye to them. It just hurts. Does that make sense to you?"

Crab waited a moment to answer.

"I thought you said you were gonna get me food."

"Jesus Christ."

"Who is that?"

"Just get on the boat."

Crab skipped lightly over the gaps in the dock as Ben slipped his dirty brown socks and rotting shoes back on and slung the backpack over his shoulder. Approaching from the slip, he could see the deck of the craft come into view. It was a glorious vehicle, outfitted like a luxury yacht. There was a leather banquette that wrapped around the main deck, all trimmed in curved, lacquered walnut. There was a separate tanning deck toward the bow, with sturdy lounges and block stools. In the center of the deck, there was a set of white sliding doors with tinted windows, beckoning passengers into the craft's interior. Ben stepped aboard, unlatched some of the storage compartments under the banquettes, and found all the necessary maritime safety equipment: life jackets, flare guns, fire extinguishers, deep-sea fishing rods, and more.

He walked through the sliding doors and was greeted by a main interior that was larger than his home. It was like an indoor peninsula, with a panoramic view of the sea that stretched around from port to starboard. There was a full galley kitchen and two dining tables and, dead in the center of the room, a fully stocked surf-and-turf buffet. The food all looked freshly prepared, as if an entire staff of servants had put it out and then disappeared the moment Ben stepped aboard: mountains of peeled shrimp, freshly shucked oysters and clams, lobsters perched atop silver tubs of crushed ice. A bottle of Dom Perignon sat in a chilled bucket, legs of cool condensation running down the side . . . beckoning him to come and drink. Ben walked up to the raw bar and took a whiff.

"How can this food all be fresh?" he asked Crab.

"I dunno."

Ben then wandered over to a big bowl of cracked crab claws. Stone crab. Ben had heard about stone crab, but had never tasted it. He looked at Crab for approval.

"Don't even think about it."

"All right, all right," Ben said. "Someone had to have put this food here. Someone must be on board."

He was paranoid now, feeling eyes around him. He imagined some race of creatures with X-ray vision staring up at him through the floorboards.

"Come with me," he said to Crab, and Crab scurried behind as Ben went below deck to the staterooms and opened every closet and turned down every top sheet. He checked every last cupboard and latrine, but there was no sign that any other living being was gracing them with his presence. This stuff was all just here somehow. Conjured.

He went back up to the buffet.

"Are you hungry?" he asked Crab.

Crab bobbed up and down.

"Then let's eat."

Ben grabbed a plate (it was warm) from a side stack and loaded up on everything: giant dollops of caviar and whole lobster tails and warm slices of flank steak from a hotel pan and oyster after oyster after oyster. Then he popped the champagne and started drinking it right from the bottle.

"Damn," said Crab. "You like to party."

"Someone may aff well enjoy thisth stuff," Ben said, his mouth full of beef. And then, just past Crab, he saw an outlet with a thin white wire running out from it. It was a charger. For his phone.

*I can charge my phone.*

He took the phone out of his shorts pocket and plugged it into the jack. The outlet was dead.

"I have to turn on this boat," he said to Crab.

"How?"

There was a spiral staircase in the center of the main cabin. Ben grabbed the charger and bounded up the staircase with the excitement of a child running around the inside of a 747. At the top of the staircase he entered the bridge. There was a full 360-degree view of the surrounding sea and coastline, a sonar monitor, a console with hundreds of little buttons and knobs, a main throttle, and a ship's steering wheel. It was a regular steering wheel, not the wooden one you spin around on a pirate ship. Ben was hoping for the wooden wheel.

The ignition still had the key in it. He grabbed it and turned hard enough to break it off.

The craft's engine sputtered to life behind him and then began to roar. Little rectangular lights bleeped and blooped all over the console. The craft rose up in the air and blew a wake in every direction, creating a hydraulic force field around itself. The sun was setting now. And quickly. As the darkness set in, Ben saw two parallel lines of phosphorescent algae begin to glow and stretch out into the water. The path wanted him to go straight out into the ocean.

There was an AC outlet resting flat on the front of the console and Ben plugged the charger in with his phone attached. The phone booted back up, but with no logo. No spinning wheel. No white screen. Instead, Ben saw an old woman spring up on the screen. She was sitting in a white room in a plush chair. She was wearing a white frock and a bright red overcoat. Ben remembered her right away.

"Mrs. Blackwell?"

"Find the Producer," she told him.

"Who is the Producer?"

"Stay on the path, and find the Producer."

"*Where* do I find this Producer?"

"At the end of the path, of course."

"Is my family alive?"

"The Producer will answer all of your questions. Go now. The beach will sink into the ocean in two minutes, and it will take you with it if you do not leave immediately."

The phone flicked off. Ben pushed the power button again, but there was nothing. *Find the Producer.* He threw the phone across the bridge and kicked the console.

"Uhhh, Ben?" said Crab. "You're wasting time."

Ben turned and saw the water beginning to envelop Courtshire. It crept up the sands and was rising to meet the wooden dock slip. They had to leave. Ben grabbed the throttle.

"Wait!" Crab yelled, "You forgot to . . ."

Ben rammed the throttle forward, paying no heed to Crab. The twin propellers started to hum, and then shriek. But the craft wouldn't move. The water continued rising. Ben realized his mistake immediately.

"The craft is still moored!"

He ran back down the staircase, Crab skittering behind, and flew out the sleek double doors of the main cabin. The roar of the propellers was drowning out everything as he grabbed the rope stretching out from the cleat anchored to the frame of the dock. It was pulled firm and taut, the full force of the propellers bearing down on it. Ben tried to reach down and slip the rope off the cleat, but immediately realized his folly in leaving the throttle on. The loop wouldn't budge and he could see the sandbar sinking down into the ocean, ready to take the craft with it. It weighed down on the rope and now the craft was tilting upward, like a plane ready for takeoff. In a few moments, it would flip entirely, capsize, and be pinned against the ocean floor.

"We have to cut the engine," Ben said. He went back into the cabin as Crab started to pinch the rope. He wasn't the biggest crab, but his pincers could do some damage when the situation called for it. The rope began to fray, strand by strand.

Ben ran up the staircase as the hovercraft tilted farther upward, the spiral staircase leaning and flattening to horizontal. Once Ben reached the top, the pull of gravity was so strong that he found himself pressed against the back window of the bridge, the controls virtually impossible to reach. He threw himself to the floor and began scaling it like a wall as the craft went up and up and up. He wasn't going to make it. Whoever this Producer was, he would never see his face. He would never see Teresa or the kids again. All those days and years with them, and he just needed one more *second*. Not even a second. Just a frame. A twenty-fourth of a second. A final snapshot of everything he loved, before the sea claimed him. He reached for the throttle one more time but it was no use.

And then, without warning, the ship broke free and soared up in the air. Ben flew back against the hard glass and felt it shatter from the force of impact. Now he was falling out of the bridge tower, the broken glass shredding his skin, and he slammed hard against the fiberglass shell covering the twin propellers as they blew the hover-craft up and way.

Now came the *really* mean part, because gravity was asserting itself once more, and the craft started to flatten back out. And in 3, 2, 1 . . . BOOM. It splashed back down in the ocean like a humpback whale, displacing thousands of gallons of seawater and throwing Ben to the deck. Before he could recover, the acceleration kicked in and he was thrown back and to the side and then, finally, overboard.

Ah, but the rope. There was a frayed end of rope hanging off to the side, cut loose from the dock thanks to Crab's diligent work. Some-how, Ben found the rope in the dark. He clung to it as the hovercraft picked up speed and jetted out into the great wide blue. It was at cruising speed now, and Ben felt his feet dragging along the surface of the ocean, the water pounding away at him as he biffed and bashed into the rubber skirt of the craft. He wasn't going to be able to hold on much longer. He called out for Crab, not knowing where he was, or if he was even still aboard.

"CRAB!"

Crab peeked over the edge of the main deck. "What?"

"Cut the engine!"

"Why?"

"Just cut the engine!"

Crab scurried back to the cockpit, but he was too small to push down the throttle or turn the key. Under the console was a series of connecting wires, so he found a wire under the ignition and gave it a good, hard pinch.

The mighty roar of the propellers and the engine died down, and the rope finally slackened in Ben's raw hands. His feet were dipping into the calm waters now as he swung forward and found himself dangling straight down the side of the craft. He began to scale the rope, drawing from a reserve of energy he never knew he had until this moment. It would cost him his last ounce of strength. Cost him everything, really. Dying here would have been just as fine as dying later on, but still he pushed on, pulling himself upward and feeling the sting of the wet and salty rope as it dug deeper into his wounded hand. This would be the last time he'd be able to use his hands for a while.

He pulled himself back on board and flopped across the deck like a reeled-in marlin. Nothing but furious breathing for a good long time. After a while, he felt a tickling on his belly. In the moonlight, he could see the outline of Crab.

"Thank you," he said to Crab.

"I think I broke the boat."

When Crab moved out of the way, Ben noticed the moon. Well, one of them at least. There were two of them in the sky now.

Two moons.

CHAPTER ELEVEN

# NIGHT ON THE OCEAN

"**Y**ou need to get up," said Crab.

"I can't," Ben said. He was all wet and bloody. Breathing was the only thing that didn't hurt right now. "I can't move."

"Get your ass up. We're drifting off the path."

That got Ben back on his feet in a hurry. Sure enough, he could see the hovercraft was floating off course, with one of the lines of glowing algae running straight underneath the ship and at an odd angle. If they drifted completely out of bounds, a sperm whale was probably going to come and swallow them whole. He raced back up to the cockpit and turned the key. Nothing.

"It won't turn on."

"I told you," Crab said. "I broke the damn thing. I clipped the wire."

"Which one?"

"I don't know. The right one."

Ben looked underneath the console and found a frayed end. He frantically searched for a matching wire as the craft drifted farther to the . . . Christ, what direction was it?

Finally, he lucked out and found the match. He sparked the two wires together and the resulting shock offered his hands one final, painful insult. But it worked. The engine kicked up, and Ben moved the throttle forward ever so slightly to get the craft back on course. Within a few moments, she was comfortably within the boundaries of the path, cruising forward into the twin moonlight. The lights in the bridge cockpit were illuminated once more and now he could see Crab sitting up on the dash and the worthless phone deposited over in the corner of the room. He picked the phone back up and tried the power button again, but there was nothing, not even after he plugged it back into the working socket. He looked up to the heavens.

"I don't know if I'm talking to God, or to this Producer I'm supposed to find, but I need a favor," he pleaded. "I need my family. Let me at least see their faces. If you have an ounce of compassion . . ."

The phone flickered to life. It gave him one picture. Just one. It was the five of them at a Chuck E. Cheese's for Rudy's sixth birthday party. Ben was in the center of the frame, one arm wrapped around an indifferent Peter, the other arm clutching the birthday boy tightly as he tried to wriggle away and go back to eating his chocolate cake. Flora was peeking out behind them. She was making a face, because a nine-year-old never smiles for a camera with sincerity. And then there was Teresa on the right. As always, she was beaming and trying to wrap her arms around the familial mass to hold them together. She was rubbing her gold wedding band with her thumb, an old nervous tic of hers.

Then the screen went back to black. Ben looked up again, tears down his face.

"Thank you."

"What do we do now?" Crab asked.

Ben knew the answer right away. "I need a shower. You stay here and make sure we don't veer off course."

"What if we do?"

"Come tell me."

"Why do I have to sit here and do the patrol duty?"

"Would you prefer to shower first?"

"No. I guess not."

"I'll bring you something. What do you want?"

"I could use some barnacles and fish parts."

"Parts?"

"Yeah. Not the whole fish, man. Just some parts. Sharks get the fish first, usually."

"Oh."

"And worms."

"I don't know if the buffet had worms or fish parts."

"Well, then, whoever made that buffet is a dick. You go shower, and when you get back, I'm gonna hop in the water and find some dinner. On my own. Fat lotta good you humans are."

Ben went back down to the staterooms below deck. They were fully furnished, with crisply made beds and a vase of flowers on every nightstand. Each stateroom had a private bathroom stocked with fresh towels and washcloths and bathrobes. He tore off his wet shorts and tattered shirt and hopped in one of the showers. The second the fresh warm water hit him, he wanted to melt into the tiles. He shut his eyes tight and let the showerhead blast his face, then he opened up his slashed hand and watched the blood drain out of it. There were superficial cuts and scrapes all over the rest of his body from his little window plunge, but nothing that would require him to stitch himself up or cauterize a wound with a flaming arrow.

He stepped back out of the shower and put on one of the fluffy white robes, the soft terry cloth tickling his skin. He was remembering, albeit slowly, what it was like to feel *good* again. It was still possible.

There was a first aid kit under the sink, with a bottle of hydrogen peroxide and some gauze and medical tape and ibuprofen. He doused his hand in the peroxide and watched it bubble. He kind of liked the sting. Then he wrapped it all up, swallowed three of the pills (he prided himself on being able to swallow pills without the aid of water), walked upstairs, grabbed himself a lobster tail at the buffet, and chewed on it like a corn dog on his way back up to the cockpit. He found a roll of electrical tape under the console and used it to patch the ignition wire back together.

"You look refreshed," said Crab.

"I have to sleep."

"What about my food, asshole?"

Ben cut the engine. The craft slowed and began to drift. "Go now."

Crab hurried down and splashed into the water. Seconds later, he was back.

"That's it?" Ben asked. "Already?"

"Look at me, man," said Crab. "Do I look like I need two pounds of food to go on?"

"Right."

He sparked the engine back up and looked out at the glowing algae as they converged at the vanishing point.

"I have to sleep, Crab. But we need to stay on course."

"We'll take turns, then. I'll watch. You rest. If I need you to steer, I'll pinch you on the ass to wake you up."

"Okay."

He went back down to a stateroom and tried sleeping on the bed but it was no use. His brain refused to shut down. He was aching to sleep. Just a few hours away from this was all he wanted. *Sleep. Stop thinking. Just fucking sleep.*

And yet, his eyes remained open. He pulled the comforter off the bed, grabbed one of the pillows, and trudged back up to the bridge.

Then he swept away the last bits of broken glass from the back window and laid down on the floor. The air was warmer out here by the ocean. Wherever he was, it was no longer November.

"Why are there two moons up there?" he asked Crab.

"I don't know."

"Am I dreaming?"

"No."

"Do you know this Producer that the lady was talking about?"

"No. How'd you get that scar?"

"What?"

"That big scar on your face. Where'd that come from?"

Ben was annoyed by the question. "I was in a fight," he replied. *"With a shark."*

"Bullshit."

"You're right. That is complete bullshit. A dog did it."

"What kind of dog?"

"A Rottweiler."

"Ah shit, I'm sorry."

"Don't do that. Don't say you're sorry. People always say they're sorry when I tell them. It does nothing for me."

"All right, then. Screw that dog. Is that a better way to react?"

Ben laughed. "Yeah, that's closer."

"You like dogs?"

"Not really."

"You own a dog?"

"Hell, no."

"Why'd you come back up here instead of staying in one of those fancy bedrooms?"

"I couldn't sleep," Ben answered.

"Why not?"

"It was a long day. Making friends with a talking crab was somehow the least weird thing about it. I have a lot to process."

"Where are we going?"

"I have no idea. My fucking hand kills."

"Think about your family, then."

"What about them?"

"Nothing. I just figured thinking about them would take the sting away."

"Yeah, well thinking about them hurts, too."

"Maybe that's a better kind of pain."

"Maybe."

And so he thought about the picture that flashed on his phone for just a moment. He could close his eyes and trace his wife and kids on the back of his eyelids. He could make a photo negative of them in his mind. The pizza parlor. The cheap red tablecloth. Teresa awkwardly rubbing her ring. He was coloring the image in when he finally drifted off.

————

When he woke up, he was in a bed. *His* bed. The queen bed upstairs in his house, white nightstands flanking either side. He looked over at the clock. 5 A.M. *Weren't you on that boat just now? Boat, what boat? There's no boat. You're home. Home just as you are every day . . .*

He was alone in bed. No Teresa. She was still working the night shift at Shady Grove Hospital. He got up to piss and looked out the bathroom window at the moon. One moon only. He heard the front door downstairs open. So he walked out into the upstairs hall, clad only in his boxers. The other bedroom doors were closed, the kids fast asleep.

He could hear crying coming from the living room now. He

tiptoed downstairs and saw Teresa slumped on the couch, still in her nurse scrubs and black clogs. She wasn't moving.

"Teresa?"

She let out a deep moan. He sat down next to her and put his arm around her, running his fingers through her hair.

"Are you okay?"

"I can't talk about it," she said.

He patted her leg gently, doing his best to walk the fine line between compassion and smothering.

"It's okay," he told her. "You don't have to say anything."

She had a rule about never bringing work home with her. It was a deal they had made long ago—to keep work at work and not burden each other with those miseries. She lost patients regularly, but never told him about it. And her policy worked. She was so smart to implement it. They were comfortable in silence together. It was the nicest part of their day sometimes, given how goddamn loud the kids were. They were good at silence.

But she looked different this morning. Devastated. He took her hand and kissed her cheek and she curled into him, still not saying a word. They sat for an hour before she finally spoke.

"Oh, Ben . . ."

"Just this once, you can tell me."

"I can't," she whispered. "I can't tell you or it'll kill me."

"You saw someone die."

She said nothing.

"More than one?"

A slight nod.

"I'm so sorry, T."

She kept her eyes shut tight.

"It's not your fault," Ben said.

"It was my fault," she said. "I killed them."

"No, no, you didn't kill anyone."

She started to cry. "I can't talk about it."

*Wait a second, you remember this night, don't you? She canceled a few shifts after that, remember? And then she stayed stone silent for a couple of days afterward: barely saying a word, only getting out of bed to go paint in the basement. Took her a week to become herself again. Worst night she ever had on the job. Don't you remember that?*

———

When Ben woke up, the hovercraft had hit an iceberg.

# CHAPTER TWELVE

# THE PACK

The front deck crumpled like a cheap sedan. Ben was awakened in midair, with no time to boot up his mind before he slammed into the front of the console. His ribs were the first thing to feel the pain.

"CRAB?!"

"We hit ice."

"It was eighty degrees when I went to sleep!"

It was no longer eighty degrees. A hard, frosty wind blew through the busted bridge window. Ben stood and saw the iceberg jutting out overhead, a floating tower of blue cliff faces, with just enough melt along the bottom to keep the ice from puncturing the rubber skirt of the hovercraft. But the engine had died on impact and the skirt was starting to deflate. She wouldn't stay afloat for much longer.

The cliff of the berg hung over the wreck, raining melt down onto the main deck in fat, heavy drops. It was like standing under a wet tree and then shaking it. There was no possible way to scale the side of the thing. Surrounding it was a loose, dangerous pack of ice: random polygons bunched together and swirling around. There was no solid land of any kind. The berg itself was a massive edifice of wiper-fluid blue glacier. The hovercraft looked like an ant compared to it.

Ben could feel the craft settling down into the water, the air whistling out of the bottom.

"The lifeboats," he said to Crab. Crab jumped off the console and down the stairs. Ben grabbed his phone and the charger then rushed back to the stateroom, where he had dumped his belongings. He grabbed his backpack and stuffed it with two robes, four towels, and two washcloths. It all fit. Then he opened up a stand-alone closet and, to his shock, found it stocked with cold-weather gear: boots, wool socks, thermal underwear, sweaters, gloves, hats, crampons, ice axes, goggles, Gore-Tex pants, and a weatherproof shell jacket. All clean. All his size. None of it had been there the day before. He took everything, along with a nearby pen and blank notepad from a nightstand.

Outside the porthole, he could see the frigid ocean rising. He got dressed in the gear as fast as he could, ran back up to the main cabin, and dumped an entire bowl of wrapped saltines into the bag, plus a dozen extra bottles of water. Then he ducked through the double doors.

The craft was succumbing now, listing forward, with water rushing up the limp skirt and into the crushed front end of the hull. Off the starboard side of the deck, toward the stern, Crab pushed a button that automatically hoisted up one of the orange fiberglass lifeboats. The stubby vessel dangled from its davits over the edge of the ship, waiting to drop. The hovercraft was tilting starboard as well, turning into the berg, eager to smash back into it on its way down.

"Hurry the fuck up!" Crab yelled as Ben ran over and popped the lifeboat hatch. The water was creeping up the tanning deck, sweeping the lounge chairs back and gushing through the tears in the fiberglass. Ben jumped through the hatch and found himself inside a diesel-powered rescue boat designed to hold twenty-four people, with a rudimentary cockpit sticking up at the stern. Ben examined the ceiling and found a large red pull tab with a RELEASE label.

He gave it a yank and the boat came free from the davits, dropping barely an inch into the surf.

"We gotta hurry," Ben told Crab. The sinking craft was still turning back into the berg, with the lifeboat sandwiched between the two. Inside the cockpit he found the thick plastic key to gun the engine. He turned it and pushed the throttle back to get away from the wreckage.

"Can you see the path?" he asked Crab.

"What fucking path? It's an ice field."

"The path continues somewhere. Look for it!"

Crab perched on the cockpit's windowsill. This boat didn't offer the same kind of sweeping, majestic view as its mother ship.

"There's ice every goddamn place. The pack must have closed around us," Crab said.

The lifeboat slammed into one of the flat polygons of the surrounding mass and Ben tumbled down the cockpit stairs into the cabin. He was a rag doll at this point. He had to train himself to be a six-year-old again, all rubbery bones and fearlessness. Crab shot back up the side of the cockpit tower and glanced out the side porthole.

"Are we sunk?" Ben asked.

"No, but the good boat is. Too bad. That was a much better boat."

Ben dragged himself back up the stairs and looked out to see the sleek yacht surrendering to the churning water. The waves reached the bridge of the mother ship and poured through the broken windowpane, gradually swallowing the craft whole, a snake unhinging its jaws for a big meal.

Meanwhile, the lifeboat had taken a blow, but its engine was still humming. Ben moved the throttle back to idle and gave the hovercraft a final salute as it went down, down, down . . . and then gone. Past the site of the wreck was a tiny opening between the berg and the rest of the pack, enough for an experienced mariner to circumnavigate.

Ben was *not* an experienced mariner. He piloted a Sunfish in summer camp when he was a kid, one of those sailboats that had a little chrome handle at the bow so you could drag the hull into the water. It didn't even have a sitting area. You had to lie on top of the thing and pray you didn't fall off. And you had to stick a daggerboard right through its heart, then steer it with a crappy wooden rudder at the back. Ben was terrible at every last possible task aboard. His knots always came undone. The daggerboard would get stuck. Whenever the boat had to come about, he would get nailed in the face with the swinging boom. He was not a mariner. He could swim, though. If you can't sail, you better be good at swimming.

There was a radio mounted to the cockpit dash. Ben grabbed the receiver and turned the knobs every which way, switching channels and shouting out distress signals. The compass on the dashboard spun endlessly, refusing to give a clear direction.

"Mayday! Mayday! Can anyone hear us?!"

After the radio crackled and buzzed for a bit, there was an answer.

"Hello?" It was a female voice.

"MAYDAY! MAYDAY! We're stuck in the ice pack!"

"Well, that sounds bad."

"This is an emergency. PLEASE HELP. The compass and coordinate measurements on this panel are all screwy. I have no idea where I am."

"Aw, you sound sweet."

"*Can you help us?!*"

"Oh, sure. What the hey. Just head around the iceberg and the path should open back up."

"Who is this?"

"I'll see you on the other side. Can't wait to meet you! Later!"

The radio went dead. Ben eased the throttle forward and moved carefully around the floating monolith.

"Pop the hatch," Crab said.

"Why?"

"So I can fucking see! I'm a crab. I gotta get close to stuff to see well."

He pulled the release and Crab jumped off the cockpit roof and down into the water. The wind came roaring through the hatch and unloaded a flurry of jabs on Ben's face. Crab quickly resurfaced and climbed back inside.

"Is there more ice below the surface?" Ben asked Crab.

"You're good. The berg retreats underwater. It doesn't stick out."

"Can you close that hatch back up? It's freezing in here."

"I can't."

"Why not?"

"I shouldn't have to remind you that I'm a crab."

"Right."

Ben walked down the steps and pulled the hatch closed. They were making slow progress around the berg now. It must have been over two miles wide, its own island. And it was gorgeous: a living slab of frozen history, moving, sweating, its facets shifting from every possible vantage point. It had presence. Photos of it were worthless in conveying its awesomeness. It was more beautiful than any object Ben had ever seen.

The surrounding pack kept threatening to close in on them, but there remained just enough room for the orange lifeboat to safely pass through. Ben tried the radio again.

"Hello?"

The female voice came back on. "Hey! You're doing great!"

"You can see us?"

"No, but you're not dead. That's pretty impressive. Keep going, you superstar, you."

The voice clicked off.

"That chica's kinda flirting with you," said Crab.

"Shut up."

"She might be cute."

"I'm not really interested in that right now, Crab."

"Yeah, but you could sure use it. And she might know some lady crabs."

"Shut up."

As they wended their way around the berg, the sun came into view, blasting down on the walls of the floating mountain and the surrounding ice patches. It was right on top of them now. Blinding. It felt as if they were surrounded by suns. Even with his goggles on, it took Ben a few moments to recover. Stretching in front of them was a clear path straight through the ice field. No sign of land anywhere.

He gunned the throttle. Then he kept one hand on the wheel and used his free hand to open up his backpack and take out a loaf of bread. He ate every last crumb. No other accompaniments. Then he took out the pad and pen and ripped the pen cap off with his teeth. He put the pad on the dash and began scrawling out a note to Teresa. He wasn't a great writer. The copy guys his bosses hired to write brochures were all more lively and persuasive. Ben was the money guy. The hammer. He figured out long ago that when he met with vendors face-to-face, he could knock down their prices by an extra 10 percent. His scar did all the bargaining for him.

He never wrote Teresa when he was on the road. It was always just a few phone calls—always short, always down to business. And that would be it. He should have written to her more—long, florid love letters, like a Civil War soldier to his beloved. Something she could keep in a box somewhere. Something that had meaning, well beyond just a phone call asking if she needed some shit from the store on his way back. They were both great at the day-to-day business of love. They helped each other. They planned. One was calm when the other was pissed off, and vice versa. They were good like that.

But they were both too old and busy and tired for grand romantic gestures anymore. If he never got home, there would be no box of letters for her to remember him. There would only be pitted-out T-shirts and half-eaten bags of pork rinds.

> *Dear Teresa,*
>
> *I love you so much. Don't worry about me. I'll be home soon.*
>
> *Love,*
> *Ben*

Crab walked up Ben's shoulder and peered at the note.

"What'cha writing?"

"None of your business," Ben said.

"Sorry."

He took out a water bottle and emptied it. Then he stuffed the note inside the bottle and tossed it through the hatch and into the sea.

The radio crackled again.

"Hello?" the female voice said. Ben grabbed the receiver.

"Hello."

"You're almost here. That's really great."

"Are you the Producer?"

"The who? I have no idea what you're talking about."

"Where are you?"

"Look ahead."

Ben looked out the windshield and saw it: a jagged, snowcapped mountain peak in the distance. Not ice. Real land.

"Nice, isn't it?" said the voice. "Hurry up. Get here soon."

"Why?"

"So I can kill you, silly! Ta!"

And the radio shut off.

"Well, I guess she wasn't flirting with you," Crab said.

# CHAPTER THIRTEEN

# THE MOUNTAIN

B en had never worn crampons before. They made for intimidating footwear: all sharp steel spikes and hard rubber straps, like lashing a spider to your foot. He slipped them over his boots and stepped out of the lifeboat, which had run aground on the shoals of a cold, gray, rocky beach. Before disembarking, he had grabbed a flare gun, flashlight, and first aid kit from the lifeboat's emergency supplies and tucked them into his backpack.

Past the beach, he saw an icy path run through a patch of short evergreen trees, then continue up the mountain. He'd need the crampons. And the axes. They were left for him for a reason. This Producer fellow was extremely well prepared, almost like his own wife. For Teresa, there was a reason for everything. If Ben walked into a room and saw a pile of laundry on the ground, he knew Teresa had put it there deliberately: for washing or donating to Goodwill or whatever. Anything that looked out of place in his home was in that place for a good cause. She was strategic, wise beyond her years. She was not a woman who left loose ends.

"You wanna scout this out for me?" he asked Crab.

"What do you mean?"

"You skip ahead and report back to me about what's up there."

"Why the fuck would I do that?"

"Who's gonna notice you?"

Crab furrowed his beady blue eyes. "Who's gonna notice me? Boy, I dunno. Maybe one of the hundreds of thousands of potential predators that I have to spend every day fending off? Birds? Octopi? Fish? Stingrays? Turtles? Otters? Other crabs? Oh, and *humans*. Were you not aware that humans eat crab? Did you not see the fucking buffet on that hovercraft? *You* wanted to eat it, you big shit. So, yes, I think I'm a bit more noticeable than perhaps you realized, amigo. I don't bury myself in the sand all day long because it's *fun*."

"You're right. I didn't mean to impose."

"You're lucky I don't just go back into the sea and leave your candy-ass alone on this beach."

"Well, why don't you?"

Crab said nothing.

"Crab? Why don't you?"

"I don't have to explain anything to you."

"Hey, I wasn't trying to grill you."

"Another way humans consume crab. Thanks for reminding me."

"I wasn't trying to . . . hurt you," Ben explained. "I just wanted to understand."

"There's nothing to understand. I'm a crab, and you're a clueless human, and I just like seeing you show your ass to the world. It's a nice change of pace. Usually when I see humans, they're waiting for me with a net and a stick of butter. Or some dipshit kid wants to throw me in a pail and poke me with a stick."

Ben felt awful now. "You can stay here if you want. You don't have to go with me. I can come back."

Crab sat up on his back legs. "That path ain't taking you back here. Or, if it does, it won't for a long time."

Crab started walking up the path, the soaked rocks giving way to a sheet of ice running through the squat forest. Ben followed behind him, digging into the backpack for some water and crackers. As they passed into the dense patch of woods, Ben smelled something awful. Putrescent. Crab, who was just a few yards ahead of Ben and had made it through the trees, suddenly came skittering back.

"Don't look," Crab said.

"Why?" Ben asked.

"Just don't."

"What's up there?" He could already venture a guess.

"I'm just saying: I'd shut my eyes tight if I were you."

"Are there any dead crabs ahead?"

"No. Good for me. Bad for you."

Ben kept walking. The smell grew worse, then quickly intolerable. He shut his eyes and felt along the ice with his crampons. Then he stepped on something thick and cylindrical. The crampons sank down into whatever it was and made a gushing sound.

"Crab," Ben asked, his eyes still shut tight, "am I still on the path?"

"Yeah."

"Do I wanna know what I'm stepping on?"

"No."

He took a step forward. Another thick, soft object—thicker than the one before it. He loosed his other crampon out of the putrid material and walked a hundred yards through more of it, laboriously uprooting his spikes before plunging them back down into the soft, fleshy path. It was wildly uneven. Sometimes he would hit something hard and slip forward. Other times he would lose his balance on something that was as thick and round as a bowling ball. *It's all mud. Mud and sticks and rocks. Nothing more.*

He kept his eyes closed, which wasn't as easy as he thought it would be. His brow grew sore. His eyeballs craved air. The smell overwhelmed him and he unwrapped the scarf around his face so he could vomit off to the side.

"Watch it!" Crab yelled.

"Sorry."

"Just warn me next time."

"Got it. How much longer?"

"There's more. Keep going."

*Mud and sticks and rocks. Mud and sticks and rocks. Mud and sticks and rocks.* He fought through it all and eventually felt his crampons strike solid ice once more. With a few more steps, he was past the horrors at the base of the mountain.

But his toil was only beginning. When Ben finally opened his eyes, he saw the grade of the path steepen sharply. In another quarter mile or so, it went vertical, up the cliff face, and then spiraled around the mountain and entered a gaping cave perched halfway to the summit. He sat and opened his pack and ate more of Mrs. Blackwell's beef stew. It was the protein he needed, although he wasn't enthralled to be eating hunks of flesh with the stench at the base still lingering.

He stood back up and stared at the cliff: two hundred feet of sheer ice that had melted and dripped and refrozen again into thick bundles. It looked like the inside of a cavern wall. He had never scaled a cliff before. The past three days were a fine reminder that Ben was not a capable outdoorsman. He couldn't sail. He couldn't camp. He couldn't climb. He had apparently spent most of his life an inert vessel for consumer goods and services. It was a good thing that he was at the stage in life where applications rarely asked about hobbies, because he would have been at a loss to put anything in the blank space.

The ice axes were beautiful, intimidating tools. Each handle was painted bright yellow and made of reinforced steel, with Kevlar straps and a carabiner at the ends to attach to his jacket sleeves. He could hack into the ice sheet with the short side and then bury the claw side into a freshly dug hole.

He began the hard climb up. He knew to anchor his feet into the ice first and let his lower body support most of his weight, but his arms were still dead by the time he had climbed up twenty feet. His upper-body strength was just a daydream. His bad hand was screaming to be put down for good. Crab effortlessly walked straight up beside him, pausing to wait for Ben. Ben gave him dirty looks.

"What?" Crab asked.

"Nothing."

"I don't get many advantages over you humans. Give me this one."

"Fine."

He stopped frequently on the way up, but the stops were hardly restful. He could feel his toes giving out as he dug them into his boots, desperate for the crampons to stay locked into the cliff face. Fifty feet up, he looked down and saw the field of decomposing body parts he had waded through: limbs, heads, bones, torsos. No whole bodies. *Where did they all come from? How did they all die? Did the woman on the radio do this?*

"Jesus, Crab."

"Why'd you look back? You kept your eyes closed that whole time for nothing, you dummy."

Past the forest thicket, he watched as the surf reclaimed the lifeboat, picking the little orange vessel up and taking it away, as if it were merely a loose buoy. He pressed his face against the mountain, desperate to adhere to it.

He remembered the last time he climbed a mountain. It was in South Dakota when he was five years old. His dad said they were going on a little hike. In reality, he took Ben up Hornet Mountain, which was nearly as steep as the cliff face he was now scaling. There were iron ladder rungs pounded into the side of the mountain that made for "easy" climbing. It was not easy. Little Ben screamed the whole way up, his mother silently fuming. For his part, Ben's father expressed no concern about the situation at all. The old man could distort reality so easily. He could say that things were going very well and that everyone was having fun, even when the precise opposite was true.

Ben's arms continued to burn. A twinge in his neck sent a ghastly round of pain down his arm, pain so severe he nearly let go of the axe. His knee was giving him trouble now, too. Everything was giving him trouble. Thanks to the marvelous levels of pain he was experiencing, he found himself introduced to the deeper wonders of his body's mechanics: the little muscles behind the bigger muscles, the dense network of nerve roots in his joints and hinges and fingertips, the miniature tendons that could only bear so much strain. Prior to this hike, he had been blissfully unaware of these parts of his body, and how they had all worked in harmony throughout his life without him noticing.

But now he noticed. The wound on his hand opened up inside his glove and sent blood running down the inside of his jacket sleeve. In the thin air, he would probably need that blood. That was important blood.

He began to feel faint. By the time he was 150 feet up, his body was eating itself. The lactic acid was building up in every muscle, chewing away at the fibers. He let out a deafening grunt with every step. He wasn't going to make it. He would fall, and this time he would not land safely on a magical resort beach. He would land exactly where he expected to land.

"Push!" Crab yelled.

"I can't. Crab, I can't breathe."

"You're almost there. Don't puss out on me."

Ben pressed on. The movements were automatic now, an afterthought in his mind, given all the neurological fires his brain had been tasked with putting out. He reached the lip of the cliff face and rested, gathering his last few scraps of energy before heaving himself up onto the ledge. The last part of any journey is always the longest.

"I wish you were bigger," he said to Crab.

"I was wishing that long before you were, Shithead."

Ben hoisted himself up and rolled onto the vast ledge halfway up the mountainside and then lay flat on his back. He made it. He started to laugh. At first a chuckle. And then, a guffaw. Crab backed away.

"Fuck you!" Ben screamed over the edge. "I did it! WOO-HOO!"

"Hey," said Crab.

"What?"

"I know you're having fun trash-talking a mountain and all, but you better move."

Crab stuck a pincer out. From the right, there was a thick black cloud approaching. It swept along the sea like a ghost unshackled. There was only one place for them to find shelter: the gaping cave mouth above them, a winding ledge leading directly into its maw.

CHAPTER FOURTEEN

# FERMONA

Crab and Ben did two laps around the mountain, ever so slowly, finally arriving at the cave mouth. Ben could see skulls and large femur bones strewn about the entrance. He could see the pores in their surfaces. All the bones were broken open, the marrow inside frozen black.

They ducked into the cave. Ben only got a few feet in before he realized there would be little in the way of natural light to guide them. He slumped to the ground, opened up his rucksack, and choked down more of the stew, plus some hard cheese. The cave entrance grew five shades darker as the clouds pounced and the pelting rain fell outside in wide, dense sheets, as if the sky itself were now entirely underwater.

Ben slid down onto his side and rested his head on a family of spiders. They burst apart like a firework and ran mad dashes across his face. He stood and shook them off, the sensations of their little legs lingering all over him.

"You're here!" a voice called from deep inside the cave. It was a woman's voice. Warm. Friendly. "Come on! Let's go. Don't keep me waiting forever."

Ben looked to Crab. Crab threw his pincers up.

"No idea."

"You should stay here," Ben said.

"Why?"

"In case I need you."

"It's boring here," Crab said.

"People get bored because they're boring." Ben must have said this to his children a thousand times.

"I'm not a person. I'm a crab. I'm allowed to get bored sitting here in a shitty cave."

"Just wait here so you don't die. I bet death is even *more* boring than this."

"It better be."

"Shut up."

Crab planted himself down by the cave wall and covered himself in grime. He was impossible for Ben to see now.

"What if we don't see each other again?" Ben asked Crab from the darkness.

"Then it's been real, I guess."

Ben unstrapped his crampons and tucked them back into his bag, and then he began walking along the path into the growing darkness. It was damp here. You could feel it in the air and smell it in the rock. Fungi thrived in the cave. . . . They were probably growing inside Ben's nostrils already. He clicked on his flashlight and saw the path curve to the right. There was a hint of light coming from around the bend. Or was that just his flashlight? He walked farther along as the cave bent gradually, painfully.

Suddenly, a bat with a six-foot wingspan flew right over his head. Ben screamed and collapsed to the floor, crying and shaking. His body was no longer equipped to handle sudden shocks. The bat shattered him. He wept on the cave floor and begged, "Please, no more. . . . No more. . . ."

"Hey!" the female voice said to him from deep inside the mountain.

"Hello?"

"What's keeping ya?"

"Go away. Leave me alone."

"Are you okay?"

"NO."

"It's not much farther. I swear. You're doing really well."

"Go fuck yourself."

There was a long silence.

"I'm gonna chalk that up to general crankiness," the voice said. "But just this one time. Now get up and come on over here, you lug."

Tired as his body was, Ben had little choice but to obey. He got up and began walking again in a half crouch in case another bat came roaring his way. Soon, the prick of light he initially saw deep inside the cave became more definite: a warm, golden glow creeping along the walls and making the fetid tunnel feel drier, homier.

He rounded the great bend and found himself at the entrance of a chamber that was easily a hundred feet high, a naturally formed ballroom of limestone walls and icicle-thin stalagmites and stalactites. Some of the jutting formations met in the center and formed columns that dotted the room. Past the chamber lay a small blue lake, its surface smoother than a television screen.

In the center of the chamber was a rug the size of a football field, piled high with human goods: backpacks and old pants and shirts and pocket watches and whole boats and canoe paddles and suitcases and shoes. There was a CB radio on top of all the loot. To the side of the rug was a vigorous bonfire with a black metal cauldron perched atop it, bubbling away.

On top of the pile sat a woman thirty feet tall. She had ruby red lips and long, curly chestnut hair, and she wore a gray burlap dress that crested right at her knees. She crossed her legs and kicked out her feet, clad in thick wool socks and boots big enough to house a little old lady. She looked to be in her thirties, although who knew how giants aged. When she saw Ben, her face lit up. She couldn't have been happier to see him.

"You're here! Why, look at you. You're as cute as a button!" She pointed to a spot in front of her great pile of goods. "Stand over there."

"Why?"

"Because if you don't, I'll just stomp on you and mash your little man-guts right into my rug, you goofball. What a question to ask. Go on. The light's best in that spot. Let me get a good look at you."

Ben did as he was told. The giant uncrossed her legs and leaned forward, putting her elbows on her knees and resting her chin on her hand. She was attractive. He couldn't help but think it. She studied Ben for an uncomfortably long period of time.

"There's a big scar on your face. Did you know you have a scar on your face?"

"I did."

"How'd you get it?"

"I slayed a giant."

"HA! I don't think so. Nice try, though."

Ben looked over at the roiling cauldron. It smelled like curry.

"You want some?" she asked.

"What's in it?"

"People, of course! No bones, though. I promise you won't choke."

Ben threw up. She shooed him off the rug.

"The rug! The rug! Get off the rug, you big jerk!"

He spilled out more used beef stew onto the cave floor.

"Please don't kill me," he begged her. "I have a wife and children and . . ."

"Oh, blah blah blah. You know how many times I've heard that? People with families are so arrogant. Just because they have a family, they think they *matter*. They're all boring. For once, I'd like a man to beg for his life and scream out, 'Save me, Fermona! I have no kids and my life is insanely fun!' No one ever does that."

Ben opened his eyes wide. "I'm not the only person who's been on this path."

"You've seen my front yard. Does it *look* like you're the first gentleman to come knocking on my door? Only the choice cuts go in the stew."

"I don't know how I got here."

"Donnnnnnnn't carrrrrrrrrre. You're losing me."

"Why would you want to kill me?"

"Why *wouldn't* I? You're eminently killable. Now, take off your clothes."

"What if I say no?"

Fermona frowned and sat back on her pile. Then she took out a sheet of paper the size of a large window and began drawing.

"Would you like to see your death matrix?" she asked.

"My death matrix?"

She turned the piece of paper around to reveal a simple line plotting:

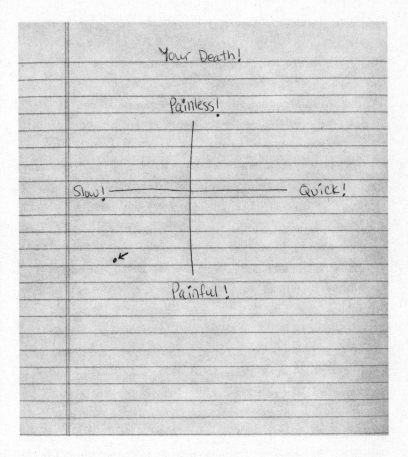

"You see that dot there in the left-hand corner?" Fermona asked him. "That's you, right now. You're practically off the chart already!"

"Oh."

"Now, if you want to die any other way, you should, you know, play ball. And I think you can do it. I think you can nudge that dot jusssssssst a bit up and to the right, okay? I believe in you. I'm not asking for much here. I just want to see you naked. Let's go. Clothes off. Hop to it."

Ben walked back onto the rug and began to disrobe: his boots, pants, jacket, sweater, thermals . . . everything but his underwear.

"Put all your stuff on my pile."

He left everything at her feet except his bag.

"You forgot something," she said.

Reluctantly, Ben took the bag off his shoulder and tossed it on the pile of booty.

"And your underwear, please."

"How could that possibly be necessary?" he asked her.

"This is strictly for evaluation. You shouldn't feel awkward about this at all. My gosh, you're not . . . *excited,* are you?"

"No."

"It's fine if you are. It's happened in the past, you know. Not a big deal."

"Yes it is, and no I'm not."

"Oop! Looks like someone's dot has crept a little bit farther off the ol' death matrix!"

"Fine." Ben dropped his underwear and exposed himself to the giant. She nodded solemnly and then gestured for him to put his boxers back on.

"See? That wasn't so bad now, was it? You're gonna be super happy we did that. This is gonna be great."

"What is?"

"Watching you fight! Now, you're pretty scrawny. We're gonna have to beef you up. You sure you don't want the stew? It's packed with protein. How do you think *I* got so big and strong?"

"I'll pass."

"Okay. Fine. Your choice. I'm not here to make you do anything you don't want to do, apart from a few extremely dangerous and potentially lethal things." She plucked a small burlap poncho off the pile and threw it at him. "There. That should be comfortable for you. I think you're gonna really enjoy the time you spend in my hole."

"Your what?"

"My hole! I have a *great* hole that just opened up a day or two ago. You're lucky you stumbled upon me when you did. Now let's get holing."

She clapped her hands and stood up, beckoning him into a darker, torchlit corridor that led them deep into the bowels of the mountain. He followed behind in his scratchy burlap gown. After a while, they came across a series of arched wooden doors on either side of the corridor. Ben swore he could hear muffled shouts coming from behind them. Fermona dug into her pockets, took out a set of clunky keys, and fumbled through them.

"After all these years, you'd think I would know which key opened which door, but here we are. This is just the worst."

"What kind of name is Fermona?"

"A beautiful one." She finally opened the door. "You've had a long day. Come on in. This is one of the more spacious holes."

Ben stepped into the doorway and saw nothing but black. The giant gave him a firm kick and he tumbled twenty feet down the steep side of the hole and onto the barren floor, rolling his ankle and crying out in anguish. Fermona posted a torch on the wall above and looked down at him one last time. She was smiling. There wasn't a hint of menace in her expression. She was the sunniest homicidal giant you could ever wish to meet. She batted a flap at the bottom of the door.

"Food and water come through here. Make sure you eat, or else I'll have to weigh you, and then kill you."

"Who am I fighting?"

"That's a surprise."

"What if I lose?"

"Then I eat you."

"What if I win?"

"Then I *don't* eat you."

"And I go free?"

"No. I just don't eat you. Let's not go crazy here, kiddo. Sweet dreams!"

And she shut the door on Ben and locked it tight.

# CHAPTER FIFTEEN

# THE HOLE

He had no concept of night or day. He had only the torchlight to go by, and if he stared at it long enough, everything around it started to flash bright white, and the flame itself became a black spot, eating deep into his brain.

He had suffered depression as a teenager, and the worst thing about it was that he knew when it was coming. He could feel the dread wafting in, a soft breeze through a cracked window. One little taste of the hopelessness and he knew that more was on the way. It was unstoppable. In human form, it would have been twice Fermona's size and just as charming. He was hopeless to resist it and, at times, he didn't even try. It was *seductive*, the way it urged you to stop caring. It could overpower him so easily, which of course was one more thing to be depressed about.

Like Teresa, Ben's mother was a night nurse at a local hospital. Her very *job* was despair, and she could tell when the depression was hitting Ben. He looked just like any of the terrified family members she saw sitting in hospital waiting rooms. Sometimes, after a twelve-hour shift, she would come home and find him in bed. And then she would take his hand and just hold it. No words. No orders. Sometimes she would stroke his hair and run her fingers along his neck. That was usually enough to get him out of bed and head off to school with the depression still perched on his shoulder.

Three times a day, Fermona would stop by the hole to open the door and dump some turkey legs and water down for him. Her visits were all he had to look forward to. She was going to murder him and suck on his bones, but at least she was pleasant about it. Neighborly, even.

On the seventh day, she opened the door and looked down at him.

"How are you?" she asked.

"Not good."

"Talk to me."

"My head hurts. And my knee. And I miss my family, although I know that bores you."

"No, no. I understand. Perfectly normal to miss your family when you know death could come for you at any moment."

"Right, yeah."

"Tell me about them. Your family."

"Well, my wife's a nurse."

"Noble profession. God bless her for that. Not easy work."

"Um, my daughter loves foxes."

"Ooh, I bet she's a little spitfire. Hang on. I might have something for you."

She left the door open and Ben tried scaling the wall of the hole to reach it. He was a bit stronger now, after a week of food and rest. His hand was scarring up, too. But it was no use. After four steps up the side of the hole, he lost his grip and fell back to the floor. Fermona poked her head back through the flap.

"Did you just try to escape?"

"Yes."

"That's fantastic. You're getting your strength back. You should be ready soon. Here . . ."

She threw down a plush fox toy. It was fat and round, like a beach ball, with two little ear flaps and four little balled paws. He could see the fox smiling at him in the darkness. Flora had a fox like this. She kept it in her bed at night, along with fifty-seven other small stuffed animals, each one arranged in a precise order. She slept with a Greek chorus observing her. Ben clutched the fox to his chest and wept.

"Thank you."

"Don't mention it."

Fermona closed the door and he lay back down on the ground, closing his eyes. The flashing white from the torchlight grew wider and wider behind his eyelids, glowing bright.

———

He opened his eyes and found himself lying on a hospital gurney. Cheap, thin sheets were covering him. *How'd you get here? You were just in the cave, weren't you? Cave? What cave? There's no cave. Don't you know where you are? You're at Ridgeview Hospital. Ridgeview, Minnesota.*

He sat up on the gurney. There was no scar on his hand. *But why would there be a scar? You never cut yourself. You're thirty-five years old and perfectly fit.*

Over on the other side of the room was a fat, bald doctor in a white lab coat, presiding over a table littered with assorted trinkets sealed in very small Ziploc bags. He looked over at the wall and saw a bunch of stainless steel doors, each one about the size of an oven.

*I know what kind of room this is.*

The doctor turned to Ben, looking surprised.

"Ah! You're awake. Good. Now you can give me a positive ID."

"A positive ID?"

"Yes, of course. You never did come and lay eyes on him, did you?"

"No. I didn't."

"Come on over here. I'll show you."

Ben got up. He was wearing a dress suit with no tie. The doctor waved him over to the table and showed him a handful of blackened objects spread out on a cloth: a gold ring, a watch, a pair of charred shoes.

"Do you recognize these objects, Benjamin?"

"Yes."

"Do they belong to your father?"

"Yeah. They do."

"Do you want to see his body?"

Ben shook his head. "I don't think I want to."

"Just for a second. Look at his teeth. Help me out."

"I can't . . . I don't . . ."

"You don't want be here, do you?"

"No."

"That's all right. No one ever does."

The coroner walked over to one of the steel doors and opened it. Ben felt the blast of icy air come from inside the refrigerator. The doctor reached in and pulled out a sliding steel tray. The corpse was covered in a blue sheet, with two blackened, crumbling feet poking out at the front. The toes were nearly gone. There was barely anyplace to hang the ID tag.

"Would you like to see the whole body, or just the face?"

"The face," Ben said. The coroner reached for the top of the sheet to turn it down. Ben braced himself, like he was ready to fend off a punch.

His father's head was pure anthracite. Nothing but dark bone.

There were some stray hairs left, but the old man's face had been fully incinerated. His teeth were his only remaining discernible feature, with one gleaming white incisor—the product of a dental implant—parked between its yellowing, nicotine-stained partners.

"Well?" asked the coroner.

"Cover it."

He did as Ben instructed.

"Is it him?"

"Of course it is."

"He died quickly in the blaze. Became highly intoxicated, dropped his cigarette . . . probably didn't suffer for very long, if that counts for anything."

"It doesn't."

"How do you feel right now?"

"I don't know."

"It's okay. It's okay to be *glad*. You're glad now, aren't you?"

"Don't put words in my mouth."

"He was a piece of shit, you know."

"Yeah. I know."

"Remember that boat he got after the divorce? That lousy boat of his?"

"Yeah."

"Remember those 'fishing trips'? You would beg your mom to switch shifts at the hospital so you wouldn't have to go on them. He'd send you out on that crappy white Boston Whaler to bake in the sun while he threw down can after can of Schmidt beer out on Halsted Bay. That old man barely ever put a hook in the water."

"We never did catch anything."

"And he always brought along those shady friends of his, remember? The burnouts, and the divorcees who spent every waking minute after 11 A.M. getting shitfaced at Lord Fletcher's. Nothing you hated more than that boat, right?"

"I did. I hated it."

"It's okay to be glad, Benjamin. You built a whole life for yourself even though he did nothing for you. Paid your way through school. Got a job. Got a wife. That was all you and your mother. You got everything you would ever need from him. And yet he still demanded you come out to see him. To that shitty apartment in Mound. It's okay to be glad that's all over: to have him *out of your way,* to know you can finally get on with your life. That's why you never bothered to come look at his body or go to his memorial, right? I bet you looked forward to him dying."

Ben started to cry. "I did."

"You were *hoping* he'd die."

"I was."

"Fell right off you when you heard the news, didn't it?"

"Yes."

"That's all right. Perfectly natural."

"No, it isn't."

"You have an appetite for grief like a cow's rumen, Benjamin. You have chambers inside you for all that grief and rage, don't you?"

"I do."

"Tell me: What would you do with all that space if it were empty? Aren't you tired of putting everything in there and leaving it?"

The coroner grabbed a scalpel.

"What are you doing?" Ben asked him.

"Let's free up some space."

"Get away from me. . . ."

"Let's see if we can get all that sadness out of you."

The coroner charged at Ben's abdomen with the gleaming blade and jammed it into his stomach. There was no pain, only a great easing. Everything went slack. His jaw went soft. His muscles unknotted. He exhaled as if doing so for the very first time.

————

He woke up in Fermona's hole. On the ground, three feet next to him, he saw a blackened lump. He reached out for it. It was a ring. His father's class ring, still covered in soot. He wiped the soot off and the pock-marked brass gave off a dull shine in the torchlight. Then he slipped it over his right ring finger.

He heard the flap in the door slap open and shut.

"Psst!"

"Who's there?" Ben asked.

"It's me, Shithead."

"Crab?"

"Shhh!"

"How'd you find me?"

"Gas station gave me directions. How do you think I found you, you nitwit? I snuck around."

"For a week?"

"Eh, I might have taken a few detours," Crab said. "Lotta good fish parts down on that beach."

"You let me stew here for a *week*?"

"I came back, did I not? Quit your bitching. You should have seen some of the other guys I found. You're the picture of health by compar-ison. Besides, I found something of yours on the beach. . . ."

Crab bolted from the door and then pushed an old water bottle through the slot. It was the same water bottle Ben had used to send the note to Teresa. But the scroll wasn't inside. *Maybe she got the letter somehow. Maybe she's summoning forensic experts as we speak to analyze the salinity of the water trapped in the paper, to pinpoint my exact location, with a joint Coast Guard/Navy convoy setting off on the high seas to rescue me from this mountaintop: gunboats and warships and fighter jets with impossibly destructive payloads. . . .*

"Another crab probably ate the letter," said Crab.

Ben looked up, annoyed. "I need my bag," he said.

"Where is it?"

"On that pile of crap the giant sits on."

"She sleeps on that pile, too."

"She does?"

"Sure as hell does. How am I gonna get the bag?"

"Grab it when she's asleep."

"Easy for you to say. She'll squash me like a bug if she catches me."

"What other option is there? I can't help you *get* the bag if I don't *have* the bag. You see my problem, Crab?"

"What's in it for me?"

"Nothing. Absolutely nothing at all."

Crab thought about it for a moment. "All right. I'll do it. Stay there."

Ben sank back down. A few seconds later, he heard the flap in the door. Another few seconds later, a flying backpack hit him in the back of the head.

"Ow."

"Sorry," Crab said. He was not sincere about it.

"That was fast."

"I'm not gonna take my time in there when the lady could wake up at any moment and stomp the shit out of me."

"You could have had me out of here *days* ago."

"I don't know what you're complaining about. This is a nice cave. I was wrong about it being boring. It's got mud, centipedes. . . . I could hang out here for a while."

"Shut up and make sure no one is coming."

"You're fine. She's still asleep."

Ben rooted through the bag and then let out a heavy sigh.

"What?" Crab asked.

"My boots. My boots and pants and jacket . . . those are still on the pile. They're not in here."

"So?"

"I need the boots to put on the crampons to climb out of here," Ben said.

"You're kidding me. I gotta go back and bring you more crap? That bag of yours was heavy!"

"Yes."

"What if she wakes up?"

"She didn't wake up the first time."

"Yeah but she *could* wake up this time, you asshole."

"I need the boots."

"You need a lesson in manners, is what you need."

Ben took the ice axes out of the bag and started climbing in his bare feet, jamming his toes into the crumbly dirt walls of the hole.

"What are you doing?" Crab asked.

"Coming up there so that I can kill you." Ben made it halfway up before falling back down again.

Crab looked down on him, a principal disappointed in his student. "I'll get you your boots. But you need to make me a promise, you whiny baby."

"What?"

"Don't give up. I know that's not easy given the fact that you're trapped in that fucking hole and she wants to kill you, but don't give up. No matter how long it takes. No matter *what* it takes for you to keep going. Promise me you won't stop."

"Why?"

But Crab didn't answer. Instead, he scampered away from the door and came back with a boot, the laces gripped in his tiny pincers. Then he left again and came back with the other boot, then the jacket, then the pants, and then the sweater. Ben put everything back on, including the boots and crampons. He was about to crawl up the side of the hole when he paused for a moment and took the phone out of his bag. The screen was dead and black. He tried to turn it on but nothing happened. He gazed up to the earthen dungeon ceiling.

"I know I said just that one time, but please . . . Please, let me see them again."

There was no answer.

Ben dropped the phone into the dirt and pressed a crampon spike through the screen, the glass shattering and the guts of it cracking up inside. Then he took the stuffed fox that Fermona had gifted him and put it in the sack instead.

He scaled the side of the hole effortlessly. His muscles had rebuilt themselves. Nagging pains aside, he felt fitter than he'd ever been.

"I promise you that I won't stop," he told Crab.

"Good."

"Let's go."

At the end of the dungeon corridor, he and Crab found a dead end. When they turned back and entered the main cavern, a very large and very awake Fermona was waiting for them. She had nothing but welcoming smiles for Ben.

"Well, I think you're strong enough to fight now!"

# CHAPTER SIXTEEN

# THE FIGHT

C rab buried himself in the dirt as Ben ran up to Fermona and planted one of the ice axes in her foot. She howled in pain as she pulled it out with one hand and smacked him down the stone hallway with the other.

"I'll have to make a new death matrix for you just for that. Some sort of z-axis."

"Fuck you!"

"You know, I've been more than nice to you, and I have yet to see that friendliness reciprocated."

"You want to kill and eat me."

"Well, *duh.* But who said that had to be a drag? I'm doing my best to make it a memorable experience for you. You've been a downer about it the whole time."

Ben held up his remaining axe. "I'll kill you."

"No you won't. But I like your determination. I think it's really fantastic that you're trying so hard. You should be proud of that."

"Go to hell."

"Try all you like, but I will overpower you. You are quickly running out of ways to make up for your surliness, so I suggest you give up now, and make the best of an unfortunate situation."

He dropped the axe.

"Good," she said. "Now gimme all that stuff again."

He threw her the bag and stripped down to his underwear.

"Your underwear, too."

"Come on."

"Drop 'em!"

He stripped off the boxers and she wadded everything up in her palm, which was the size of a kitchen table.

"These are going right into the fire," she said. "Sorry to inform you, but you've lost pile status. Now get back in the hole."

He walked through the door and slid back down the hole. Naked. Defenseless. She poked her head through the door and stared down at him.

"One man or five dwarfs?" she asked him.

"What?"

"Do you want to fight one man, or five dwarfs?"

Ben had no idea how to answer.

"You know what? Sleep on it," she said. "Tell me in the morning. I'm not gonna put a gun to your head over it."

She slammed the door and Ben was left in the pitiful torchlight. Ten seconds later, the door opened again. There was Fermona's big, jolly head.

"Oh!" she said. "They're unarmed."

"What?"

"The dwarfs. And the man. Either one you pick, they will be unarmed. And they possess average hand-to-hand skills, much like yourself. Dunno if that helps you winnow down your selection, but it only seemed fair to tell you. Adieu."

And the door slammed shut again. He lay down and curled into a ball. After a while, he pawed the dusty floor for the phone he'd smashed, just so he could curse at it again. There was a skittering coming from the hallway. Crab poked through the flap.

"Psst!"

"Hey," Ben said.

"She's burning all your stuff."

"Yeah, she said she would do that."

Crab crawled down the wall of the cave and rested in front of Ben's face, his eyes bobbing on their stalks. "What did she say to you just now?"

"She said I had a choice between fighting five dwarfs or one regular human."

"Wow, that's fucked up."

"Fucked up is my new normal."

"So which one are you gonna pick?"

"I have no idea. You said you went into some of the other holes?"

"I peeked around, yeah."

"And what did you see?"

"A bunch of sad, naked guys in each one."

"Did they look, you know, jacked?"

"Jacked?"

"Muscular."

"Not really."

"Did you see any dwarfs?"

"You're humans. You're all fucking enormous to me."

"Did you see anyone who appeared to be smaller than normal humans, despite being relatively large compared to *you*?"

Crab thought for a moment. "I'm not sure."

"This is some kind of trick. She probably thinks I'll take the dwarfs, but the dwarfs will all have the power to fly."

"Then pick the one man. Oh, but that could be a trick as well. He could have fire breath or something like that."

"You're not helping," Ben said.

"You were thinking out loud, so I started doing likewise, you prick."

"So who would *you* pick?" Ben asked.

"The one guy."

"Why?"

"Well, because it's *one* guy, isn't it? Only one set of pinky toes for me to clip off."

"All right, so I pick the one man."

"You know how to fight?"

"My wife taught me a little."

"Your wife taught you to fight? She cut your steak for you, too?"

"Shut the fuck up, Crab. So I beat the one man, and then . . . what then?"

"You're asking me?"

"Yeah. How do we beat Fermona after that?"

"I dunno, shitbird. Sounded like she was really big on killing you."

"There has to be a way. The path wouldn't lead me here just to have me get eaten by some giant."

"Why wouldn't it?"

"Because it just wouldn't."

"You're assuming there's a reason behind all this."

"I am."

"No offense," said Crab, "but you're a real sap if you buy that."

"Why don't you crawl up out of that door and go get fucked by a turtle?"

"That's completely unrealistic, anatomically speaking. That's not even something the turtle would *want*."

"Shut up and go away."

Crab slipped back through the door as Ben dug up the cracked phone and stared at the punctured screen. He was so used to grabbing at the thing that even now, with it busted and caked in filth, his first instinct was to pick it up and stare at it.

Minutes later, Crab was back.

"Maybe you don't beat her," Crab said.

"Come again?"

"She's a giant, right? She'll crush you no matter what. So maybe you ask her to help you instead."

"I'm not gonna do that. She's a cannibal."

"Doesn't matter."

"It matters to *me*."

"But if you befriend her, maybe she won't eat *you*."

"This is your strategy?"

"Yeah," said Crab. "I mean, it probably won't work. She'll probably impale you on a fork and then rip your heart out and then eat it like it's a chicken nugget. But hey, you never know."

"Go to sleep, Crab."

"I don't sleep. I'm a crab. I only lie dormant."

"Why don't you sleep?"

"Because things will kill me if I do. I need to be in a state of constant awareness. Even if you think I'm sleeping, I'm not. I'm saving my energy so that I can fuck you up. Heads up 24/7."

"Then lie dormant, or whatever it is you do."

Crab rested his belly on the lip of the hole and froze like a stone, his pincers folded. Ben rolled over onto his side and hugged himself for warmth. His determination came and went down in this pit. Those periods of steely resolve that welled up in him were usually followed by moments of sloth and despair. He was in one of the valleys now. *Search parties only search for forty-eight hours, you know. It's been much longer than that now. You're dead. Or the world is dead. Your family will never find you. You'll never find them. The time has come for shock to become grief, no?*

He wondered about the man he was going to have to fight for Fermona's pleasure. In his mind, he played a game of Guess Who? with a million face cards in little plastics slots. *Is your opponent blond? Does he wear glasses? Is he black? Does he wear a hat?* He slapped the cards down one by one until, via the process of elimination, he had his guess. Looked a whole lot like the man who punched him in the airport parking garage. He remembered telling Teresa about the incident after it happened.

"You're coming with me to the gym," she told him.

"It's fine. It's not that big a deal."

"Yes, it is." She sent the kids to her mother's house that weekend and dragged Ben to the ratty jiu jitsu place across the street from her hospital (Ben always found it telling that the two facilities were adjacent to one another), where she trained. She had gotten into fighting a couple of years earlier, right around the time she had that nervous breakdown after losing (killing?) a patient, and started to work out at the gym three times a week—either before a day shift or after a night shift—willing to write off the lost sleep as a sunk cost.

There, on a cheap gym mat that had whole chunks gouged out of it, she drilled him on arm bars and knee locks and other basic moves. He was fatigued after four minutes. Exhausted.

"Can't we just go back home and nap?" he begged her.

"No. *Focus.* What if you see this guy again?"

"What are the odds?"

"What were the odds that guy was gonna hunt you down and punch you in the first place? You learn this stuff so that you never have to use it."

She charged at him as if she were holding a knife. He responded by mimicking her first demonstration, pulling her lead arm across his body and holding it fast against his chest.

"Good," she said. "Now lock it."

"I can't hurt you."

"I'm a big girl."

"I don't want to."

"You can't waver."

She yanked her arm out of the lock and wrapped her leg around his. Then she shoved him to the ground.

"Focus!" she said. "What if this guy never stops? What if he keeps coming back again and again? What if you're so stunned by it that you have no defense at all? You need to be ready, Ben. Do you understand? Just *try.*"

"Okay," he said, out of breath. "I'll try."

"Good. Now get your hands up. I'm gonna punch you in the face."

———

He fell asleep in the hole. No visions. No coroner. No Annie from college. Hours later, Fermona opened the door and threw a bucket of cold water on him.

"Wake-up time!"

"Huh?"

"Special breakfast!"

She showered Ben in breakfast goods: cartons of hard-boiled eggs, boxes of sugary cereal, bunches of bananas, hot sausages, and a thermos filled with hot coffee. Then she rolled a gallon of water down the side of the hole. Ben feverishly unscrewed the cap and started guzzling.

"How are you feeling? Trim? Fit? I like watching you eat and drink. You do it with real gusto."

"When do I fight?" he asked her.

"Are you finished eating?"

"No."

"Then finish eating. We'll get you up here and struggling for your life in no time. It's gonna be fun. Lotta people are hesitant at first, but once you get into it, you really understand what it's all about, I swear."

"I don't believe you."

"Huh. Don't really care. Eat up, scarboy!"

She slammed the door shut. Crab came out of hibernation and crawled down to the floor, cutting open a banana and nibbling at it.

"You're gonna have to help me kill her," Ben said.

"Like hell I will."

"I assume she watches these fights intently. She won't be paying attention to anything else. Go into that pile and find me a weapon." There had to be a proper weapon in there, perhaps many: guns and rifles and knives and halberds and lances and long, curved, unidentifiable weapons designed to open up bodies and empty them out.

"There are no weapons in the pile," Crab said. "I've already rooted through it."

"A gun. All I need is a gun."

"A gun might not bring her down."

"A gun brings everyone down."

"There won't be one in there."

"Then find me SOMETHING!" he screamed at Crab. "Find me a way out of this."

"I already suggested a way out."

"On the off chance that you are wrong, look in the pile again. You made me promise to keep going. This is what I need to keep going."

Crab pushed the banana aside. "I'll turn up something for you."

"Thank you."

The door swung open again. Crab quickly hid himself. Ben envied his ability to disappear any time he pleased.

"Would you like thirty minutes to digest?" Fermona asked. "I'd hate for you to get a cramp."

"I'm ready now," Ben said. Fermona reached into the hole and plucked him out with her bare hand. It took no effort at all. Her palm was as thick as a mattress. Her fingerprints circled around in wide corduroy swales. It was quite a thing to be carried in the hand of another creature. He felt light, as if he were being swept away by a strong wind.

She set him down in the corridor and handed him a pair of white canvas shorts.

"You can wear these," she told him. "You shouldn't have to fight with your stuff hanging out."

"Okay. Where do I fight?"

"Oh, back in my living room, of course. Right this way."

She pushed him forward along the row of thick dungeon doors. He heard more muffled cries and moans. In the center of Fermona's main chamber, there was now an octagonal cage made of chain-link fencing. In the middle of the octagon was a 200-pound man wearing a Rottweiler's face as a mask, ears and all. Ben turned around and tried to run away from the cage. Fermona held him in place with her huge paws. It was like holding back a baby.

"You tricked me," Ben said to her.

"How did I do that? He's roughly your size. And his fighting skills, frankly, are pedestrian. Won his last twenty fights, sure. But there was very little in the way of showmanship."

Ben could hear the dogface laughing at him. The menace was back.

"Get in the cage," Fermona said.

"No."

"Don't be so defeatist. You can beat this guy. I have faith in you."

"You're sick."

"No, I'm not." She pointed at the dogface. "Now him? He might be sick. I mean, what *normal* person wears a dog's face like that? Something must have happened to him that just . . . just took away his *soul*, you know? It's such a shame that there are monsters like that in this world. I think you'd be doing us a real service by defeating him, and giving us a champion to look up to. A role model. Now hold out your hands."

Ben did as he was told. Fermona handed him a roll of athletic tape.

"For your fingers," she said. "It'll help protect them."

He wrapped the tape around his wrists and the meat of his palms. He taped his forefinger to his middle finger and his ring finger to his pinky, just like he did before football games. He hadn't forgotten anything about the ritual. Fermona walked over to the cage and swung the gate open.

"He won't attack until I ring the bell," she said. "First one to die loses."

Ben stepped inside and she locked the cage behind him. No escape now. He tried to contain his fear but it was already eating away at his mind and body. He could see Crab skittering out from the corridor entrance and along the side of the chamber. No one else noticed. Fermona went over to her pile and picked up a bell the size of the Liberty Bell. The peals rang out loud enough to make the limestone formations above tremble.

*Focus.*

"Go!" she cried. The dogface ran at Ben and, ever the running back, he juked out of the way and scampered over to the other side of the octagon. The dogface barely spoke. It only let out grunts and moans and horrid laughs, like an ogre. Ben slipped out of his way two, three more times.

"Come on!" Fermona said. "You're ducking him!"

"I'm thinking!" Ben cried.

"Punch while you think."

The dogface made another charge and this time Ben dropped to his hands and knees and rolled into the maniac's legs, cut blocking him. Then he leapt on top of the dogface and wrapped his hands around his throat.

"That's it!" Fermona yelled. "Now you're fightin'!"

Ben hadn't been in a real fight since the angry man had punched him, if that could even have been called a fight. He forgot how uncomfortable it was, how disturbing it was. He got into a fight in school once and wanted it to be over the second punches were thrown. It was an overbearing sort of conflict. Tiring, too. Exhausting. Fighting was the most exhausting thing in the world.

Ben pressed down hard on the dogface's throat and began yelling at him, like he was a cockroach Ben was trying to kill. "I fucking hate you," Ben seethed. "Fucking die. DIE."

But the dogface grabbed Ben's right arm and bent his forefinger backward. Once he was compelled to let go, the dogface acted quickly, slipping out from under Ben and whipping around him, standing up and holding Ben's arm fast to his chest, trapping Ben in an armlock. He pressed down on Ben's elbow and Ben could feel it begin to snap—the bones and nerves and tendons all on the verge of coming undone. Ben turned toward the killer and dug his free hand into his face, jamming his fingers into the dogface's eyes like he was gripping a bowling ball. He tried to rip away the dog mask and found it impossible to remove. It was either glued on, or it *was* the man's face.

He dug in deeper, pushing the dogface back and mashing his head into the chain-link fencing like he was trying to strain it through a sieve.

The dogface stomped on Ben's foot, then wheeled around and pushed him to the ground, jumping on top of him and exulting at his newfound positional advantage. He grabbed Ben's wrists and held them down to the ground, as if he were preparing to violate him. Then he laughed.

*"I've been waiting for this since . . ."*

Remembering another trick Teresa had shown him in that ratty gym, Ben brought his knees to his chest and lifted the dogface up in the air, then flipped him to the side and punched him in the face with a solid right jab, his father's class ring opening up a gash above the maniac's eye that half blinded him. The dogface shrieked in agony. Ben quickly held his left forearm to the killer's throat and punched out his other eye with the lethal ring. The bleeding dogface struggled and wheezed as Ben tried to keep every part of the man held fast to the ground. He needed more arms to pin the dogface down. Four arms. Maybe six. But the end was coming now. The struggle grew less and less difficult to contain. He could see the life give out of the dogface's eyes. Eventually, the dogface stopped moving entirely. Still, Ben pressed. He pressed so hard he could have taken the dogface's head clean off.

"Stop," Fermona said.

Ben fell off the man.

"It's over now," she said. She reached down into the cage, plucked the dogface's limp corpse off the ground, and bit his head clean off. As she chewed on the head, she tossed the man's body into the bubbling curry stew. Ben wailed in terror.

"Too hairy," Fermona said, picking at her teeth. "Such a pain to shave you guys down before eating." She saw that Ben was still inconsolable, so she knelt down by the side of the cage and reached in to stroke his head with her index finger.

"Ever kill anyone before?"

"No," he whimpered. It was true. He had never killed anyone.

Never came anywhere within orbit of killing anyone. This was not an act that was ever intended for him. There were no other covenants left for him to break.

"You did well," Fermona said. "You make a fine champion."

"Why are you doing this?" Ben asked.

"Because it's awesome. Don't you feel alive? I have one more surprise for you."

"No, please don't. . . ."

"I know I said you had a choice, but you actually don't. You're gonna fight five dwarfs right now."

"What?!"

She snapped her fingers and here came five men, all three feet tall. They rushed into the octagon and piled on top of Ben, biting his legs and twisting his arms and ripping away at his ears, attacking him like a pack of dogs. He tried to shake them off, but they were dense, powerful little creatures. And they were coordinated. Ben could hear them openly discussing which parts of him needed more punching and grabbing. *"Hey, this shoulder needs more work."* One man had indeed been the correct choice.

He was rapidly giving in to the pack of dwarfs when suddenly Crab came into the cage and shimmied around and over the mass of stubby, angry arms. He crawled up Ben's stomach and dumped a leather pouch on top of his chest. Ben freed his arms momentarily and opened it.

Inside the pouch were three hard seeds. Ben grabbed one and immediately slammed it down, praying a wolf wouldn't appear. Instead, there was now a gun in his hand. *Ohhhhh, a gun.* Just the sweetest, loveliest gun you could ever want to lay hands on. God bless guns. He had never become infatuated with anything as quickly as he became infatuated with that gun. He raised it and fired it into the air. The dwarfs instantly ceased their attack and backed away from him.

Ben stood, gun in hand. The door to the octagon was still wide open.

"Get out," he said to the dwarfs, and they readily complied, forming a single-file line and running straight down the massive stone hallway. He stepped out of the cage and turned the gun on Fermona.

"What are you gonna do with that?" she asked.

"Nothing," Ben said. "I don't wanna kill you. I don't like feeling what I felt just now."

"That little gun couldn't kill me anyway."

"I think it could. I think you're bluffing. I don't know much, but I know that little bullets can do big, big things."

She said nothing. Ben could have sworn she was about to break into a smile.

"I want you to set everyone in here free," he told her. "The men in the dungeon, the dwarfs, all of them."

"The dwarfs won't go," she said. "I don't even keep them in a hole. They have their own party room in the back. I don't know what they do in there and I don't *want* to know."

"Fine. Then set the rest of them free."

"Why would I do that?"

Ben cocked the hammer and smirked at her. Crab crawled up on his left shoulder, like a parrot would.

"Because it'll be awesome," Ben told her. "I think you're gonna be *great.*"

# CHAPTER SEVENTEEN

# THE SPLIT

Fermona crossed her arms and tapped her foot on the floor.

"Let me keep a few guys," she said. "I don't wanna have to start from scratch. It takes a lot of fuel to keep me going. I eat nine meals a day. Not grazing either. Usually a full man every time."

"No," said Ben, keeping the gun on her. "Let them all go."

"Fine."

She grabbed her keys and went into the back corridor. Ben could hear her unlock all the massive bolts and swing open the wooden doors. Moments later, a succession of terrified, naked men and women ran out of the corridor like rats scurrying down a subway track. They had all gone mad, babbling in incoherent tongues and sprinting past the lake, presumably out of the mountain. One man was so distressed that he jumped right into the bonfire underneath Fermona's cauldron. Ben covered his ears as the man screamed out in agony like the dog-faces that had been chewed down to nothing by the wolf at the base of the iron tower. The rest of the prisoners were gone before he could even wave to them.

Fermona stomped back into the cavern. Ben kept the gun held high.

"What do you want now?" she asked. "You cleaned out my pantry. That's not what good houseguests do."

"I want all my stuff," he said.

"I burned it."

"Then I need whatever supplies you can turn over."

She sighed and let Ben scavenge the pile for anything he needed to continue onward: boots, pants, clean socks and underwear, flashlights, shirts, a jacket, a paintball gun (any kind of weapon seemed useful to him), and pounds of nonperishable goods—cans of soup, packaged snack cakes, jars of pickled vegetables, and more. Then, when he was finished pillaging, she plunged a mighty fist down into the pile and pulled out the bag Ben had carried with him into the mountain.

"I did burn *most* of your stuff," she admitted. "But you can have this back."

She tossed the bag to Ben and he found the old hot dogs, the bottled water, along with the plush fox, smiling at him. Flora's fox. He nearly dropped the gun because he was so overcome at the sight of it.

"Thank you," he said, pointing the gun back at her.

"You don't need to keep pointing that thing at me," she said. "I get the gist, you know. I do something wrong . . . *gunny gunny shoot shoot.*"

He put the gun back down. "How do I get out of here?"

"Past the lake. Where the mental cripples went. Are you gonna shoot me?"

"Are you gonna eat me if I don't?"

"I'd like to, but there'll be more where you came from. And they won't be as stubborn about not dying as you are."

"So we're cool, then? Crab and I go, and you don't follow?"

"I was gonna ask," said Fermona. "What's with the crab?"

"I dunno," said Crab. "A few days ago I was asking him, 'Hey, what's with the freaky giant lady?'"

"Oh, he's got a smart mouth on him."

"If we leave here, will you track us down?" Ben asked her.

"No."

"Where did you come from?"

"What do you mean?"

"Who are your parents?"

"I don't have any."

"Do you know who the Producer is?"

"No."

"How did you get in this mountain?"

"I've always been here. At first, I was nowhere, and then POOF! I was here. And that's how it's always been, you silly little man."

"But how? Why?"

"I haven't the slightest idea. I simply *was*. What does it matter? I was happy here before you sent all my food running. When you're happy, you don't question how that came to be."

"What about the people you imprisoned? Where did they come from?"

"From the path."

"Did they tell you how they got here?"

"No. What do I care? Borrrrrrrrringgggggggg. If I'm not eating you, you're boring me. Like now! I'm bored now. And hungry. So go, before I put my grumpy pants back on and take that gun away from you."

"What's on the other side of the mountain?" Ben asked.

"I don't know," she said. "Unlike most people, I'm comfortable exactly where I am."

She pointed them through the cavern and past the eerily still waters of the underground lagoon. Ben could see rainbow swirls on the surface of the water spreading in every direction, like leaked gasoline. Past the lake there was yet another gaping mountain corridor, wide and tall enough to accommodate a locomotive. Ben backed into the tunnel slowly, his eyes still on Fermona as she let out an annoyed snort and sat back down on her treasure pile. The soft torchlight of the cavern faded away as Ben kept walking backward, Crab on his shoulder. Soon, he turned around and they were enveloped in wet darkness again, walking for miles through the heart of the mountain. Fermona never came after them. She probably could have taken that gun from Ben if she had really wanted to. He couldn't shake the feeling that she had *let* him win, but he wasn't quite sure why.

They made their way through the cavern and finally emerged into the daylight. Ben had to shield his eyes from the glare, but once he adjusted, he could see nothing but a flat, open prairie in front of him. The path sloped gently down the base of the mountain and into the warm, lush fields, lined on both sides by a wooden split-rail fence. Among the clovers and tall grasses and bursting dandelions, he saw herds of wild horses galloping across the grasslands. They were gorgeous animals, with slick auburn coats and visible muscles rippling everywhere. Two weeks ago, he couldn't have given half a shit about horses. Teresa was a fan of them. He thought horses were for rich girls and old men. But Christ, it was nice to lay eyes on them now. The fresh air and sunlight from the prairie acted as a kind of atmospheric Xanax, blunting his trauma, gently numbing the thought that he was now a killer. Not a murderer, per se. But he *had* killed a man with his bare hands. A young foal went up and nuzzled against her mom and Ben had to look away for a moment. It was all too much.

Off in the distance, he saw a house. The path ran right past it, but maybe there was a turn into it. He broke into a run, and Crab nearly fell off him.

"Hey! Watch it!"

The house sat fifty yards behind the fence. No driveway. No gap in the fence to walk through. It was just there, in the middle of the grass, with no surrounding infrastructure. It was two stories high (three if you counted the basement poking out from below), made of faded white-painted brick, with a red front door. Ben recognized the fuzzy brown couch peeking out above the living-room windowsill.

"That's *my* house, Crab."

"It is?"

It was very much Ben's house, down to the last detail: the shoddy black rails on the concrete stoop, the black shutters, the small section of the chimney that had to be knocked out and patched back up with fresh red brick, and the neatly trimmed bushes dotting the front—just the way Teresa's mom liked trimming them when she would come over and do some landscaping for kicks. It was all there.

And then the door swung open and there was his youngest child, Peter, in his little crocodile pajama pants and a red T-shirt with a rocket on it. He never changed out of his pajamas. Normal clothing was worthless to him. He would have worn pajamas to a funeral. Every effort that Teresa and Ben made to get him to dress properly was an exercise in wasted energy.

The boy looked like he had just been napping, his face all marked up from the creases in the sheets. His cheeks were red. He looked so warm and soft to hold. Peter grabbed a nearby garden hose and began to water the grass. The boy loved doing that. He could stand outside the house with a hose for hours, drenching the concrete. Now he walked around the airlifted residence, blasting away at the small front lawn and the flowers and the walkway, until everything was saturated and his feet were muddy all over. Then he turned the hose on himself and got drenched. He saw Ben and waved.

"Hi, Dad!"

Ben put his hand to his mouth, aghast. It was really his son.

"Peter?"

"Hi!"

Ben walked to the fence and leaned into it. Peter remained in the doorway.

"Can you come here?" Ben asked him.

"No, Dad. I can't go *there*. I have to stay *here*."

"Is anyone else in the house? Rudy? Flora? Mom?"

"No, Dad. I have to go back inside now. I'm alllllllll wet. You do work, Dad."

"Just come here for a second. Let me hug you."

Ben was standing on the lower rail of the fence now, leaning over. *Oh, why won't this fucking fence just go away?* He swung a leg over the top rail and now he was sitting on it, staring at his youngest child.

Crab whispered into Ben's ear, "Don't do it."

"Shut up, Crab."

"It's not real. It's bait."

"Shut up."

Peter smiled and waved to Ben. "I have to go, Dad!"

Ben was falling apart now. "Okay. Okay."

"Love you, Dad!"

"I love you, too."

Peter shut the red front door. Ben could see the top of his son's head bouncing across the bottom of the living-room window. He ran to the other side of the path and leapt onto the fence rail, screaming.

"FUUUUUUCCCCCCKKKKKKK!!!! God damn you, you fucking asshole shithead path! FUCK!"

"It's not real, man," Crab said.

"*This* isn't real!" Ben cried. "Every bit of this is an insane fiction, and now you're telling me I can't go and hold my son, MY SON, because he's somehow the only bullshit thing in it? What is this? Is it God doing this, Crab? I didn't even believe in God before this. I just figured if God existed, then He was an *asshole*. This only clinches it. This is cruel and vile, and I did *nothing* to deserve it. I never betrayed a friend, Crab. I never committed a violent crime. I loved my wife and family the way a man is supposed to love his wife and family. I waded through enough shit jusssssst to get where I was before I stumbled upon this godforsaken road. And even then, life was still *brutal*. I had bills and children and a sick mother. I don't even know how I've survived it. I don't know how anyone does. It was already a trial by fire. And now I can't even walk across that field and have *one* moment with my son? What kind of fucking animal God lets that happen? What exactly does He want me to prove? I'll kill Him myself, Crab. I will find this God . . . this Producer, and I will drive a knife right through His fucking brain."

He grabbed his bag and trudged down the road, still steaming. Crab followed along silently. After a time, Ben's house grew smaller on the horizon, until it vanished entirely. When he turned around and saw it was now gone, he took out the plush fox toy from his bag and clutched it to his chest.

"Are you all right?" Crab asked.

"No."

"Listen, there's . . ." Crab hesitated.

"What?" Ben asked.

"There's something up ahead."

"How do you know?"

"Just keep walking and I'll show you."

Eventually, they came to a grand split in the path, nothing but fences and prairies and horses either way. Crab jumped off Ben's shoulder and walked up to the edge of the fork.

"Which way do we go?" Ben asked him.

Crab turned to him. There was something different in his expression now. Crab was not his usual, well, *crabby* self.

"You have to go to the right," Crab said.

"Why is that?" Ben asked.

"Because *I* have to go to the left."

"Why do you have to go left?"

Crab sighed. "Because I've already been down *that* road."

And then it dawned on Ben. He felt like a complete fool. It should have been so obvious.

"Wait a second," Ben said. "You've been on this path before."

"I have."

"You're not just a crab, are you?"

"Very perceptive. The fact that I can fucking talk maybe clued you in."

"You were a person."

"Yes."

"What was your human name?"

"You don't wanna know."

Ben took out the gun and aimed it at Crab.

"I'm faster than that gun, muchacho," Crab said.

"Tell me what your human name was."

"Hang on. This is not easy for me . . ."

"SAY IT."

Crab quivered. After a long time, he looked down and said softly, "It's Ben."

"What?"

"Ben. My name is Ben."

Ben dropped the gun. He couldn't feel his hands anymore. He couldn't feel anything. His body began to wobble.

"It's not possible."

Crab reared up and traced his pincer down a faint, virtually invisible line under his eye. Ben had never noticed it until now.

"Ninety-seven stitches. We got ninety-seven stitches from that dog."

"Oh, God."

"I'm sorry, man."

Ben felt as if he had just been sentenced to life in prison. He was going into shock. Knew it, really. This was going to be the *least* painful part of finding out Crab's identity. The pain and despair would soon coalesce and then mushroom.

"What happens to me?" he asked Crab quietly.

"This."

"How long have you been on this path?"

Crab turned his back to Ben. "I can't say."

"Has it been a month?"

Crab wouldn't answer.

"A year?"

No answer.

"Five years? *Ten* years?"

Crab turned back around and looked at him with a pity that bordered on unbearable.

"No," said Ben, shaking his head. "Ten years?"

"More or less. I lost count."

Ben crumpled to the ground, flopping onto his back. The sky above was utterly empty. *He* was empty. His body, his mind, his whole history: All of it felt vacated.

"What happens to me for ten years, Crab?"

"I've probably told you too much already. And you promised to keep going."

"I can't. Ten *years*, Crab. Ten years and you can't even tell me if I get home."

"There's no point in doubting. It'll only slow you down."

"Did you find the Producer?"

"Still looking, kid."

"Why didn't you tell me all this before?"

"Because you wouldn't have made it this far if I had."

"How can you know we won't be on this path forever?"

"Does it matter? How long would you walk to see them again?"

"Forever."

"Exactly. There's no other way."

Ben stood up. "I'm coming with you. I'm going to the left."

"No. No, you're not. I didn't put in over a decade of suffering just to watch you short-circuit all of it."

"You can't stop me."

Ben charged to the left and bashed against an invisible barrier that kept him from continuing down the path. He smashed against the wall again and again but it wouldn't budge. And there was no going around it either, unless he wanted to leave the path and get himself killed. Now he was slamming against it out of anger, trying to *hurt* the bubble.

"It isn't easy to accept," said Crab. "I know that."

"You go to hell."

"This is where Crab left me back when I was your age. There's a certain way this has to play out, which means you can't take any shortcuts. Whatever you find down that road will prepare you for what's next."

Ben grew angry. "How do you know that at all?" he spat. "How do you know that following this little infinite loop serves me well? For all I know, you did this all fucking wrong. Look at you! You're a crab!"

"It's not all bad."

"How the fuck can you say that?"

"There are things I can do that other crabs can't."

"Like what?"

"You see me talking here, right? Ben, I believe in the path because I have no other choice. Like you told me, right? Remember, on the beach? You said the same thing. I have to have faith in it, even though I am now very much its prisoner, Ben. I have doubts every second but all I can do is move forward. And now *you* have to believe in the path, even more than you did before."

"What if I just run back to that house and hug our son and let death come? Why wouldn't I do that?"

"Because it's not real, and you know it. When I get to the end of this thing—and I will get to the end of it—I will see Peter again. Flora, Rudy, Peter, Teresa: I'll see them all. And it'll be real. I won't have to go looking over my shoulder, waiting for the hammer to fall. That will be *my* eternal salvation, and yours."

Ben began to cry. "Please don't leave me here. Don't leave me all alone. I have no one."

"You won't always be alone. You'll have company."

"Who?"

"You'll find out. But the first thing you'll need to do is go back to the giant."

"What? Why?"

"She can help you."

"She tried to kill us."

"Eh, you learn to forgive. Besides, there are ways of dealing with her. Take out the seed bag."

Ben did as he was told. Two hard brown seeds remained.

"Throw one of them down the next time you see Fermona," ordered Crab. "It won't grow if you do it now."

"What does it turn into?"

"That's a surprise. It'll make managing the giant a bit easier for you. You can always use the gun on her, too, if you have to do her in for good."

"I won't go back to her."

"Well, you don't have to do it *now*. You can have a snack first, if you really want."

"That doesn't make it any better."

"You can bargain with Fermona. Fun fact: She's only ever eaten humans."

"So?"

"Just think about it, and then you'll have your strategy."

Ben looked to the fork in the road. "Do I have to kill more people up ahead?" he asked Crab.

"Yes."

"I can't do that," said Ben.

"Yes, you can. You've already killed one man. You'll kill again. It's a slow burn."

He crawled up on Ben's shoulder a final time.

"Like I said, it's not all bad," he whispered.

"How can you say that?" Ben asked.

"I adjusted. You can adjust to anything if you're willing to live on. There's a tent lying to the side of the road a mile down or so. You'll see a castle past that, but you won't be able to get in it without going back to the giant first. When you need a break, just spend the night in the tent. You'll have your work cut out for you, but you can beat him."

"Who's him?"

"That's another surprise. But you can beat anything. I promise you."

He hopped down and waved a pincer at Ben.

"Do you want to take anything?" Ben asked him.

"I don't need anything. One day, you won't need anything either."

And then Crab passed through the invisible barrier like it was nothing, and scurried down the road that Ben would hopefully travel down himself a decade from now.

**II.**

CHAPTER EIGHTEEN

# TONY WATTS

B en sat on the path and watched Crab fade into the soft waves of buffalo grass. *What does it feel like to be a crab? Does it hurt? Will my brain get shrunk down to nothing? Will I stay a crab forever after that? I don't wanna stay a crab forever. Don't do that to me, God. Don't leave me that way.*

He was draining. He could stay there on the road until all the blood and fluid leaked out of his body, until he was flat as a pancake, and then his skin would slowly biodegrade, and he would become like shreds of an old paper towel: little bits that the wind could pick up and scatter about.

The peak of Fermona's mountain was still visible behind him. The walk back would take hours. And what about the house? What if Peter was outside again, playing on the stoop? If Ben saw Peter again, he would jump over that fence and be ready to die. He couldn't bear to go back. Not yet.

So he decided to sleep on it. Like Crab told him, there was no need to rush.

It took twenty minutes to walk down the gentle slope to the right and see the red tent collapsed on the side of the path. To the right of the tent was a small duck pond. In the distance, Ben saw the forked path carve out great big loops up a *second* mountain (another one?), across a series of natural arches, to a tall, black castle. The sun was setting now, and in the purple twilight, the castle's façade took on a menacing appearance: all sharp spires and peaked arches, as if it were made entirely out of fangs.

Suddenly, he heard a piercing scream come from the castle, like the sound of a man tortured. He looked up and saw the wings of a great and terrible creature unfurl from atop one of the sinister, barbed turrets. It was too far to make out its face or body. All he could see were those devilish black wings, stretching out wider than a house. They began to flap, kicking up a cyclonic wind behind them. Soon the creature, carrying something large in its hands, vanished behind the castle.

He felt an immediate need for shelter.

Once Ben had the tent staked and zipped open, he ducked past the loose flap and discovered that it opened into a library with cathedral ceilings reaching twenty feet high. Thousands of leather-bound volumes lined the dark-stained oak shelves. There was a small desk over in the corner, with a stained-glass lamp and a gold pen and legal pad arranged neatly on top of a green felt desk pad. Next to the desk was a king-sized sleigh bed with a white duvet. The duvet was fat and poofy, like a dollop of marshmallow fluff. The whole chamber looked like the library of an 1890s robber baron. Ben could smell the glue from the old book bindings lingering in the air.

He walked over to the desk and grabbed the yellow legal pad. His handwriting was garbage. Teresa always wrote the thank-you notes in the house, because his handwriting made everything look like a ransom note. But there were no laptops or tablets to use in this library, as far as he could tell. He took one of the pens from the slot in the desk pad and began writing as neatly as he could:

*Dear Teresa,*

*I don't know if you got my last note, but all I can tell you is that I've been imprisoned and I may stay imprisoned for a very long time. I don't quite know how to explain what has happened.*

Ben paused in the draft. *What would you think if you got a letter like that? You would think your husband ran off.* He threw the pen against the wall. Then he went back and retrieved it. Ben did this a lot with inanimate objects: throwing them or kicking them, and then trying to make it up to the object by fixing it or picking it back up and setting it gently back down. He was a serial object beater.

*Dear Teresa,*

*You aren't going to get this letter, but I'm going to write this to you anyway for the sake of my own sanity because something awful has happened. Just know that I love you. This terrible thing that's keeping us apart may keep us apart for a very long time. I know that you know, deep in your heart, it's not something I chose. I haven't fled. I haven't lost my mind. The path I stumbled onto accidentally is now holding me hostage in a faraway land. But I would never be away from you if I could help it. Never. Not for a day. Not for an hour.*

*I will come back. Stay where you are and hold on, because I will come back. I love you.*

*—Ben*

He drank a bottle of water in one gulp and stuffed the letter inside. When he walked out of the tent with the bottle, a nearby crow snatched it up from his hand and absconded with it. *Really? A crow?* The crow was probably delivering the letter to Satan incarnate. He went back inside, ripped off a sheet from the legal pad, and wrote DAYS at the top. Then he made fourteen marks. Tomorrow night, he would mark the fifteenth. Off came the boots and socks and pants and shirt. Ben set them by the bed and then slipped under the soft duvet, which swallowed him up and seemed to heal all of his superficial pains. He was resting inside a fog of opiates. Quickly his eyelids went limp and there was nothing but sweet, thick blackness.

———

He felt a nudge on his shoulder.

"Ben. Ben. You awake?"

*Was that Tony? Tony Watts? That's what Tony Watts always said anytime you slept over at his house. You'd just trade "You awakes?" until the morning broke and you hadn't slept at all. But that was twenty-five years ago . . . no wait, twenty years . . . no wait, five . . . no wait, what were we talking about? It's Saturday, right? You've been looking forward to this sleepover all week.*

Ben woke up in a tight, red sleeping bag. He was wearing striped boxers and a loose black Metallica T-shirt. They were in a basement. Not some magical tent library, but Tony Watts's mother's basement. Burnsville, Minnesota.

1990. Yes, the year was 1990. That sounded right. Ben felt around his body. He was younger. Softer. *No wait, you were always this young and soft.* No scar on his face. *But why would you have a scar on your face?* He turned and there was Tony, with the floppy black bangs, lying right beside him in a bag of his own.

"You awake?" he asked Ben again.

"Yeah," Ben said. "You?"

"Yeah. My old lady's asleep now. I gotta show you something."

Tony stood up and shook off the sleeping bag. This was how any thirteen-year-old exited one: They never zipped down and stepped out. They just stood up and walked out of the thing, like popping out of a shopping bag.

Mrs. Watts's basement was unfinished except for the small guest room the boys could use anytime Ben slept over. The guest room had everything they needed: two sleeping bags, a tape deck (Tony had the best tape collection. . . . Ben liked to crack open the cases and study the clear plastic cassettes, memorizing track times), a crappy TV, and a Nintendo console. Mrs. Watts let them bring down pizza and snacks and pop if they wanted, because she was cool like that. Tony's dad was always away, maybe for good. Tony said his dad was in the Middle East, inventing a new kind of Coke can that had a special insert that would turn the Coke ice cold the second you opened it. No refrigeration necessary. Ben thought that would be awesome.

Outside the guest room was a typical utility space, lined with a workbench and all of Mr. Watts's tools, which went unused for long stretches. There was also an old pinball machine over in the corner. They played it for hours at a time, so focused on the game that Mrs. Watts often didn't even bother to bid them goodnight during sleepovers. She would just leave them in their gaming trances.

But on this night, Tony wasn't interested in the pinball. He led Ben up the shaggy carpeted stairs and into the living room, over to Mr. Watts's liquor cabinet. Then he bent down and grabbed a bottle of clear liquor out of it.

"Peach schnapps," he said triumphantly.

"Whoa."

"That's not all." He reached in deeper and pulled out a flimsy plastic shopping bag, then held it open for Ben to see. "Check it out."

Black cats and bottle rockets. A whole *shitload* of them. They could blow up a car with that much ammo.

"We can't use them close to the house because my old lady will wake up," Tony said. "But we can go to the park."

"Shit, yeah."

Their sweatpants were still on the living-room floor, right where they left them. Mrs. Watts had been too tired to pick them up or to nag the boys to do likewise. They quickly got dressed and slipped on their sneakers (always pre-tied—the back of Ben's sneakers were ripped apart because he kept smashing them with his heel, trying to wedge his feet in without bothering to untie the laces) and Windbreakers.

"Do you wanna hold the booze?" Tony asked. It was an important question. The *most* important question.

"I'll hold the fireworks," Ben said. "You hold the booze."

"Don't drop the fireworks, yo. The ground's probably wet."

"I won't. Swear to God."

"All right. Shhhhhhh!"

They cracked open the front door. The Watts family cat didn't make a scene of it. Then they slipped out into the seemingly endless subdivisions of Burnsville. It was a utilitarian suburb. The rich asshole kids didn't live here. This hood was for the average white kids, and it went on for miles. You could walk block after block without ever hitting a highway or major boulevard. In this neighborhood, late at night, everything felt possible, especially to a thirteen-year-old.

At the end of Cobble Drive was a small playground shielded by a tiny creek and some woods. It would give them just enough cover. Along the way, Tony paused at a random house and ripped some flowers out of the ground.

"Watch this."

He stuffed the flowers into the mailbox and the two of them ran like hell down the hill toward the park.

"Dude!" Ben whispered. "That was fucking crazy."

"You gotta try it. It's fucking sweet."

So Ben did. Right before the park, he uprooted some more flowers and then threw them on the hood of a BMW parked outside a house. They couldn't stop giggling.

"Oh, man," Tony said. "That car is totally *shit on* now."

"Yeah."

At the park, Tony opened the bottle of schnapps. "You wanna sip first?"

"Nah, man," Ben said. "Your booze. You get the honors."

Tony stared at the bottle. "I dunno, man. My old lady will freak out if she notices."

"Don't be a puss. Drink it!"

"All right! All right! But when I give it to you, don't drink, like, *too* much. Like, my mom shouldn't be able to tell any was gone."

"Are you gonna drink it or not?"

Tony took a sip and made a face. "It's not bad!" he lied.

"Wow, you really drank it."

Tony passed the bottle to Ben. He hesitated.

"Do it, bro," Tony said.

"This is crazy, man."

"Who's the puss now? You gotta drink."

Ben took a swig. As first liquors go, it wasn't so terrible. He had sniffed his old man's vodka once and recoiled. But *this* . . . At least someone tried to give the liquor some flavor, you know? It really did taste like peaches. Now Ben was feeling mellow and loose.

"Dude, I think I'm fucked up," Ben said.

"Dude, me, too."

"This is so awesome."

Ben took a really big swig from the bottle. A Mrs.-Watts-will-notice swig.

"YO!" Tony shouted, grabbing at the bottle.

Ben was cracking up. "What? I just wanted a little more."

"You fucker."

"Pour some water in it. Your mom won't know."

"My ass, she won't. I'll have to pour some booze into it from another bottle." He swiped the bottle back from Ben and took a big swig of his own. Off to the side of the playground, there was an empty Coke can lying on the ground. Tony went over and picked it up.

"Is it time to fuck some shit up?" he asked Ben.

"Oh, yeah."

They loaded a dozen bottle rockets into the mouth of the can and twisted the fuses together. Then Tony took out a small cardboard matchbook that he had snagged from a complimentary basket at the local Perkins. He tried lighting three matches in a row, failing on every attempt.

"Shit, man."

"Lemme try," said Ben. He grabbed one of the matches and flicked it against his thumbnail. It blazed up instantly. Tony was in awe.

"Dude, how did you do that?"

"It's my little secret." He handed the match to Tony, who lit the megafuse. It burned bright and metallic and now the rockets were flying out of the can, whistling up into the trees and out into the field. They didn't expect the fireworks to be quite so loud. Thirteen-year-olds are poor planners that way.

Tony screamed out, "Holy shit!" and fled up the hill, with Ben close behind. They couldn't stop laughing. Ben looked back at the exploding can and could have sworn he saw a living-room light go on. They turned down a new street and the explosions died down. Then Tony took out the black cats, all neatly packaged together in one bundle, ready to light. They found a tin mailbox with nothing inside it.

"You do the honors this time," Tony said. So Ben did the thumb trick (he'd learned it from his old man), and then threw the lit bundle into the box, cracking up as they sprinted away from it. When it blew, it sounded like someone had dropped fifty pots off the side of a building. They were dying laughing now. Ben could barely run with his stomach muscles pulling double duty.

And then . . . *sirens*. They heard them and saw the flashing lights reflecting off the cheap aluminum siding off one of the houses at the top of the hill. Now they panicked.

"Oh, *fuck*," Tony said. "RUN!"

The sirens grew louder as the boys zigzagged through the hood, aiming for the darkest lanes to duck into. The cops were hunting them. At one point, Ben turned and saw the headlights of the cop car shining on him, boring into him like a pair of all-seeing devil eyes. Ben and Tony made one sharp turn and then another and then ducked between two small ranch-style houses on a darkened Lafayette Road and ran deep into the trees, deep enough to get Lyme disease five times over. They huddled behind a huge maple and sat there for minutes as the sirens grew closer and then more distant and then closer and then more distant again, with the occasional flash of red and blue light coming off the leaves. But after a while, everything calmed back down. The cops were gone.

"Holy shit, dude," Tony said.

And then they cracked up again.

Back at the Watts house, they performed an easily detectable bit of alchemy, pouring a small amount of vodka and cognac into the schnapps bottle and then pouring some rum into the cognac to make sure everything came out even, and then carefully replacing the all the bottles where they found them.

They were too full of adrenaline to sleep. They needed a few rounds of Nintendo for a cooldown period.

"Dude, I'd bang Jenny McDowell so hard," Tony said, mashing his controller.

"Me, too."

"How many thrusts you think you'd last?"

"Two."

"No way, dude. Not a chance. I wouldn't even get a thrust in. I'd just be *near* her, and then *thpppppppppp....*"

"Give yourself more credit."

"And what about Tina Hansen? Oh, my God, dude. Tina Hansen, dude."

Ben laughed as the two basked in their collective triumph. They had boozed and blown stuff up and no one had caught them doing it. They had pulled it off.

*Or had they? That's not really what happened that night, was it? You didn't get away. Quite the contrary. Remember? On that night, you two ran between the houses and past a Rottweiler on a chain, and then Tony screamed at it for kicks. Turned out the chain gave that dog a considerable amount of slack. So it jumped up and bit your face off. That's what happened. The animal pounced on you and mauled you, digging into your lower eyelid and ripping straight down. And you begged the dog to stop, praying it could understand your commands. You were screaming for mercy at the top of your lungs, and yet Tony didn't help at all. No, Tony kept running. In fact, Tony ran away even faster because he was scared the dog would attack him as well. Then the cops burst into the yard and shot that dog dead.*

*That's what happened. Remember now? You could feel your face being torn away until there was a loud POP and the Rottweiler slumped down on top of you, dead and bleeding. Remember how it filled your nose with its last few hot breaths? Next thing you knew, you were inside an ambulance, blind in one eye, the paramedics openly discussing whether or not you'd ever see out of the bad eye again. After the fact, the doctors told you that if you had arrived at the hospital ten minutes later than you did, they wouldn't have been able to save it. Ninety-seven stitches. They threaded ninety-seven coarse black stitches through you. Remember how prickly they felt? Your face was a cactus for five days.*

*The cops got Tony, too. They tracked him down and delivered him back to a very angry Mrs. Watts, who pulled Tony out of school the next Monday. Then the police cornered you in your hospital bed, asking you about the flowers, and about how much you had to drink. And they didn't give a shit about your face being ripped off either, because cops are dicks. There were gonna be lawsuits: against the Watts family, and perhaps against the police for killing the dog. You never saw Tony again after that, remember? That was the last night you two ever hung out together. That happened, didn't it? Wasn't that how it all went down? Wasn't this . . .*

Ben woke up in the massive tent library, his teeth clenched tight. He felt his face and drew his finger along his scar, which still remained. Next to his bed, he saw a half-drained bottle of peach schnapps.

# CHAPTER NINETEEN

# THE CURIOUSLY UNDEAD

That wasn't all. High up among the stacked shelves of ancient volumes that lined the walls, one faded book was sticking out, the kind you might yank on to reveal a secret passageway. Ben got out of bed—he felt oddly hungover—and walked over to the shelf. There was an old wooden ladder, mounted to a top rail, that slid back and forth across the stacks, so you could reach the highest shelves. He pulled it over and climbed up to retrieve the book:

*Dr. Abigail Blackwell's Gallery of the Curiously Undead.*

"Mrs. Blackwell?"

The tome was in rough condition—the pages tattered to the point of falling apart. But there was one page that was dog-eared. The spine cracked open to the marked page naturally, as if the book had been resting open on it for years and years.

It was a reference section, divided into categories: Lords, Sentients, Brainless, etc. He read through some of the descriptions on the page:

**Regenerators**—Normal-looking humans who have the ability to grow back anything that's been chopped off, including their heads. Cannibalistic.

**Smokes**—Small black clouds that have bright white eyes. Can roll over a man and asphyxiate him to death with their poisonous ash. Mute but highly intelligent.

**The Skinless**—Zombies who appear as skinless human beings. Deaf. Blind. Turn the living skinless merely by touching them.

**Jellies**—Gelatinous organisms that aim to absorb and smother.

**Head Spiders**—Spiders that possess human heads in the middle instead of a body. Possess a poisonous bite that causes paralysis. Once paralyzed, they slowly devour the body until only the head is left, which then sprouts spider legs. Brainless.

**Mouth Demons**—Vile creatures with multiple mouths all over their bodies. One bite from a Mouth Demon causes a mouth to grow where the wound once was. Brainless.

Each entry included strategies for killing the creatures involved, but here the text grew faded and illegible at certain points. He could make out only some of the defense techniques. Regenerators, the tome said, could be killed only with fire. The Skinless could only be killed by throwing salt on them. The Jellies were vulnerable to hot liquids, even plain hot water. And the Head Spiders had to be stabbed, or doused in a mix of "thyme and gingerroot and monkfish liver oil." Stabbing seemed easier. Mouth Demons needed their mouths filled with something, but the ink disappeared before Ben could figure out what that something was.

But the entry that really caught Ben's attention was the description of a creature named Voris.

Lord. Eyes are pitch black, save for the pupils, which Voris can use to shine a light bright enough to burn through virtually any living being. Winged. Bloodless, but possesses skin so hot to the touch that it can cause victims to burst into flames. Will kill or possess any human who gets in his way.

*I just saw something that had wings come out of that castle.*

The only way to kill Voris, the book said, was to kill him in his sleep by feeding him a "glowing solution." A poison. Ben looked at the ingredients:

- Curry powder
- The dead tissue of another undead being
- The dead, stewed tissue of a human

The next ingredient on the list was illegible, but the final element of the poison was not:

*A drop or two of peach schnapps.*

Ben dropped the book onto the floor.

"Oh, God."

He knew a place where he could find curry powder. He knew a place where he could find the dead, stewed tissue of a human. He knew exactly where he needed to go, and he remembered the seed bag and the hint Crab gave before deserting him:

*She's only ever eaten humans.*

———

Back to Fermona's mountain he went, with the book and the tent tucked neatly into his bag. There was one merciful part to retracing his footsteps: The mirage of his house was now gone. He didn't have to watch Peter spraying the lawn in his jammies and drenching his own shoes, laughing gaily all the while. Whoever put him on the path had spared him that torture, and for that he was grateful.

As he reached the mouth of the cave, he realized that he hadn't seen the split in the road where Crab had left him. The other path was gone now.

He walked briskly into the mountain, through the corridor. This would not be his last time inside Fermona's cave. Not at all. He would have to come back once more. Three times in here, with the torchlight and the musty floors and the smell of simmering human bones. Three times was too many. He took one of the seeds out of his small leather pouch and pocketed it.

She was sitting on her pile, filing her nails. Ben could see the sloughed-off bits snowing down to the floor. The cauldron bubbled. Her eyebrows went up at the sight of Ben. As she stood, her mammoth shadow swept over the chamber like a storm system.

"Oh really," she said. "You again?"

"I need you to do me a favor," Ben told her.

"A favor? HA! Bring back my livestock and then I'll do you a favor, you poacher."

"I won't do that, but I will make a trade."

"What is it that you need from me?"

"Some of that stew you made."

"Ooh, you wanna try it now!"

"No. I don't want to try it. I need it."

"Well, I need it, too. You've left my cupboards bare."

"I don't need much."

She crossed her arms and tapped her enormous foot, considering it. "Very well."

She bounded deep into her dungeon and returned with a clay pot the size of a steamer trunk. She set it before Ben, and then grabbed a ladle the size of a shovel from the cauldron and began dumping the stew into the massive pot. The curry powder in the stew smelled good, which frightened him.

"I don't suppose you have a smaller vessel for it," Ben said.

"Oh, the pot gives it flavor. You store humans in it long enough, and it seasons the clay. That's the secret."

"I didn't need to know that."

"Don't be such a prude about it."

Ben took a pickle jar out of his bag and dumped the pickles into the bonfire, then held the jar out for her.

"That's all you need? A pint?" Fermona asked.

"Yes."

"Oh." She let a couple of drops from the ladle fall into the pickle jar, spattering Ben's hand and burning him.

"Sorry," she said. She seemed to mean it. "Let me get a towel to . . ."

"It's fine," Ben said curtly. He added a couple of drops of the schnapps to the jar. Three ingredients down, two to go.

"Hey!" she said. "You're messing with the flavor profiles."

"It's not for me."

"Where's that crab you were hanging out with? Your little accomplice."

"He had to go ahead."

"Where?"

"Back home to Maryland, where my family lives."

She licked her lips. "More humans? Are they nice and fat and fleshy and well confined?"

"Don't get any ideas."

"You owe me more food. Why, this cauldron will only last me the month! And what then? I'll have to go down the mountain and cook up old parts. You know how long it takes to get those parts tender? You said you were here to make a trade. You better produce something."

He dug into his backpack and held out a can of tomatoes. Fermona stomped her foot and fumed at him.

"I gave you those from my pile, you little weasel!"

*Meat. It needs to be meat.* Ben panicked and scoured through the bag as the giant grew more impatient and angry. Suddenly, he spotted one of the old packages of hot dogs he found at Annie Derrickson's campsite. He held it up for Fermona.

"What are those?" she asked.

"You ever eaten cow?"

"I have not."

"These are sausages made from cow," Ben told her. "They're very good. I eat them myself."

"If it's not people, I don't want it."

"You know what? I don't think you've ever tried any food that wasn't people."

"I have so!"

"Okay. What was it then?"

She paused for a moment, thinking. "Well, the stew has coconut milk in it."

"That doesn't count. I don't even think you *like* eating people all that much. You said it yourself: They're hairy."

"I'm not eating your weird cow tubes, dear. They don't look natural."

He held out the pack. "They're hair free. Just try expanding your palate for once. I have children who are picky eaters, like you. And we don't make them eat anything they don't want to. But we do ask that they at least try a bite before they say no. Just one bite."

"Just one, eh? These better not be poisoned."

"They're not. I mean, they have nitrates in them, which aren't great but . . . You know what? I've probably said too much. They're fine."

"And you promise you won't come back here with that stupid gun of yours?"

"I swear it," he lied.

She grabbed the package.

"Take the plastic off first," he told her.

She ripped open the little package of franks with her fingernail and the water inside dripped onto her foot.

"Ew! There's water in this!"

"I'm sorry about that. Hot dogs are always packaged with a bit of water."

"These are made of dog?"

"That's just an expression."

She tried one. A second later, the whole package was gone. She held her hand out. "More."

"Oh, you like them?"

"More. More more more."

"I have more in my bag."

"Then gimme the bag," she said.

"I'm keeping the bag."

"I want the bag."

"Stay where you are."

"Bossing me around in my own cave? I won't have it!"

She started walking toward Ben. He quickly reached into his pocket. When he slammed the seed on the ground, he saw a tranquilizer gun with a note taped to it.

*SHOOT YOURSELF.*

Fermona closed in.

"I've been too nice to you. I think I'll take your magic food bag, and then eat you anyway."

Ben grabbed the tranquilizer gun, turned it on himself, and aimed it at the meaty part of his thigh. Fermona was so baffled that she paused for a moment.

"Hey, what are you doing with that?"

He squeezed the trigger and the dart from the gun hissed into his leg, stinging him. Now he doubled over and grasped at his thigh as the skin around the puncture wound began to swell. Suddenly, he felt full, like he had just swallowed a hippo. His fingers began to elongate. The hair on his head unspooled, as if released from a kite reel. He could feel his arteries dilating, his limbs growing thick and long. The swelling on his thigh metastasized throughout his body, as if an army of wasps had descended upon him and stung every square inch of his body. His liver swelled. His head swelled. His genitals swelled. He grew and grew and grew until the floor beneath him had shrunk down considerably.

When he stood back up, he was twenty-six feet tall, his clothing and his bag growing with him. Fermona stared at him in wonder.

"Goodness gracious!" she cried.

"I think I'm still shorter than you," Ben said, dazed.

"HA!"

There was no more time to recover from the shock of his transformation. He dug into his bag and took out the real gun, now large enough to mount on a battleship.

Fermona backed away. "This has all been a terrible misunderstanding. . . ."

"I'll give you the hot dogs, but I need to rummage through that big pile of yours in return."

"Only if you promise to never come back here. Do you promise?"

Now, Ben wasn't much of a liar. He had neither the creativity nor the energy to lie. He didn't even like playing pranks, because keeping the lie up wore him down so quickly. Tony Watts could lie his face off, especially when he had to tell the police that no, he had never provoked that dog. Ben wasn't skilled enough to lie like that.

But that was before all this, before the path kidnapped and coarsened him. *Much easier to lie in a world that doesn't seem real to begin with. Maybe Crab was wrong. Maybe his path won't be exactly the same as yours. Maybe you never have to come back here. Yeah, that's it. That's not out of the realm of possibility.*

"I promise," he told her.

"Good. Now make with the cow tubes."

Ben grabbed the second hot dog package from his bag and tossed it at Fermona's feet. They were the size of logs now. She clapped her hands in joy, like a child.

"Take anything you want," she said, "and then go away."

Ben knelt down by the pile and rooted around, grabbing more packaged food that the giant had ignored, along with bags of sand and iodized salt, now as small to him as beanbags. As he scavenged, Fermona guzzled some extra stew from the clay pot. He could hear her smacking her lips, moaning with satisfaction, spitting out the occasional stray bone. He was nearly ready to retch on her carpet again when she stopped feasting and called out, "I'm finished!"

He turned around. Fermona was wiping the sides of her mouth with a dress strap.

"You missed out on a good batch," she said.

"I'll take your word for it."

He grabbed two torches off the wall and snuffed them out.

"Hey!" she cried. "I only said you could take from the pile."

"You said I could take anything I wanted. I want these."

"Bah! You'll clean me out of house and home if I let you. Just like a giant to think he can do whatever he pleases."

"I'm finished. I swear."

"Then get out."

"One more question . . ."

"Going back on your word already, eh?"

"Have you ever heard of a creature named Voris?"

That caught her by surprise. "Where did you learn that name?"

"From a book. Do you know him?"

"In the dungeons," she said, "some of the people I've found, they would say that name—Voris—over and over again. Didn't mean a thing to me. It meant quite a bit to them, though. But then I would eat them and they wouldn't cry about it anymore."

"So you don't know who Voris is?"

"Nope. But I bet you get to find out. Oh, that's gonna be so fun. I almost wanna come with you, to see your face when it happens."

"But you won't."

"No, I won't. I'm precisely where I should be. Maybe you'll find a place like this for yourself one day."

"Maybe."

"Or maybe this Voris will kill you and rip your guts out. You just never know!"

"Yes, thank you for that, Fermona. Good-bye."

"Good-bye! See you never."

He slung his backpack over his shoulder and turned back down the mountain tunnel. Back to the castle, on a path that would return to this very mountain again one day.

But first, Voris awaited him.

# CHAPTER TWENTY

# THE CASTLE

He walked between the split-rail fences, his new size making the journey considerably shorter this time. The horses looked like squirrels beneath him. The ground itself felt bouncier. No wonder Fermona was always in such a cheery mood. Being a giant felt fantastic.

The house never materialized again, allowing Ben to push his family out of his mind, if only for a moment. Pining and yearning would do nothing for him now. He would have to be like a reporter dropped into a war zone, in a place to observe it, but not *of* it. Maybe he could keep it together if he was clinical about his plight, if he acted as if he elected to be there for a work assignment. *Be at a remove. Be analytical, distant, unemotional. Keep yourself busy and the burden of time eases.*

But thinking clinically wasn't going to be easy for him. The shock waves were wearing off, the dread laid bare. There were so many years left to go, the mere thought of them heavier than pure lead. He ruminated on the final, terrified utterances of Fermona's victims, some of them crying out the name of the creature up in the castle ahead. *Maybe they were also lost on this path and Voris was the fate that awaited them. Maybe Voris is the Producer and this path feeds him his* victims. "*Eyes are pitch black, save for the pupils, which Voris can use to shine a light bright enough to burn through virtually any living being.*"

As he got closer to the castle, Ben smelled something faintly metallic. One of the tiny, wild horses came galloping over and gazed at him from behind the fence, a trail of blood running down its chin. He reached into his bag and pawed his gun.

He bypassed the stallion and hurried to the foot of the winding, arched road leading up to the blackened castle. Between the rocky cliff edge where he stood and the massive castle gate was a moat sitting a hundred feet below. It ran blood-red, as did the nearby pond. A bevy of purple swans cruised through the moat, the blood dampening their feathers and slicking them black. The air reeked of iron. Ben hiked his bag higher up onto his shoulder and began the hard trek up the walkway, stopping in the middle to sit and rest, letting his legs dangle off the rocky arch. The purple swans passed under the arch and dove into the blood, emerging again and turning rust brown. Up ahead, the walkway came to an end at a large gap, with a raised heavy wooden drawbridge blocking the castle entrance on the other side.

Ben buried his head in his hands and rubbed his eyes hard, as if he had shards of glass stuck in his irises. His body was altered now. In a few years, he would find himself in another altered form, perhaps with many transformations to be experienced in between. There was no guarantee he would, at the end of this, revert back to his normal size, his normal proportions, his normal *self.* Maybe there was a wheel of fate with a cutout of his stupid head pasted to the center, with all his possible new body types crudely marked all around it, and someone Up There was spinning it at random intervals just for the pleasure of watching Ben grapple with becoming a giant, a crab, a centaur, a dishwasher, a loaf of bread. Nothing about this land was permanent, not even him.

The only concrete thing he had was his memory. He dug into the backpack and grabbed the legal pad and pen, which had grown with his bag and his body and remained perfectly usable. He tried to sketch his family, going from the memory of the photo from his phone. He could see it clearly in his mind: the table at Chuck E. Cheese's, Flora's purple fleece jacket, Teresa awkwardly rubbing her wedding band.

But he couldn't draw it. Teresa was the artist. In her limited spare time, she would paint wonderful things: vivid landscapes; chestnut horses with shimmering, muscular coats; harrowing self-portraits. She knew all about light and shadow. She could see the composition of things that Ben couldn't. He drew like a kindergartner who'd been asked to sketch a murder suspect. The more detailed he tried to be, the worse the portrait looked. Hilariously so. Flora would have made fun of this most recent attempt relentlessly. She would have looked over his shoulder and, with characteristic bluntness, told him, "You are not good at drawing, Dad."

He laughed. He could forge memories like this now. He could put himself back in his house and daydream about Teresa and the children and make those daydreams feel like real remnants of his past. This kind of daydream was the precise opposite of life before the path, when he would sit at home with the kids losing their minds and imagine fly-fishing alone in some fucking river somewhere. All the fantasizing was reversed now. The most mundane things seemed so remote and foreign.

Ben crumpled up the paper and tossed it off the bridge. Just before it hit the standing blood, another crow (or the same one?) swooped in and grabbed it. He wadded up another sheet from the pad and chucked it at the bird, but missed.

The castle gate beckoned. He came to the considerable gap between the end of the rock bridge and the narrow ledge under the gate and looked down into the stillness of the moat below. God only knew what happened to you if you fell into that pool of chum. *Is that where the Jellies were? Or the things with the mouths?*

He leaned over the span and pressed his hands against the castle wall. It was an awkward position. If he stepped clean over to the ledge, he'd have no room to pull the drawbridge down without his gigantic body getting in the way. So he dug his thick right hand into the top of the drawbridge, braced against the wall with his other hand, and then ripped the bridge back down toward his feet, regaining his balance at the edge of the span as the chains went taut and the bridge slammed down onto the end of the walkway in front of him, just narrowly missing his toes.

Past the drawbridge lay not a stone chamber, but a set of glass double doors, each eight feet high. The windows were tinted, so Ben couldn't see inside. Yellow stickers that said CAUTION: AUTOMATIC DOORS were plastered on both sides. They looked like hotel doors.

Ben was just about to step onto the drawbridge when suddenly the chains holding it began to creak and moan. The bolts keeping the right chain fast to the stone castle wall came flying out, and the chain smashed down onto the wooden bridge with a heavy THUD, splintering the wood and sending bits and pieces of it down into the blood moat below. Soon, the entire bridge began to crumble and fall, heavy shards of oak plunging down and smashing the bevy of purple swans. The part of the bridge spanning the gap was all but gone now, the swan bodies floating on the surface of the plasma. All that was left was the small ledge in front of the automatic double doors.

Inside his bag was the extra-large can of whole peeled tomatoes that Fermona had initially rejected. Ben took out the can—the label boasted that the tomatoes contained "extra lycopene"—and squeezed it into his mouth, like he was drinking from a juice box. Then he tossed the can into the moat, took ten steps back, and ran toward the expanse separating the arch and the castle gate, jumping as far as he could.

He smacked right into the double doors upon landing and had to carefully regain his balance on the rebound to keep from plummeting into the gorge below. Just as he was steadying himself, he doubled over in pain again, turning away from the castle walls and clutching at his leg. Everything went taut: his skin, hair, fingers, and toes. He felt as if he had become a fist. His mighty giant hair spooled back into his head. He slumped down on the narrow ledge as his chest and stomach and legs and arms shrank back down, the serum from the gun wearing off.

He was six feet tall again, which would have been a welcome development except that all his writhing and spasming had caused him to roll right off the mountain.

He grabbed hold of the ledge just in time to avoid falling into the red abyss. His hands were in better shape now, but his full body weight was bearing down on them and he could feel his fingers getting sweaty and losing friction. He was slipping away. In one desperate motion, he pulled himself up and swung his foot onto the ledge as all his hand muscles cramped and seized.

The doors in front of him parted silently to reveal a stark, modern hotel lobby: pristine white marble floors, black light fixtures, a large black fountain in the center of the lobby with water falling down the sides of a black granite cube, and a series of elevated tables with sleek black bar stools. Two escalators ran up to a generic white mezzanine.

Ben swung his other leg over the ledge and rolled to safety, gasping for air as he gazed into the lobby. At the back, to the right, there was a long white counter with a short old man standing behind it, staring at Ben but not saying a word, never blinking, not offering to help the traveler lying prone at the hotel's doorstep.

Eventually, Ben got up and walked inside, the doors sealing shut behind him. When he pressed down on the floor mat and waved his arms around, the doors failed to reopen. There was no leaving the hotel now.

# CHAPTER TWENTY-ONE

# THE HOTEL

H e was just a man once more, everything about him now in correct proportion to his environs: his body, his clothes, his bag. It was vaguely disappointing.

Between Ben and the clerk was a small, circular stone table with a fruit basket sitting on top: complimentary apples and pears and oranges. He grabbed an apple on his way to greet the creepy old clerk, who looked like a wax figure: his face caked with foundation makeup, each strand of hair on his head discernible to the naked eye, occupying its own little patch of real estate on his pale scalp. He looked as if he had been crafted by a twisted dollmaker. Ben approached him with caution.

"Hello?"

The clerk said nothing, and instead reached into a drawer to pull out a plastic key card, the kind you find in any twenty-first-century hotel. He placed it against a magnetic reader until it beeped, then bundled it inside a little pamphlet and scribbled a number—906—on the inside in blue pen. He left the Wi-Fi password space blank, then slid the pamphlet over to Ben.

"Is this my room?" he asked.

The clerk answered only with a leering half smile. There was a bank of elevators behind him to the right. He pointed Ben toward the bank, but Ben wasn't in a rush. The lines demarcating the path were gone now. He had free rein to explore the hotel as he pleased. To the left of the cube fountain was a sleek, open lounge with a full bar. No one was there. No bartenders. No patrons. There was a smattering of tables, but all of them were covered in overturned dining chairs, as if service had ended. Ben walked up to one of the place settings and unfurled a cloth napkin, watching a fork, a spoon, and a thick steak knife all tumble out. He grabbed a second bundle from another place setting and tucked it into his backpack. The clerk, who remained conspicuously silent, slowly ambled over behind the bar and rested his frail, rotting hands on the cold marble countertop.

The bar, apparently, was still open. Whatever this place was, it at least had better liquor laws than Pennsylvania.

Ben walked to the bar and hung his backpack over a stool. He didn't bother asking for a double rye. He knew the clerk wasn't going to ever speak. Ben pointed at the bottle and held up two fingers. The clerk nodded and filled a tumbler. Then he dug up a scoopful of ice and held it over the glass, awaiting further instruction from Ben. Ben held up one finger and the clerk let a single rock fall into the tumbler, then placed the drink on the bar. He stared at the glass until streaks of condensation ran down the side, pooling at the base and forming a suction ring.

"Money?" Ben asked.

The clerk shook his head. Ben dislodged the tumbler from the wet bar and took a sip. It was real booze. No tricks. No poison. Real, honest-to-God booze. His socks were digging into his ankles and now even his leg hairs were sore, like wearing a snug baseball cap for too long. His body and mind moaned with every blissful sip. It tasted like home in the wintertime.

He gestured for a refill. The clerk obliged.

At the far end of the bar was another set of tinted double doors. After a couple more sips, Ben stood up and walked toward them, then looked back at the clerk for approval. The clerk gave a nod and Ben stepped onto the floor mat that made the doors slide open automatically.

Outside, he came upon a flagstone patio. In the center of the patio was a small, black-tiled pool with deck chairs arranged in a rectangle around it. Rolls of complimentary towels were stacked on built-in shelves over to the side. To the right of the pool was a raised fire pit, made of stone, with a circular slab running along its perimeter for bench seating. The pit was surrounded by wrought-iron outdoor furniture with firm cushions and little side tables where patrons might rest all manner of fruity, fifteen-dollar cocktails.

The entire patio was enclosed by a black aluminum rail fence that was five times higher than Ben was tall. In the distance, he saw that the patio overlooked a vineyard at the base of a series of rolling, sunbathed hills. It looked like paradise: the fat grapes hanging in bunches from vines that were held up by wooden stakes. (*Stakes, eh?*), the wizened olive trees that dotted the hillside, the way the fading sunlight seemed to embrace all of it and give it a visible aura. He walked to the fence and grabbed one of the cold rails with his free hand, the second rye cocktail in his other hand nearly finished. He wanted a third. He wanted a hundred.

The clerk was outside now as well, perched by the double doors, which remained open to the hotel lobby. Ben took a final sip of his whiskey and then grasped the fence with both hands, bracing his foot on the rail, ready to climb. He looked to the clerk for approval.

The clerk shook his head.

So Ben picked up the tumbler and gave it a shake. The clerk nodded and went to get another refill. The sunlight faded to purple and Ben looked down into the stone fire pit, which was filled with tiny blue rocks and had two small gas pipes jutting out. When the clerk returned with a full drink, Ben pointed to the fire pit. The clerk nodded once more and walked over to a white switch on the side of the patio. The flames kicked up and toasted Ben's skin the way the liquor toasted his insides. He slumped into one of the chairs ringing the pit and gazed into the fire. He didn't want to think about Annie Derrickson, but he couldn't help it. It was okay now. A few drinks always made it okay to put guilt aside for a moment.

Then he thought about Teresa and the children. No SWAT team or Special Forces agents had found him. They wouldn't find him, of course. They could sweep every square inch of the Earth and not find him. *Maybe they had a funeral already.* He hadn't had time to write a will or make any sort of proper burial request. He was at that age where he used work as an excuse to put off other pressing matters, like personal finances and filling out life insurance forms. He preferred making the small amount of money he made to figuring out how to take care of that money.

But Teresa would know what to do. She would be practical. After the proper amount of time had passed, she would accept that he was gone, and then hold a small memorial service in their home, with platters of sandwiches and bowls of dip (she made excellent dips) set out for the bereaved. She would keep her shit together until everyone had cleared out of the house, and then she would cry and wail privately, just to herself. After a year, maybe she would begin dating again.

Maybe she would get married. The kids would have a new dad. And slowly, they would all forget about Ben, wouldn't they? Life would move forward, without him. He didn't want to be gone, but now he was. Just like *his* worthless old man. A whole new ecosystem would soon grow and thrive over his grave site.

He squeezed his glass angrily and left it on the edge of the fire pit, unfinished. He fell asleep right in the deck chair, his clothes still on. In the dead of night, the clerk gave him a gentle tap on the shoulder and he slowly opened his eyes. He didn't like the clerk touching him. His touch felt like it could infect others.

The clerk pointed up. It was time for him to go to his room.

# CHAPTER TWENTY-TWO

# 906

Through the double patio doors, across the lobby, past the desk, and into the elevator bank Ben went. Alone. The clerk didn't follow this time. In this confined part of the lobby, he could hear a tinkling of Muzak coming from the speakers embedded in the hotel ceiling: the darkest of jokes.

The elevator opened and Ben consulted his key card packet, which was festooned with stock photos of smiling children and young couples holding hands on the stone patio. *906*. His room was on the ninth floor.

He pressed the 9 button and watched the doors seal shut behind him. When they reopened, he found himself in a standard hotel hallway, with generic framed photographs lining the walls and cheap sconce lights mounted between them. The whole hallway smelled like wallpaper glue. He came to room 906 and dug out his key card. The black sensor under the door handle flashed red when he placed the card against it. He tried again. Red. He tried a third time, turning the handle. Red. Then he kicked the door.

When he turned to walk back to the elevator, there was a Mouth Demon right in front of him.

All mouths. Its eyes were mouths. Its nose was a mouth. Its long, stringy hair was interrupted by bare patches with mouths where scalp should be. All the mouths were open and drooling green fluid and babbling incoherently. Its breath was a cloud of horrors. The voices coming from the Mouth Demon suddenly filled the hall, sounding like a throng of the damned.

It reached out for Ben, and he could see two hungry mouths embedded in its palms, and more mouths lining its forearms. He backed up so quickly that he fell to the ground and the Mouth Demon pounced on him. Ben screamed in terror as the demon grabbed his hand and bit him on the arm with its hand-mouth, its rotting teeth plunging in, eating away at him like a living tumor.

Ben jerked away from the demon as it ripped a chunk of him free and feasted on it. He got up to run to the end of the hallway and the demon followed, slowly but with purpose. Ben's arm was festering now, the wound bleeding and widening. He saw teeth growing along the outside of the wound, and a pit forming down into his arm. Soon, there was a tongue. His arm began babbling.

The demon approached. There was a door marked STAIRS but when Ben tried to push it open, it held fast. The demon grabbed him again and bit into his clothing, and he could see more mouths lining its neck, open and waiting to be fed.

*The gun.* He needed the gun. Why hadn't he just kept the gun out the whole time? He reached into his bag with his uninfected hand and felt the grip of a weapon, but when he pulled it out, it turned out to be the paintball gun he'd filched from Fermona's cave. Then he remembered: the faded tome said you had to fill the mouths to beat the demon.

*Paint fills things.*

He aimed the paintball gun at the monster and blasted a tiny orb of orange latex into its face. One quick shot was enough to make the demon recoil. Ben fired again and again, hitting every possible open orifice at the base of its neck and across its chest. It fell to the ground in pain, covered in nightmarish bursts of Technicolor. Ben watched as the demon tried frantically to spit the latex out, making strange noises and writhing about as the mouths sealed shut.

He rolled the demon over and found more mouths lining its back and legs. He filled those mouths as well, and then filled the hungry wound blabbering on his own arm. Once filled with paint, the maw on his arm closed and the lips sealed shut, fading back into his skin, leaving a lively orange polka dot. When he wiped the paint off, he uncovered a faint white line on his skin that would not go away.

On the ground, he now saw a human corpse. Male. Sunny paint blots all over him. Ben slid down to the floor, resting against the wall, shaking uncontrollably, rubbing the new scar on his arm. He tore off his shirt, checking for new mouths, listening to see if he could hear any more unholy gibberish coming from inside him. But there was nothing.

He ran back to room 906 and frantically tried the key card again. And this time—by God—the light turned green. He turned the handle, hurried into the room, and slammed the door shut, bolting every bolt and sliding every chain. *The mouths . . . Oh, God, the mouths.* He kept seeing the mouths, smelling their toxic breath. No one would hear him in this generic hotel room. It would be okay. He screamed and banged his head against the door. He took the real gun out of his bag and held it fast to his heart.

After his fifth violent head-butt of the door, he remembered . . .

*. . . the tissue of another undead being . . .*

There was an ingredient for Voris's glowing poison right outside that door. Who knew if it would be there for much longer? Perhaps some ghoulish maid service swept through the hotel every hour to pick up remains of the undead. He was gonna need that poison.

He took out the pickle jar and unbolted the door. The man lay dead in the hallway. His nose and eyes had been restored. He looked like any other man. Ben knelt beside him and felt his cheek, which was now cold and hard.

He unfurled the napkin roll from the hotel lounge. The steak knife was serrated and razor sharp.

"I'm sorry," Ben told the corpse, as he dug into its arm and carved out a small hunk of flesh where a mouth once was. The man's blood was already coagulated and crumbly. Not a drop of liquid came out of him. Ben dropped the hunk of flesh into the pickle jar and ran back into 906. Again, the bolts and chains.

He wanted to sleep. Needed to, really. But how? He looked at the steak knife. It had cut through the man's flesh so easily, like digging into a fresh jar of peanut butter. It would be a cinch to draw the knife across his own neck and watch the blood come running out, a quick moment of pain in exchange for eternal slumber. The knife could free him. No more mouths. No more giants. No more mountains to climb or bridges to cross. And no more uncertainty.

*No.*

He wiped the knife on the cloth napkin and rolled it back up neatly with the fork and the spoon, leaving it ready for room service.

The room itself was a suite, nicer than any hotel room he'd ever been in. He didn't even know hotel rooms could *be* this open and spacious. There was a kitchen, and a vast master bath with whirlpool jets, and two king beds in the main bedroom, each turned down and adorned with a single chocolate wrapped in silver foil. On the desk in the corner of the room, there was a vase of fresh flowers, along with a cheese-and-fruit plate and a bottle of champagne chilling in a pewter bucket. There was a small envelope tucked under the plate. Ben set his bag on one of the beds and walked over to the desk, grabbing the envelope and tearing it open, reading the tiny note card inside:

*Compliments of the Producer.*

Behind the desk was a set of French doors that led to a balcony. He opened the door and saw the outline of the picturesque hills in the darkness and smelled the olive trees perfuming the fresh air. This Producer, whoever he may be, was abusing Ben in the most classic sense. There was trauma, and then there was a gift, and then more trauma, and then another gift. The pattern was unmistakable.

There was no sign of the path beyond the hotel. Whether it had abandoned him, or whether he had to figure out some mindfuck puzzle to conjure its return, he was too tired and frazzled to care.

Just then, a crow flew by and dropped a scroll of red construction paper onto the balcony. He bent over and unrolled it. There were two small handprints on the paper, made with white finger paint, and a poem cut out and pasted beneath it:

> *Sometimes you get discouraged*
> *Because I am so small*
> *And always leave fingerprints*
> *On furniture and walls*
> *But every day I'm growing up*
> *And soon I'll be so tall*
> *That all those little handprints*
> *Will be hard to recall*
> *So here's a special handprint*
> *Just so you can say*
> *This is how my fingers looked*
> *When I placed them here today.*

At the bottom, there was the name "RUDY," written by a kinder-garten teacher in black Sharpie.

"God damn you," Ben whispered softly. "Thank you, but God damn you."

He placed the paper on one of the king beds, and put Flora's stuffed fox next to it. There were a great many kiddie board books that Ben could recite from memory. So, on this night, he recited them aloud to the fox and the handprint. He asked the fox, which acted as proxy for Flora, how her day had been. He told a joke to the hand-prints. He tucked the objects in for twenty minutes before finally kissing them goodnight and covering them with the sheet and blanket. After a quick shower and change into clean boxers and a white T-shirt, he fell into the opposite bed, staring at the door, waiting for something to start banging on it.

Nothing did. He fell into a deep sleep with the balcony doors open.

----

When he woke up, he was a tenth grader. In school. The principal's office, to be exact. He was sitting in front of a stern woman.

*Oh, that's Principal Blackwell. That was her name. Hey, wait a second. . . .*

The principal had called Ben into her office and worse, she phoned Ben's mom at the hospital and made her come in as well. Apparently, Ben's teacher had read through his journal and was horrified by its contents. Now Principal Blackwell laid the open journal out on her desk for Ben and his mom to see: Severed heads. Pools of blood. Angry missives and threats to kill other students. Hideous creatures covered in frothing mouths. *You drew those. You probably don't remember that, do you? Depression has a way of vaporizing big parts of your mem-ory. Important parts.*

"Is this your journal?" she asked Ben.

"Yes, ma'am."

"Why would you put these things in your journal?"

"I don't know. Sometimes I get angry."

"Are you planning to hurt anyone, Ben?"

"No! No, I swear!"

He wasn't lying. *It's just a journal. You're free to empty out your mind in there and sort through the trash, aren't you? That's what the teachers said to do, man.* He was a depressed, only child. The *only-est* child. The fuck did they think they'd find in that journal: unicorns? He never wanted to really hurt anyone, except for perhaps himself. Wasn't that obvious? *You don't see me walking around kicking cats, do you?*

The principal gave Ben a kind pat on the shoulder.

"If you ever need to talk to anyone," she told Ben, "my door is open anytime. Or you can visit the guidance counselor, Mrs. Fazio. Okay? We know how hard it is for you, Ben. We're here to help."

*But that's not what really happened now, was it? No, not at all. The principal said nothing of the kind. When they see death threats in a kid's journal and that kid has an honorary prison scar running down the side of his face, along with a record for public vandalism . . . yeah, no, they aren't cutting that kid any slack. You were suspended for two days. Other kids found out why. Barely anyone at school spoke to you again. The rest of the football team froze you out. That's what happened. That was the real world for you. Always ready to assume the worst.*

———

When Ben woke up, Voris was hanging over him. He could tell it was Voris right away: the black eyes, the pupils bright like headlights in the dark, black wings with a span of twelve feet sprouting out of his back. His face was white. Sallow. Black gloves sheathed his seemingly endless fingers.

Ben rolled out from underneath Voris and grabbed the fox and handprint paper from the other bed, tucking them into his backpack. Voris turned his head and gazed at Ben with curiosity. The light in his pupils felt like its own distinct, separate creature. There was no need for him to explain that Ben would soon be under his complete and utter control. The pupils owned him. Voris could not be beaten.

"What do you want?" Ben asked.

Voris floated out from the bed, tucked in his wings, and came to a standing rest on the hotel suite floor. Still staring. Still curious. Ben reached over to his nightstand for the gun. By the time he had a hold of it, it was too late. Voris wrapped his praying mantis fingers around Ben and lifted him up off the ground, his lethal skin radiating through the black gloves. Ben shrieked in pain and dropped the pistol. Soon, Voris would melt through his skin and char his ribs.

Then Voris spread his wings wide and flew out the French doors and over the balcony, up into the sky, carrying Ben in his claws as easily as a crow would a slip of paper.

# CHAPTER TWENTY-THREE

# THE JOB

Dawn was breaking, and the cold air whipped Ben's face and body as Voris carried him in his burning talons between two white jet trails in the sky: the path. They were flying over the bucolic foothills now, and beyond that Californian mirage lay a red, cracked desert that stretched out in every direction. Ben's cheeks and jowls were flapping as the wind roared against him, drowning out all other sound. After an hour, he felt the cartilage between his ribs searing off, and he gasped in agony as Voris descended lower and lower into the rolling sands, gently resting him on the ground in front of a small section of the rusty desert that had been cordoned off with a thin yellow rope.

It was a square lot, covering roughly an acre of land. To the left of the square were thirty pallets, each piled high with a pyramid formation of hard white stones. Hovering above the square were two small black cloud forms, each with bright eyes, white like Voris's pupils. No mouths. These were the Smokes.

No one said anything as Ben clutched at his rib cage and groaned on the desert floor. The pain coursed through him like a steady electrical current. The sand remained cool from the night wind, but the sun was intensifying now. Soon, the desert would bake and burn. There wasn't a single living thing or piece of vegetation in sight: no cacti, no shrubs, no scorpions or rattlesnakes. It was all just one big griddle, except . . .

The path. Beyond this plot of desert, Ben saw two parallel lines in the sand, just like back in Courtshire. That wasn't all: There was a truck. A marvelous red pickup truck with a high cab and tires thick like rib eyes. Its bed was stacked with dozens of bags of dry concrete mix, pressing down on the truck and nearly making it pop a standing wheelie. The truck and the path were right there, ready for Ben.

But not quite yet.

Black, foggy pseudopods extended out from the Smokes' bodies, allowing them to grasp tangible objects. They dumped a pickax and shovel at Ben's feet, along with a pair of work boots. Ben stood up, dropped his backpack, picked up the shovel, and swung it at Voris, who dodged it nonchalantly.

"Rot in hell," Ben screamed.

Voris tilted his head and stared at Ben, yet again curious, like a doctor performing a biopsy. Voris didn't speak. He invaded Ben with his pupils, locking into his eyes, hijacking his optic nerves, and sending missives directly to his brain.

*How do you know this* isn't *hell?*

That was the thought Voris left inside him. Then he took off one of his black gloves and revealed a pale hand with grotesquely long fingers, the tips glowing red like steel coming out of a forge. Voris pointed at the square, and then at the tools provided for Ben.

"What do you want me to do?" Ben asked.

Voris pointed back to where he had carried Ben through the sky, and then raised his ghoulish hand upward in a majestic swoop.

"You want me to build you a castle?"

Voris nodded.

"Here? By myself? It can't be done. Where would I even start? It would take me years."

Voris shrugged.

"Please, no. I can't."

But Voris ignored him and pointed to the Smokes. They were to be his guards. They would supervise the project. Ben would not be leaving this worksite until the castle was finished, even with the truck and the path right there to tempt him.

"If I build this for you, do I get the truck?" Ben asked.

Voris said nothing. Instead, he spread his wings and flew off, although not back to the castle. Instead, he flew in a straight line directly over the pickup truck and the path, disappearing into the west, or whatever direction it was.

The Smokes continued to hover. Ben unpacked his tent and staked it at the eastern edge of the worksite. The Smokes made no move to confiscate it, or to take his bag. He ducked into the tent library with his backpack and drank a bottle of water, ripping up a white T-shirt and wrapping it around his aching rib cage. He gazed at the bag. The pickle jar full of poison for Voris was still there. And his seed bag. He needed to hide them, but not here.

The Smokes poked through the flap. One Smoke was holding the shovel and pickax, the other a pair of canvas pants and a plain white shirt.

"You want me to start now?" Ben asked them. They advanced forward, the tools and clothing outstretched. He brushed the apparitions off.

"Gimme a moment," he said, "and I'll think about it."

That wasn't what the Smokes wanted to hear. They dropped the equipment and descended upon Ben, holding him down and burning his retinas with their halogen eyes. One of them raised a cumulus fist and plunged it into Ben's face. The ash filled his nose and mouth and flooded the back of his throat with hot bile. He couldn't breathe. His sinuses began to burn away, as if he had snorted pure fire.

"Okay! Okay!" he cried. "I'll do it!"

The Smokes backed off him. He gulped the fresh tent air and hacked out the ash, coughing in berserk fits as if flu-stricken on a winter morning. He was ready to cough out all of his innards. The Smokes seemed unconcerned. They dumped the clothes on top of him and watched him dress.

Outside the tent, Ben took his shovel and dug into the loose sand. For hours, he piled it high off to the side of the rope, and then watched with great discouragement as a stiff wind came in and blew some of it back down into the tiny hole. There was a whole acre of this to go, and no telling how far down he had to dig before hitting bedrock. Mrs. Blackwell's garden seemed much more appealing by comparison.

The next day, he dug a bit more. A skinless hand reached out of the ground, swiping at his ankles. Another ghoulish hand popped out, and soon a full-on skinless zombie rose out of the desert: a grotesque piece of walking meat. Its eyes bugged out as it stalked Ben, sending him scurrying back to the tent for a bag of salt. It came within ten feet of the flap—dripping hot mucus and reaching for Ben with its veiny, swollen hands—when he threw a handful of salt at it and heard it moan in agony. Its muscles shriveled and its veins hardened. The white cartilage of its nose turned to stone and its ghastly exposed jaw locked shut. Within minutes, it was a lifeless piece of jerky on the ground.

The Smokes carried it away.

It would not be the last Skinless he would have to deal with. They rose up and attacked every few days or so, a plasticine anatomy exhibit come to life, stripped of all dermatological tissue and displaying only the monstrousness of the human framework beneath.

Weeks passed. Every morning, the Smokes barged into Ben's tent at dawn with the tools and sent him out into the searing hot desert skillet. He would wrap a shirt around his head for sun protection and go to work immediately, stopping only for a blip of a lunch break. The Smokes would hand him a metal tray of gray meat and lukewarm potato cubes and then prod him back into hard labor the moment he was finished. If he took too much time between spoonfuls, he got a fistful of black ash.

His progress was glacial. Every so often, he would come across a boulder and have to break it up with the pickax. His back ached. His arms became saddle leather. Massive sun blisters formed on his neck and shoulders: brown spheroids filled with burning hot plasma. The sweat would collect in the folds of his brow and then drip down and sting his eyes to the point where, by the afternoon, he was digging through a blind haze. The red sand burned like coal in the sun. When the wind kicked up, it would shower Ben in a fiery squall.

Every three days, Voris would pass directly over the site, never landing. Instead, he would fly from the western horizon back toward the hotel/castle, and then back again three days later. Ben made note of it. Every time Voris flew by, Ben hurled curse words and invectives at him from the ground, fuming at him like a disgruntled employee.

The Smokes let him keep his tent, and so he spent every night in the fluffy white bed, sleepwalking through corrected versions of his past: lost football games that were now triumphs, a car wreck he was once in that now never came to pass, bad dates that now went right.

He never saw his family, though. They were kept away from him, even when he prayed to the sky above for one more glimpse. The fluffy fox and handprint paper remained on the other side of his bed and he tucked them in every night.

One day, in the pit, he found a stray rock and slipped it into his pocket, then went into the tent and stared at it. If he stared at it hard enough, he could see eyes.

"Peter."

After that, he tucked the rock into bed at night as well. He would kiss the rock, and stroke the top of it. When he closed his eyes, he could feel his fingers running through the dense thatch of hair on Peter's ample skull.

———

The weeks turned into months. Ben marked so many days on his pad that he was running out of pages, and the paper was too precious to waste on counting. He laid the marked sheets of paper on the floor and began making notches into the hardwood to continue the tally. There were hundreds of notches. Perhaps more. But he had his routine to keep him sane. And he knew there was something after this. Crab. Meeting up with the Younger Ben. There was a *next* to this. That was important.

The truck and the path were so achingly close, but Ben shut out the idea of hijacking the truck for now because the Smokes seemed impossible to distract. They never slept. Ever. Sometimes at night, he would wake up and they would be in the tent with him, staring. Silent. Hovering in place even when Ben threw a shoe at them.

His hands grew thick with calluses and his skin red with sun damage. His fingernails became hard as quartz, with months of crimson sand and dirt built up underneath the cuticles. And soon he found that his entire temperament had grown calloused. Nothing surprised him much anymore. Nothing bothered him, not even fighting off the Skinless. He didn't curl up and cry thinking about the dogfaces and rabid Mouth Demons. A hard shell was forming over him.

The Smokes would bring him more food and water as he needed it. His shoulders grew broad. You could have parked a car on top of them. Despite being enslaved, he didn't mind the physical transformation. He felt stronger, more confident in his ability to withstand misery. In time, he excavated six feet down into the pit. He could see the results of his work, and it pleased him.

He consumed almost the entirety of the library inside his tent. There was an ingredient missing from his recipe: a final component for his pickle jar. He read Mrs. Blackwell's reference book over and over, and scoured the library for related materials. He kept hoping he'd find another book written by her somewhere in the stacks—some companion volume that gave him the secret to the poison and a way of defeating the Smokes. But there was nothing. Many of the books were unfathomably dull: long treatises on peat moss, encyclopedias printed in Armenian, turgid histories of Olde England. A select few kept him rapt: old works by Chaucer and Ovid, the occasional Bible passage. Every book was a door; every page a new place to hide. He read Dante and began to wonder if he was truly in hell, and what he had done to deserve it. He used to curse and yell at his kids. One time he left a scratch on another car in a parking lot and drove off instead of leaving a note. He pleasured himself a lot. He had sex with an old flame in a time warp.

But those seemed like minor offenses. Mostly, his sins were within him, terrifying impulses that he had quashed at every turn over the course of his youth. His depression would lead to rage, and his rage would lead to fantasies of . . . well, Mrs. Blackwell had seen all of it in his journal now, hadn't she? The violence. The blood. What if God had seen all that as well? What if God *knew*? One night, the thought of it made Ben weep uncontrollably, and he sat up in his bed, with the Smokes' eyes on him, and began to apologize:

"I'm sorry, God. I'm so, so sorry for the things I've thought. I'm sorry for the things I've done. I'm sorry for the hurt I've caused that I don't know I've caused. I'm sorry, Mom. I'm sorry, Teresa. I'm sorry, children. Please, please know that I'm sorry. Please forgive me."

There was no reply from above.

"I SAID I WAS SORRY. WHAT MORE DO YOU WANT FROM ME? Didn't you hear me? Can't you see how sorry I am? What is WRONG with you? Get me out of here. GET ME OUT OF . . ."

The Smokes rushed over and snuffed his cries out. He passed out that night in a fog of soot.

Like any other prisoner, he found rituals and small moments to make the intolerable tolerable. He got better at drawing, remembering everything Teresa had mentioned to him about light and shadow. Contours and perspective. Every day he gazed out at the dead plain and took note of how the shadows crept along. He scratched drawings on the library floor. He took out many of the leather-bound volumes lining the stacks, and if the books bored him, he would draw right over the text. He summoned the picture of his family from his phone in his mind and painstakingly drew it again and again, the same image a hundred times over until it began to roughly resemble the real thing. He talked to the drawings and felt along the faces.

Sometimes at night, he would walk out into the serene desert breeze and even the presence of the Smokes couldn't ruin his view of the stars. They weren't normal stars at all. There was no Orion's Belt. There was no Big Dipper. He could make out all kinds of bizarre constellations that had nothing to do with basic astronomy: ampersands, topsails, a human foot. Someone had shaken the heavens and let the universe resettle above him. And of course, there were the two moons. Equal in size. Always full. Never waxing. Never waning.

One day, he finally struck bedrock and knew his foundation would soon be complete. He had unearthed ten feet of hard desert spanning the acre, a gradual slope at the front allowing him to climb in and out of the hole. He celebrated with a sip of peach schnapps in the tent. A few days later, Voris flew above him and he saw the Smokes look skyward. Just for a minute or so.

A week later, during a water break, while the Smokes looked up at Voris, Ben quickly bored a hole in the sand near his tent and stashed his pickle jar inside, the poison still missing its last, vital ingredient. He threw the seed down hard on the ground and nothing happened. It stayed a seed. Panicked, he threw the seed into the hole with the pickle jar and covered it up. The seed wasn't ready to sprout right now. It worked on some kind of existential time release. But he had learned how to be patient. After all, he had years to play with. He could wait until he had the timing exactly right.

Every so often, he'd scream unholy things at the Smokes, or make a frenzied run at the pickup, and they would push him down and fill his lungs with enough toxins to make him beg for mercy. They made for horrible company. He missed Crab. He even missed Fermona, in his own twisted way. He missed the sound of another living being. A truly living being, and not the spooks haunting his every waking moment.

———

Six years passed.

One morning, Ben was mixing the concrete powder with water in a wheelbarrow (provided by his captors) when a stiff wind came and triggered a sand slide. He watched the wall of the foundation hole quiver and then quickly collapse, a metric ton of sand crashing back down right at his feet. It would have to be re-excavated. He picked up a nearby shovel and hurled it across the pit. The Smokes immediately descended upon him.

"Fuck you!" he screamed at them. "You mute *fucks*! This thing would get built three times faster if you ever bothered to help. But do you? No. No, you sit there like the fucking puds you are and ride my jock. One day . . . one day I swear to God I will find a way to end you both."

And they were just about to hold him down and choke him to death when they abruptly changed their minds. No, they had a better idea. They flew silently over to his tent perched on the edge of the pit. His home.

"Wait!" Ben cried. "I'm sorry. Listen, why don't we talk about this? Please don't."

But it was too late. One of the Smokes produced a white flame from inside its noxious vapors and set the tent ablaze. The books, the drawings, the fox, the handprint, the bed, his bag and everything it contained—all of it burned. A plume of black smoke rose high up from the desert and it may as well have grown two eyes as well, it looked so malevolent. Ben fell to his knees and watched helplessly as the wind blew around the tiny, blackened bits of his former abode. The black ash fell softly down into the pit like hell-spawned snow, covering Ben in tatters of the only things left that he had held dear. He screamed at the Smokes until his face was ready to fall off.

The Smokes stared back at him. Ben was just about to charge at them when Voris came flying over the worksite.

He wasn't alone.

In his fearsome talons he was carrying something. A man. Voris swooped into the hole and laid the man gently on the bedrock, ten yards from Ben, then unfurled his wings and again flew out to the west, as he did every six days. The man clutched at his ribs in anguish, just as Ben had all those years ago. Ben rushed to help him up and lifted him to his feet, perhaps against his better judgment. The man stood barely five feet tall, with long black hair and a single gold tooth and thick bushy mustache. He wore leather boots and short pants and a puffy white tunic.

He also had a scabbard attached to his belt. And when he saw Ben, he drew his sword upon him.

# CHAPTER TWENTY-FOUR

# CISCO

"Who are you?" the man asked in a thick Spanish accent. "FIEND, I'LL CUT YOU TO PIECES!"

"I'm not one of them," Ben answered. "I'm not with Voris. I swear." He stretched his arms wide, offering no defense against the sword. The man lowered it and began to tremble. Then he thrust the blade into the ground and fell to one knee, bowing before Ben.

"*Dios mio.*"

"What?"

"My Lord, I am Cisco del Puente, explorer and emissary of the king and queen of *España*. I was hired as mate aboard the *Santa Maria de Vincenze*. But Sir Edward Black, the British swine, captured our ship, and forced us to sail with him to this land. The ship ran aground. Many men drowned. Savages, *cowards*, shot arrows at us. I was the only one to make it to shore, and that is when I came upon this path. And I have followed this path ever since, oh, Lord."

"Wait, hold up. . . ."

"I have followed it and endured the mysteries of this new land, knowing that our Holy Father sent me here to discover it for the glory of Spain and the destruction of WHORE ENGLAND. And now I know for certain, as I gaze upon you, that I have found paradise. The path to God. I am here to serve you, my God in heaven."

Cisco pressed his forehead hard into the hilt of his sword. The Smokes hovered above them both as the embers from the tent fire glowed red at the edge of the pit. Ben could see that his rock doll of Peter was all that remained. Everything else had been incinerated.

One of the Smokes flew over with a trowel and shovel, dropping them at Cisco's feet. Cisco was too busy praying to notice. Ben jerked him upward.

"We need to get to work," he told the Spaniard.

"But Lord . . ."

"I'm not the Lord. And you are not in paradise."

*"Qué?"*

"I'm not God."

"You are not the Producer?"

"Nope. They told me I had to find him, too. I'm lost, man. Same as you."

"Are you English?"

"I'm not English."

"Good. The English . . . They are *pigs*."

"Yeah, I think I got that from your little speech. Now get moving. The Smokes will kill us if we don't start working."

"They are with the man with the fire eyes?"

"Yeah, they work for him."

"This is not a good man."

"No. No, he isn't." He gave Cisco a shovel. "Don't say anything you aren't comfortable with those two shitbags hearing. They see it all and hear it all and they never sleep."

Ben walked over to the landslide pile and started digging in, carrying each shovelful up the ramp and dumping it far from the pit. Cisco followed suit.

"You said you came on a ship," Ben said.

"Yes."

"Was it the hovercraft?"

"Huntercraft?"

"What kind of ship was it?"

"One of the biggest and strongest Her Majesty had ever commissioned."

Ben paused and turned to him. "What year do you think it is, Cisco?"

"The Year of Our Lord 1485."

"Well, that's just fucking great," Ben said, and he kept on shoveling.

"I have kept detailed maps of this land. And I have noted many places where gold can and will be found. When I bring those maps back to Spain, they will declare me the greatest explorer who ever lived."

"Really."

"I will name this land after my mother, Antonia."

"Brother, I don't know how to explain this, but I'll give it a whirl: You are NOT in the New World."

"How do you know that?"

"Because *I* come from the New World. Maryland. I assure you that Maryland does not behave the way this place behaves. I'm from the future and you're from the past and this place is a fucking wasteland. This place is nothing."

"You are wrong. This is real. And Jesus has sent me here as his courier." Cisco looked over at the massive red pickup truck at the western edge of the property. "What is that wagon?"

"That's the truck."

"Is it yours?"

"If I play my cards right. Listen, man, you have a bag on you, right?"

"Yes."

"Does it hold whatever you want it to hold?"

"Yes. It is like magic."

"Did you get any bags of seeds?"

"No."

"What about a crab? Did you meet a crab?"

"No."

"What about a giant?"

"Yes. The woman giant. She threw me into a pit, and made me fight like a dog."

"But you escaped."

"To the house of the man with the fire eyes, yes."

"Did you get a tent?"

"No. I sleep on the ground. But I did get this. . . ."

He reached into his little bag and pulled out a rolled-up mat.

"When I sleep on this mat, it is like sleeping on silk. And when I fall asleep, I have dreams of my mother. I am a little boy, at her side in the market. I can see her and touch her, and that is how I know this mat is a gift from the Lord. This whole land is a gift from the Lord."

Ben snorted. "It's not a gift. You found a path that's cursed. And it's not real."

Cisco blanched. "Who are you to say?"

"I just know. Cisco, you and are I are probably going to spend a lot of time together in this pit, so I'm not gonna overload you with information on our first day."

They had stopped shoveling during their chat. The Smokes flew over and scowled at them angrily.

"We'd better get back to work," Ben said.

And they did. Ben and the Spaniard labored day after day, clearing the foundation, pouring and spreading the concrete slab, laying the stones, icing them with wet mortar, and building the exterior walls and battlements. Ben noticed that he was spending the majority of his working hours with his back to the Smokes. Sometimes they hovered close by, but usually they were content to linger in the background, their halogen eyes never flickering.

Every night, Ben and Cisco would sleep on Cisco's mat outside, spread out horizontally so that each man could rest his torso on the mat with his legs sticking out on the sand. The food and water provided by the Smokes grew more and more scarce. All the hard muscle Ben had built up from his early years of labor was beginning to deteriorate, leaving him with nothing but the permanent ache of every remaining joint, muscle, and nerve. His knee was falling apart, to the point where Cisco would put Ben's arm around him and carry him up the ramp at the end of every workday. At night, Ben would entertain Cisco by describing elaborate fantasies of killing the Smokes . . . shooting them, stabbing them, choking them, kicking them. Cisco had a bonus suggestion.

"The *strappado*, Mr. Ben."

"What is that?"

"You tie the man's wrists behind his back. And then, you raise his arms up. . . ."

"You do that?"

"They did it to many members of the crew. Discipline. You can hear the shoulders popping out."

"Jesus, man."

"Do not speak of the Lord in such a manner."

Cisco told Ben more stories of his life at sea, all as valuable to Ben as the good books he once had stocked in the tent library. From the explorer, he learned about sailing and maritime navigation, and all the horrible things old sailors did to one another. Ben learned everything there was to know about Cisco. He learned about the small fishing village outside Cádiz where the Spaniard grew up, and he learned about Cisco's seven brothers, all of whom became sailors as well. Most of all, he learned that Cisco hated pretty much everyone who was not Spanish. Cisco hated the French. He hated the Portuguese. He hated the Italians. He *really* hated the English. (Ben made sure not to tell Cisco that he himself had English blood from his old man's side.) He even hated other Spaniards, like the Catalonians. Man, did he hate the Catalonians.

"The Catalonians . . . They are bird droppings that landed atop our fair kingdom. They ooze. They are SHIT."

"Cisco, I could listen to you rag on Catalonians all night."

Cisco smiled, his gold tooth glinting in the starlight. "Good, because they are the mongrel afterbirth."

They developed a code, so that they could make plans freely without the Smokes understanding them (or so they hoped). The "barrel" was Ben's pickle jar. The Smokes were "bricks." Voris was "the slab."

One day, with his body blocking the Smokes' view, Ben made a hole in the castle wall. He left a small compartment in the masonry and secreted a tiny water bottle inside it. Then he covered it with a loose stone. Every six days, at midday, Ben would unearth his little pickle jar from the hole in the sand and pour a bit of the poison into the water bottle, then put the jar back in the hole before the Smokes turned away from Voris. There was still one unknown ingredient in the poison left to go, and he would have to find it. He would have to experiment. He tried sand. He tried his own hair. He tried bits of his rotting work clothes. Nothing seemed to make it glow. The potion sample remained inert on every attempt.

"What's in the barrel today?" Cisco whispered to him once.

"Piece of my fingernail," Ben said. "To crack the slab."

"Did it?"

"No."

Through their crude cipher, Ben explained the seed to Cisco, how it was still buried in the ground, along with the poison to kill Voris. Every twelve days, Ben would unearth the hard seed and smash it on the ground, only to see nothing come of it.

"Why would you care about something so worthless?" the explorer asked him.

"One day, it'll work. You'll see."

Cisco shook his head. The explorer seemed to believe in everything fanciful *except* that dopey little seed.

"I will eat this seed of yours," Cisco joked.

"That's not funny."

"Can I ask you something?"

"Yeah."

"This scar, on your face. How do you get this scar?"

"I was in a sword fight and won."

"This is a good and brave thing."

"Oh, I'm brave as hell, Cisco."

As the job progressed, Ben's memories became more blurred and abstract. He would speak to his rock at night, much to Cisco's confusion, and invent stories about the rock's day: what Peter wore, how his day at school was, what new friends he made, how the rest of the family was holding up. He would put the rock on his back and crawl around on all fours, giving it an elephant ride, as he did with the real Peter back at home, in his previous life. He would trace drawings of his family in the sand every night, the images growing morphed and distorted. His wife grew more beautiful. His children grew older and stronger, sometimes appearing superhuman to him. At night, the sand would get kicked up by the wind and invade their little mat, coating Ben's skin in a layer of sediment he could never slough off. Little grains of it would get trapped behind his eyeballs, driving him wild with irritation.

Some days, the Smokes would deprive them of water entirely, and Ben's tongue would grow black and hard from extreme thirst working on the desert griddle. In his savage hunger, Ben saw mirages: great lakes filled with fruit punch, supermarket aisles lining the outskirts of the desert, a smoking pit with thick sausages hanging above a pile of burning hickory.

He and Cisco talked endlessly about food and cheese and wine. One night, they made a cannibalism pact: If one man died, the other could eat him. It was all right. Whatever it took for someone to get back on the path home. They discussed this pact openly, without using the code. It wasn't as if the Smokes would care.

"Remember," Ben said, "I have to die."

"Yes," said Cisco.

"You can't start eating me before that happens."

"But what if you're asleep and you *look* dead?" Cisco joked. "Let me have just an arm. You are right-handed, so I eat the left arm. This is the dumb arm."

"Don't joke about that. Bad ideas always start off as bad jokes."

"I suppose they do."

Cisco looked up at the two moons in the sky.

"I cannot wait to go home," Cisco said to Ben. "Someday, I will find my way back to Spain. And when the people find out I have discovered this New Orient . . ."

"I keep telling you: It's not real."

"How do you know this? You insist and you insist some more that this is not real when you are here. I do not think your outlook is healthy in this way."

"I didn't mean that's it not real. It's just . . . In my time, five hundred years after you live, the whole of the Earth is mapped. Everything's been discovered."

"That is not possible."

"I'm telling you, Cisco: Where I come from, there are cameras in outer space that can look down and see everything. At home, I have a little box that can see whatever those cameras see. I can bring up any section of the world I like and get a perfect rendering of it, and I can hear a voice that tells me how to get wherever I need to go."

"This is a gift from God."

"You would think. And yet."

"If this little box of yours can show you everything, why did your little box never show you this place?"

"I don't know."

"And did you know about this second moon before?"

"No."

"Well then, I have discovered it. A new moon on the far side of the world. They'll name this new moon after me. And the continent after my mother."

"They already named the New World continent."

"And what did they name it?"

"America."

"After Vespucci? THE FILTHY *ITALIANO* PIGDOG?!"

"Relax, relax. If I get back, I'll tell everyone America is the wrong name for it."

"You don't believe you'll ever get back."

"I have no idea."

"You don't believe in God."

"If this is the work of God, I want no part of Him."

"I believe in God. This Producer is God, you know. We'll be rewarded for this. You will see. God has put us here because He loves us. I can't wait to meet Him at the end of this path. You will meet Him, too."

"I doubt that."

"Is your world a world of God?"

"I don't know how to answer that, Cisco. There are a billion Catholics in the future, if that makes you happy."

"But you are not among them."

"No."

"My friend, just because God loves you does not mean He can save you from suffering."

"Look, you still think this is all real and that the Earth is flat and that Jesus sent you here. That's fine. I think that's a great attitude to have. Me? I want no part of this. I want to go home. I *built* something there, Cisco. My father was a loser. My mom never had any money. I left cold-ass Minnesota and got myself a good job and I made a life out of the scraps God left for me. And now I'm stuck here. Whenever I think about what Teresa and I built at home, I see it rotting. Everything we ever worked for, just wasting away. Condemned. And I'm stuck with this empty fucking castle instead. Don't you ever miss home?"

"I am doing more for my family here than I possibly could at home. Men like us were born to explore. We have homes so that we can leave them. And if I die here on this path, I will have given my wife and children more glory and honor than I could ever give them by staying home, like a coward. Do you understand this?"

"We should sleep."

"We should sleep, yes."

Cisco began snoring and Ben's eyes remained wide open. Laid out in front of their sad little mat was Voris's new abode, the curtain walls finished and the stone interior of the first floor nearly complete. Ben's job at home was minding the money for a small construction firm, so he knew all about the raw materials of contract work: joists and tenons and struts. But he rarely laid hands on such things back then. Now he knew the raw materials of existence intimately.

He fell asleep dreaming of burning the castle down.

# CHAPTER TWENTY-FIVE

# THE POISON

Four more years passed. The labor and the hunger and the thirst and the soreness and the deathly midday heat and sweeping midnight cold were all working in concert to smash Ben. Every day his body stretched and compacted with the temperature, like a road about to buckle. His teeth were yellow and cracking. His skin had liver spots now. His beard had grown scraggly over the bottom half of his jagged scar. He had become a zombie himself: a hollowed-out remnant, hands now ghost white with dried mortar paste, brainless save for the urge to fulfill one primal need.

But he wasn't quite dead yet.

Still obsessed with defeating Voris, he had taken to muttering passages from his old library to himself ("Curry powder; the dead tissue of another undead being; the dead, stewed tissue of a human"), Cisco eyeing him with grim concern. The sample bottle in the castle wall hadn't yielded anything fruitful yet and Ben fell into a mania as he searched both his mind and the desert for the final elusive component.

The castle was nearing completion, the turrets and flanking towers rising forty feet high and connected by parapet walks that Ben and Cisco had finished in exacting detail. Every morning, the pair would wake up and find the truck bed stocked with whatever construction materials were required for the job: wooden joists, long corner posts, iron spikes, ladders, flexible pine studs, a forge. The Smokes never took away Cisco's bag, although the stranded explorer hadn't amassed much of anything useful inside it: some clothes, a canteen, twigs of dried rosemary (Cisco would make tea with them on special occasions), some hardtack, a Bible, half a bottle of rancid ship brandy, his maps and journals (which he curiously refused to share with Ben), salt for fighting off the Skinless, and the precious sleeping mat. Cisco scored the mat after crossing a lake filled with man-eating anacondas. Then he had a sword fight with a spider whose body was a man's head. That was what the path had decided were proper obstacles for him.

One night, the two decided to celebrate Ben's forty-eighth birthday. Bereft of a calendar, they chose the day arbitrarily and rejoiced with some extra hardtack, a sip of the brandy, and a song or two. Ben had taught Cisco modern music, and Cisco had taught Ben a handful of filthy sea shanties. They sang out loud as the Smokes watched, ruining the moment the way they always did. Emboldened by the brackish liquor, Ben stood up and talked directly to the ghosts.

"Tomorrow," he said, "I'm gonna kill both of you fuckers, and there's nothing you can do about it."

They ignored him and kept staring. They were used to him mouthing off. Immune. He couldn't kill them, so they let him run his yap all he pleased. In the end, they could always shut him up if they felt like it.

Under the rearranged stars, Ben began sketching out another mural of his family in the sand: the phone shot, at the Chuck E. Cheese's, with the family huddled around the cheap tablecloth. He was muttering to himself about the poison again when Cisco laid a gentle hand on his shoulder.

"There's nothing in that barrel, my friend. You have to let it go."

"No."

"You have tried everything. This is noble but nobility has its limits."

"There's one thing left and I can't see it. I know it's there. It's hiding in plain sight and I just can't . . ."

He drew his wife's hand as he remembered it from the photo, with her thumb awkwardly rubbing her ring finger on the same hand.

*Her ring.*

"Cisco."

"*Qué?*"

Ben pointed to the outline of Teresa's hand in the sand.

"This is your wife, yes?"

"She's wearing her ring," Ben said.

"You've tried your rings. Both of them."

"My wedding ring is stainless steel. My father's ring is brass."

"So?"

"My wife's wedding ring is *gold*, Cisco. The Producer is telling us that we need gold for the barrel. And we have gold."

He eyed Cisco's tooth. The Smokes watched indifferently as Cisco backed away from Ben.

"My friend, nothing will work."

"We haven't tried everything," Ben said. His mouth hung open like a hungry dog's.

"You cannot have my tooth."

Ben got up and walked in the dark over to the worksite, reaching into a bucket of tools and rooting around. Cisco trailed behind, gripping his sword in its sheath. The Smokes kept their distance, watching the two men for sport as the sun began to rise in the background.

Ben found a pair of pliers in the bucket. Cisco drew the sword.

"Cisco, there's no other way."

"Stay away from me."

"Please, Cisco. Please. You have to give it to me."

"My gold is mine."

"GIVE ME THE TOOTH."

He lunged at Cisco and the Spaniard thrust his sword out. But Ben dodged it, grabbed Cisco by the wrist, and pulled him closer. With a significant advantage in height and weight, he twisted Cisco's arm and loosed the sword. Cisco bit down hard on his shoulder and both men fell to the ground, wrestling around.

"You cannot have the tooth!" Cisco cried.

"We'll never get out of here! Don't you fucking get it?!"

"It's mine!"

"What does it matter if we *die* here, Cisco? I can't die here! You're my friend and I love you. Please don't let me die in this shithole, Cisco. Please. Think about God."

"You don't believe in God! You are a heathen!"

"I am a good man. If it were my tooth, I'd give it to *you*."

Cisco relented for a moment. "Then that is what you will do."

"What?"

"You're a man of your word, no? You take my tooth, and then I take yours."

"But mine's not gold."

"Show me you are a man of sacrifice. Show me how far you will go to prove yourself to God."

Ben's eyeballs bugged out as he drooled yellow onto Cisco's tunic. "Tooth for a tooth, then?"

"Yes."

"You swear it?"

"On the life of the queen."

Ben gave a reluctant nod. The Smokes approached as the two men got up and dusted themselves off. Ben held out a hand to the ghosts.

"Not now, you pricks. We're settling something."

The Smokes retreated half an inch as the men shook hands.

"Who goes first?" Ben asked.

"I will go first," Cisco said. "I can trust you, yes?"

"Yes."

Ben took the pliers and slipped them over Cisco's gold incisor.

"You must be fast," Cisco said.

"I will," Ben promised. "Do you want to give me a signal? Or do you just want me to get it over with?"

"Get it over wi . . ."

Ben clutched the pliers and gave them a firm twist and pull. The Spaniard made no sound. No screams. No cries. No groans. He fixed his eyes on Ben as the blood gushed out from his gums and made the pliers slick in Ben's already shaky hands. After sixty brutal seconds, the gold tooth was extracted. The pressure from the pliers had left a series of ridges in the soft metal. Ben dropped the pliers in horror.

"I'm so sorry, Cisco."

Cisco calmly bent over and grabbed the bloodied tool off the ground.

"Are you ready now?" he asked Ben.

But he couldn't bring himself to say yes out loud. He whimpered and closed his eyes as the explorer walked up to him and slipped the pliers over his perfectly healthy front tooth. There was a split second to dread the pull, and that dread was almost worse than what came next. Cisco yanked and the pain took over, shooting through Ben's face like pure sound, deep and sharp and maddening. He could feel the root of his tooth stretching down within him, as deep as the tomato vines in Mrs. Blackwell's garden, a seemingly endless network of exposed wiring now electrified.

He did not possess Cisco's tolerance for pain. He made sounds that shook the sands. He seized and twisted and wailed. When it was over, he lay prone on the ground for five minutes, leaking hot blood, feeling around the exposed socket with his dry tongue. Cisco felt the enamel of Ben's tooth between his calloused fingertips.

"Now you are a man of sacrifice."

The Smokes came and dropped two shovels at the men's feet.

"Fuck you," Ben said to them.

They started in on him and he quickly got back up, walking into the castle.

"I'm working! I'm working! I have no fucking joint compound here. Do us a favor and get some joint compound."

One Smoke flew off while the other prodded Cisco to start working and followed him up the inner staircase of the castle. Ben was now alone for a moment, parked close to the interior wall. He quickly moved the loose rock and found his water bottle filled with sample poison.

When he dropped Cisco's gold tooth in, the solution glowed bright green.

He quickly tucked the little bottle into his waistband. The Smokes and Cisco returned to the lower level of the castle. Ben gave Cisco a firm nod. They had their poison.

This happened to be another sixth day. At lunch, with the working poison still tenuously hidden inside his waistband, Ben saw Voris approaching, his leathery wings spread out and perfectly still, content to glide along with the wind. No flapping necessary at all. Ben took his water break and Cisco did likewise. They sat in the sand, near the little hole with the jar and the seed. The wind whistled through Ben's new tooth gap. When the Smokes looked skyward, he took out his water bottle and added it to the pickle jar, watching the insides of it light up. Then he grabbed his hard brown seed and struck it down.

On the sand now sat a handheld vacuum.

"Holy shit."

Cisco looked down at the vacuum and nearly yelped with surprise at the transformation, but Ben quickly covered his mouth with his hand.

"Shhhh!"

They threw the vacuum in the hole and covered it in a thin layer of red sand.

"We can't do anything during the day," Ben whispered.

"I agree," said Cisco.

"I think he can see through their eyes."

"Yes. We must strike at night. What is this thing we bury?"

"A vacuum."

"What is a vacuum?"

"It's better if you see it in action than if I explain it."

They went back to work, their faces still smeared with dried blood from the morning's amateur dentistry. The rest of that afternoon was a study in torture—less physical than having a tooth pulled but no less pronounced—as they stacked stones and glued them with mortar, trying to remain as productive as usual so that everything would appear normal. By the look in Ben's eyes, Cisco knew his friend was delirious, almost rapturous. Ben was *snickering* as he labored, driven insane by the idea that escape was so close for them.

"You know what? We celebrated my birthday last night," said Ben aloud. "Tonight, we celebrate yours, amigo."

"A celebration for me?"

"Shit, yeah. Why not?"

The Smokes said nothing. Darkness fell, the mean wind sweeping back over the flat desert. Again the two explorers toasted and drank from the rancid brandy bottle, although this time, Ben and Cisco only pretended to take swigs, letting their pink backwash slide back into the bottle. Cisco's bag was directly over the hole where the vacuum was buried.

As casually as possible, Ben said, "I'm putting this rotgut back. We've had too much." With one hand, he slipped the brandy back into the bag. With the other, he dug into the sand underneath the bag and grabbed the vacuum. By the time he had it out, the Smokes could see that Ben was acting with a bit too much purpose. They sailed toward him. And when they saw the vacuum, they flew into a rage.

"Cisco, RUN!"

The explorer got up and raced along the side of the castle, with one of the ghosts peeling away to capture and smother him. Just as the other Smoke was about to reach Ben, he held up the vacuum and flicked the power switch. The vacuum sucked up the Smoke within seconds, trapping it inside an opaque plastic chamber, leaving it wild with anger, practically knocking at the plastic to get out.

The other Smoke caught Cisco and held him down, stuffing his lungs with tar and ash, when Ben ran up behind it and flicked the switch again. But before he could trap it, the Smoke turned away from the Spaniard and began smothering Ben instead. Ben dropped the vacuum to the ground as the ghost blanketed him. This was the end. The Smoke had seen enough. He was really going to choke Ben to death this time. Ben's throat felt stripped. His mutilated gums burned. The Smoke was reaching deeper down inside his frail body than it ever had, ready to end him.

But it didn't count on Cisco recovering so quickly. The Spaniard hopped up and saw the vacuum sitting on the ground. He pushed the RELEASE button by accident and set the first Smoke free. It immediately pounced on Cisco, forming a brute fist to knock the vacuum away. But Cisco held on and clipped the plastic dust chamber shut. Then he flicked the right switch and sucked up the first Smoke once more, its eyes bright with fury as it disappeared through the handheld's anteater nozzle.

Then Cisco came up behind the second Smoke and sucked it right up. SHOOOOOOOOOOOMP!

There they were. The two demon fuckers, trapped in that little Dustbuster. The chamber shook and rattled with their collective outrage. If they could have screamed, they would have.

Ben was still on the ground, gasping for air. Cisco grabbed his bag, then ran over and offered a hand.

"They're gone," he told Ben.

"We can go?"

"We can go."

He shot to his feet, jump-started back to life. Then he looked at the tiny vacuum and beamed, smiling so wide that his cheeks ached.

"CISCO!" he cried, shaking his friend's shoulders. "Cisco, you magnificent bastard!"

They grabbed their shovels and dug a hole in the ground. They had grown quite proficient at digging. Then they placed the vacuum in the hole and covered it up. The Smokes would only see blackness all through this night, and for the rest of forever. Ben picked up the glowing pickle jar, then took Cisco by the collar and led him to the truck. It was unlocked. The key was in the ignition. He put a bewildered Cisco in the passenger seat and buckled his seat belt for him, then hopped up into the other side of the cab.

"My friend, do you know how to . . ."

"I sure as hell do."

Ben gunned the engine and they blasted off into the desert night.

# CHAPTER TWENTY-SIX

# VORIS

Cisco uttered prayers in Spanish as Ben stomped on the gas and the truck soared over 100 miles an hour, with the lines of the path clear in front of them and the spires of their castle sinking down in the rearview. They sped into a patch of dunes and the truck got air after each bump, landing back down with a THUD that made the explorer cry out for Jesus.

"You can drink that brandy for real now," Ben told him. Cisco did as instructed.

After a few sips of the calvados, Cisco stopped praying and began asking questions.

"Where are we going, my friend?"

"To kill Voris."

"How do you know?"

"The path will take us to him."

"You believe."

"I don't require faith for this."

"What is this vessel?"

"This is a truck."

"How does it go so fast?"

"Gas, baby. Gas."

"I must bring it back to Spain."

"When we're done with Voris, you can do whatever the hell you want with it. Check the glove compartment and see if there's anything useful inside of it."

"The what?"

Ben pointed to the underside of the dash. Cisco unlatched the glove compartment. Inside was a syringe with a handwritten label that said CORTISONE. Ben grabbed the needle, popped the sheath off, and jammed it into his bad knee.

"Holy shit! WOO-HOO!"

Now they were doing 110. Also inside the glove box they found ripe oranges and cold bottles of water and pouches of air-dried beef and fresh-shelled pistachios. And a seed. One single hard brown seed. It rolled out and Ben lunged to catch it before it hit the floor mat, the syringe still poking out of his leg. The truck swerved and tipped, and Cisco crossed himself as Ben violently pulled the wheel back to keep them on the road. He pocketed the seed in his tattered work pants. Then he pointed to the food.

"We share," Ben said. They feasted as Ben upped the truck to 120, desperate to outrun the night. When Ben slid his water bottle into the cup holder between their seats, Cisco marveled, as if the Virgin Mary had appeared before him.

Suddenly, Ben panicked.

"Cisco, did you get my rock?"

"Your rock?"

"Peter. Did we leave Peter at the castle?"

"I believe so, yes."

Ben stomped on the brakes hard, nearly driving poor Cisco's head into the windshield. There they sat, in the center of the desert, the engine growling, eager to resume its work.

"Are you all right?" Cisco asked.

No. No, he wasn't. He knew every facet of the rock by now. It had *become* Peter. Ben began to hyperventilate. Cisco gently placed a hand on his shoulder.

"We cannot go back for it, my friend."

"I know." Ben began to choke and wheeze on his tears, the kind of crying seizure you have when the tears come too fast. He felt hormonal. Unstable. "I didn't even say good-bye. . . ."

"You will see your real son soon. It is destiny."

Ben put his hand to his mouth and let the tears fall openly. "I'm okay. I just needed a moment."

"I understand."

Done with his crying jag, Ben gripped the gearshift hard enough to tear it clean off. Then he snorted like a bull and gunned the engine once more, throwing Cisco back into his seat.

They drove for hours. Ben could have driven forever. The sky was shifting from black to dark blue, the dawn before the dawn. The sandy path soon gave way to gravel, and then at long last, asphalt. Smooth, humming black asphalt. He hadn't seen asphalt in ages. He began crying again as the pickup tore across the highway. Street lamps appeared. Cacti. Shrubs. He saw a coyote stalking beside the highway and could barely contain his glee. Cisco pointed at the mangy animal.

"What is that?" he asked.

"*Life.*"

Ben's capillaries opened wide at the sight of it all, sending nutrients and oxygen to the formerly dormant parts of his anatomy. Through the windshield he watched the desert sands turn from red to light brown. In the distance, he saw the path open to a convenience store on the side of the road with a working gas pump. The lights were on under the pump shelter. The truck needed gas, so they pulled in. Cisco stepped out of the truck, gazing at the store in wonder. The doors were padlocked shut and a CLOSED sign hung in the window. Ben jammed the pump into the truck (it pumped gas for free, without any request for payment), and then began to load up the bed with bags of salt, sand, antifreeze, and motor oil. He had memorized *Dr. Abigail Blackwell's Gallery of the Curiously Undead* from cover to cover before the Smokes burned his tent down. There were things they were going to need.

No one was inside the store, and the lights were off in the mini-market. Cisco walked up to the window on the left-hand side and stared at the aisles, all lined with chips and snacks and big fat coffee urns and old hot dogs on steaming rollers and packaged Danishes.

"My friend, how do we . . ."

Ben hurled a sandbag into the window on the right-hand side and the glass exploded.

"Oh."

"That felt amazing," Ben said. "You wanna smash the other one?"

"No."

Ben stepped through the display and motioned to Cisco.

"Open your bag."

Cisco took out his little leather satchel and they looted the store: ready-made sandwiches, rope, winter gloves, lighters and lighter fluid, cigarettes (for Cisco), individually wrapped pies, energy drinks, candy bars with enough sugar to kill a diabetic. Cisco took great interest in the cheap beaded bracelets on a display rack. He emptied them all into the bag.

"What's with the bracelets?" Ben asked.

"Natives will trade for them."

Ben shrugged. On the opposite display rack hung a bunch of

tiny stuffed animals on key chains, including a fox. Ben grabbed three of them, even though he knew he wouldn't be able to keep them for very long.

"This place is extraordinary," Cisco said.

"That it is. Everything you need. Now let's get going."

Back to the truck they went. Cisco ate his first tortilla chip. And then he ate forty more.

"These are very good," he told Ben.

"More where that came from."

No other vehicles crossed their path. No other signs of human life—or unlife—were anywhere to be seen. Soon, a single glass building with mirrored windows came into view. It was sitting in the dead center of the highway: the end of the road. The raw sunlight was now breaking through, and they could see the reflection of their own truck barreling toward the building through its shiny façade, all blazing chrome and hot smoke.

They skidded to a stop outside the double glass doors at the front of the building. If the Smokes could only see darkness while buried in the sand, maybe Voris wouldn't know that daylight had arrived. Cisco got out and stared up at the edifice in awe. He knelt on the ground and began to pray.

"Heavenly Father, *Dios mio*, thank you for this. . . ."

"NO TIME!"

Ben jerked Cisco up and dragged him toward the mirrored double doors. They wouldn't open. Off to the side, there was a keypad with an inscription above it.

0, 1, 8, 11, 88 . . .

"It's a sequence," Ben said. "Cisco, you any good at math?"

"Mathematics are the language of the devil."

"You know, normally I'd disagree with you. But considering who put this keypad here, I'll roll with it." He stared at the sequence. It seemed simple enough. *Ones and eights, right?*

He punched in "III" and nothing happened.

"Is it a puzzle of some kind?" Cisco asked.

"Yeah. The next number in the pattern will open the . . ."

Ben shuddered as Cisco hurled a sandbag at the double doors. The bag bounced right off the glass and smacked down hard on the pavement, breaking open and spilling coarse sand all over the concrete. He glared at Cisco.

"What? It worked for you back at the food castle!"

"That's true," Ben said. He stared at the inscription again.

0, I, 8, II, 88 . . .

Shapes. They were shapes, not numbers. All symmetrical. The numbers themselves were irrelevant. Only the shape of them mattered. Which meant the next number was . . .

"IOI."

Ben punched it into the keypad and the double doors parted. The two men stepped into a medieval stone chamber and the doors sealed shut behind them. They would not open again. The building was the precise opposite of Voris's hotel: modern on the outside, primitive on the inside. It was cool and musty in here, the only light provided by the torches lining the wall. There was a great stone arch at the far end of the lobby. Standing under it was the old, doll-like clerk from the hotel. He wore a crisp, pin-striped suit. He gave both men a crooked half smile before advancing. This was not a hotel. He was not there to serve them. The clerk broke into a run.

"Cisco!"

The explorer unsheathed his sword, waited a beat, and chopped the clerk's head clean off with a single, gorgeous flourish. The clerk grew a new head almost instantly. It sprouted from his neck in a fleshy blob and then took its original form, pancake makeup and wispy hair and all. Meanwhile, the dismembered first head sprouted eight legs, each coated in thick black armor, with ghastly cilia running all along them. The regenerated clerk and the Head Spider advanced.

"I take the spider," Cisco said, throwing his bag to Ben. Ben dug into the satchel and found a canister of lighter fluid. The clerk ran at Ben and opened his mouth wide, far wider than his face seemed able to accommodate. There were fangs. The clerk's pupils began to glow. Ben futzed with the plastic seal on the can as he dashed away from the Regenerator. It was a hell of a time to be wrestling with retail packaging.

The clerk wouldn't relent, chasing him toward the wall and cornering him. He grabbed Ben's shirt and tore his sleeve away as Ben finally pulled off the seal and aimed the fluid canister right at the creepy old man, hosing him down like a sunflower. The torches on the wall were within reach. He wrested one off its moorings and dipped the flame into the fluid trail, then dove out of the way. A hot orange blaze engulfed the clerk. His hair singed off and his skin melted down like hot wax.

Meanwhile, Cisco held the Head Spider down with his boot and chopped off all eight legs in compact, graceful strokes. He could paint a masterwork with that sword. Ben ran over with the fluid and doused every limb, along with the head. Then, the flame. Both men retreated to the farthest wall as the undead bodies turned to lifeless ash.

"I am glad we killed this man," Cisco said. "He looked like an Englishman."

They were both weak. So, so weak. They were running out of second winds to catch. The c-store junk food and the snacks in the car couldn't restore all their lost muscle tissue and fat in a single night. They needed to find Voris and kill him *now*, and then they could finally rest.

Past the stone archway they found themselves winding up a

torchlit ramp, each man shaking with dread, ready to kill a Skinless or a Smoke or a Mouth Demon or anything else that could be lurking around the seemingly eternal bend. After countless loops around on the way up, they entered a stone hallway that progressed for hundreds of yards, well outside of the standard physical limits of the supposedly normal-looking office building they first entered. After a while, the hallway opened up to a room that was fifty yards wide, with a wall of flame towering across the center of it, offering no way to pass. The heat was volcanic; it came at both men in a powerful gust. In front of the wall of fire was a small idol, fashioned of pale white marble, with black wings and a pair of glowing white eyes. It was a statue of Voris. Directly in front of the statue was a padded prayer rail: the kind you'd find in any church pew. Scrawled in the musty floor was a single order:

PRAY

Ben started walking toward the prayer rail but Cisco held him back.

"What?"

"You cannot pray to this man," Cisco said.

"It's how the fire goes down," Ben said. "We don't have to mean it."

"It is not a prayer if you do not mean it."

"There's no choice, Cisco."

"I will not give this man my soul, no matter the cost. If I give myself to him, then I truly *will* burn."

"Hang on."

Ben took out the seed they had found in the glove compartment and smashed it on the floor. Nothing happened. He picked the seed back up and dug into Cisco's bag, throwing items from the convenience store at the flames to make them go down: more sand, more salt, a box of candy bars. Nothing worked.

"We *have* to pray," he told Cisco.

"I will pray," said the explorer. "But not to him."

Cisco turned his back on the statue of Voris and dropped to a knee. He waved to Ben to join him.

"You will pray with me," the explorer said. "Do not face the idol."

Ben did as instructed. The two men held hands as the wall of fire burned on.

"Close your eyes."

"Okay," said Ben.

"Repeat after me: When thou passest through the waters, I will be with thee."

*"When thou passest through the waters, I will be with thee."*

"And through the rivers, they shall not overflow thee."

*"And through the rivers, they shall not overflow thee."*

Cisco began yelling his prayer. "When thou walkest through the fire, thou shalt not be burned; neither shall the flame kindle upon thee. SAY IT LOUD, FOR GOD TO HEAR."

*"When thou walkest through the fire, thou shalt not be burned; neither shall the flame kindle upon thee."*

"Now open your eyes and stand up."

Ben stood and the two men faced the wall of fire. The explorer turned to Ben and cradled his face in his hands.

"God is with us now," Cisco said.

"Cisco, don't."

But it was too late. Cisco walked directly into the wall of flame and disappeared.

"Cisco? Cisco?!"

There was no answer.

"CISCO?!"

Still nothing.

Now a half dozen Jellies emerged in the hallway behind him—blobs of living mucus that rose up out of the floor as if pulled. All as formless as death itself. They crept toward Ben and their shiny, gelatinous bodies oozed a trail of milky slime onto the stones behind them. Ben could hear them slurping and sucking, eager to bury him alive inside them. Bereft of hot liquids, he needed faith in a hurry, before the Jellies could fill his mouth and leave his prayers forever unsaid.

*It is not a prayer if you do not mean it.*

He hadn't meant it the first time. He was just saying the words because Cisco told him to. That wasn't enough. He turned his back on the idol and dropped to one knee. In his mind, he saw magic seeds and living paths and the dreams of his luminous, alternative past. *The Producer could be merciful. The Producer could be forgiving. Please don't let me burn.*

The Jellies closed in, reaching for his foot.

This time, he yelled out the whole prayer:

*"When thou passest through the waters, I will be with thee; and through the rivers, they shall not overflow thee. When thou walkest through the fire, thou shalt not be burned, neither shall the flame kindle upon thee."*

Then he walked into the fire without hesitation. The surrounding flames brushed coolly against him, like a pleasant draft from an open kitchen window. He walked ten feet through the gauntlet before emerging on the other side of the wall, his flesh and hair unblemished. Cisco stood waiting for him on the other side, beaming.

"I told you we should not pray to the idol," he boasted.

"Yeah, you were probably right about that."

They stood now in Voris's crypt, a circular stone room with a grand sarcophagus resting atop a round pedestal in the center of the room. There was no sign of anyone else. It was just them and the coffin. Ben sighed at the sight of the lid. It looked extremely heavy.

"You have the jar?" he asked Cisco.

Cisco took the jar out of the bag, still aglow. The years hadn't been kind to its contents. The stew was green with rot and marbled with fermenting, bacterial fur. They opened the corroded lid and discovered that the gold tooth had made the putrefied liquid stink even worse than usual. The stench was its own monster now, attacking both men and leaving them hacking and wheezing.

Cisco set the open jar down on the floor and wiped his hand clean. Meanwhile, Ben tried kicking the lid of the sarcophagus loose. Cisco grabbed him.

"What?" Ben said.

"Might that disturb the person sleeping inside the coffin?"

"Oh! Right, yeah."

Cisco placed the butt of his palms against the lid.

"We open it this way," he told Ben.

Ben stood next to Cisco and pressed his own palms against it.

"Do we pray?" he asked the explorer.

"No. Praying is over. Now we push."

"One, two, three . . ."

They slammed against the lid and it started to give way. It felt like pushing a bus uphill. Millimeter by millimeter, they watched in both elation and horror as the top slid open to reveal a resting Voris inside. The sallow skin. The folded black wings. The white, glowing eyes, now shut. The devil's mouth was closed tight. Cisco held up the putrid stew jar.

"How do we do this?" he asked.

"His skin will burn you," Ben said. "We need gloves and a knife."

Cisco dug into the bag and handed Ben a small knife they'd taken from the convenience store. Both men donned winter gloves.

"I'll open the mouth," Ben said. "You drop the stew in."

"Yes."

Ben slipped the knife between Voris's white lips and gave the knife a twist, revealing his blood-red gums and sharp, conical teeth. Cisco tipped the jar ever so slightly, letting the stew dribble down into the opening. They could see the potion burning its way through Voris's gums as Cisco set the jar down beside the coffin.

"How long do you think this takes to work?" Cisco asked.

But Ben never got to answer, because Voris woke up and shot his deathly glowing pupils at both of them.

"Keep your eyes closed and hold him down!" Ben screamed. He dropped the knife and clamped Voris's mouth shut to let the poison go down his throat, like holding an alligator by its jaws. Cisco jumped on top of the sarcophagus and kept Voris's wings fast to his body as he tried to burn them with his eyes. Cisco's shirt rode up and his bare stomach came into contact with the devil himself, the skin burning into the explorer's flesh as he screamed and cried out for God.

Both men shut their eyes to avoid Voris's gaze, praying they could hold on long enough to get him to swallow enough poison to just *die*. But Voris kicked Cisco off the coffin and spat the hot stew right into Ben's face, causing him to fall to the ground and choke.

Voris stood up in his resting place and spread his black wings. This would be easy for him now. He was awake. The poison was out of his mouth. He could kill the two men any way he pleased. They couldn't even *look* at him without dying.

"Cisco!" Ben cried. "THE SEED!"

Forced against the wall with his eyes shut tight, Cisco reached into his bag as Voris swooped down and dug into Ben with his red-hot uncovered talons. Cisco found the seed and threw it across the room as Ben curled into a ball and prayed for a quick death.

The seed grew. From its landing spot on the crypt floor, it sprouted thirty feet high, growing legs and arms and ruby-red lips and curly hair, a great burlap dress covering its form. Above the ruckus of Ben's screams echoing off the walls, the two men heard a big, booming female voice cry out:

"HA!"

There was Fermona, towering over the three combatants, looking down at them as if she had come across a handful of rabbits playing in her backyard. Even Voris was paralyzed by the sight of her. He gazed at her with his glowing pupils but they couldn't harm her in any way. Fermona plucked the winged devil up off the ground and studied him for a moment.

"Eh," she said. "What the hey."

And then she swallowed Voris in a single, easy gulp. There wasn't even time for him to make a sound.

Ben leapt up and grabbed the pickle jar off the pedestal, holding it up for the giant.

"Fermona!" he screamed. "Have a chaser!"

She grabbed the jar in her massive hand and downed it like a shot from a thimble, then made a disgusted face as the consumed Voris and the poison sloshed around in her great belly.

"Ugh, disgusting," she grimaced. Then she looked down at Ben and pointed an accusing finger at him. "*You.* You ruined me for human meat, you lout! I've spent the past ten years looking for more of those hot dogs."

"I know a place that has them," Ben said.

"Oh, really?"

"Honest to goodness."

"How many of them?"

"A lot. I swear."

"Look at you! You're all tiny again. Bet you thought you were hot stuff when you were my height. Tell me where I can find this food and maybe I won't throw you into the sun."

Cisco stared up at Fermona, making a cross on his chest and whispering holy praises.

"Are you going to eat us?" Ben asked her.

Fermona put her hands on her hips. "What do *you* think, Ben?"

And then it hit him. "No, you're not going to eat us."

"And do you know why?" she asked.

He did. "Because we're on the path. We were told to never leave the path, or we would die."

"Ah, but there's a flip side to that now, isn't there? Which is . . ."

"If we stay on the path, we *can't* die."

"There it is. Now you know. Besides, you and the little Spanish fella are both way more trouble than you're worth. That one kept poking me with his little toothpick! There's nothing worse than a man who puts up a fight. Now, where's the food? Gimme gimme gimme."

"Back in the desert," Ben said. "There's a store that has them, straight down the road."

"Brilliant. You two: Huddle up in the corner together."

"Why?"

"Just do what I say, stupid. Quit being annoying. This is gonna be *great*. Watch what I can do."

Ben ran over to Cisco and the two weakened men clung to each other as Fermona took her left hand and placed it directly above them, forming a makeshift awning. Then, with a gargantuan right hand, she punched through the ceiling of the crypt, broken pieces of mortar and heavy slabs of rock beating down onto the floor of Voris's bedroom. Ben watched in terror as blocks of stone the size of air conditioners tumbled off the back of Fermona's hand and landed within inches of flattening them. When the dust settled, Fermona shook off a few of the boulders and plucked both of the men off the ground with her left hand.

Above, the desert sun blazed into the crypt and the room itself seemed to recoil from the light. The giant reached through the hole in the ceiling and climbed out of the desert glass building with Cisco and Ben still grasped firmly in her hand. Then she jumped off the roof, the meat of her palm protecting both men from the impact of landing on the sun-baked sands below. She set them beside the crimson pickup truck and put her hands on her hips, looking up at the sun and shaking her head.

"I don't know how you humans tolerate that thing beating down on you all day long."

"We are not as close to it as you are," said Cisco.

"Does this store you mentioned have hats?"

"Not in your size," said Ben.

"Bah! Well, you two just remember that I put my delicious, alabaster skin on the line helping you."

"We will. Fermona . . ."

"Yes?"

"Thank you," said Ben. "Thank you so much."

"Aw, that's sweet. Now I kinda wanna eat you again." Then she gave him a playful wink. "Just pulling your leg. I'm off."

And she stomped off down the desert road, in search of newer, bolder flavors.

# CHAPTER TWENTY-SEVEN

# THE VILLA

Here was another curious development in an endless series of them: After Fermona left, Cisco and Ben watched as the asphalt road leading to Voris's lair extended out of thin air, wrapping around the now-convertible office crypt and stretching out into the desert plain to the west. Ben and Cisco hopped in the pickup truck and followed the path for hours. Both men ate junk food with gusto. Cisco wouldn't stop waving his hand over the air-conditioning vent.

"How does it make the wind like this?" he asked Ben.

"Refrigerant. Freon," Ben said.

"Who is this Freon?"

"No, it's a chemical. It makes the air cold."

"This is a miracle."

"It's thirty bucks at the store, brotherman."

"This future you live in . . . would I like it?"

"Honestly, it's probably not that different from the world you know. Some people are happy. Some people are angry. There are wars. I don't know if time makes much of a difference. The world changes, but people act the way people always do."

"Do you think I might be able to pilot this truck?"

"No."

After hundreds of miles, the road abruptly came to a thick ribbon of wetland jungle. The trees rose up from the edge of the desert, reaching for the sun and forming a thick, impenetrable canopy. The path cut into the dark center of the rain forest, the canopy shrouding them in green shadow.

The jungle road grew choppy and narrow, the vegetation pressing against the truck, poised to ensnare it. A lemur jumped onto the hood, causing Cisco to cross himself, and then it jumped off onto a nearby tree. Unseen animals and insects made unidentifiable sounds around them as they rolled on. After a few moments, the truck emerged on a pristine white beach, the sand made of nothing but pure ground seashells. The sun was slowly melting into a ravishing Caribbean-blue sea, waters that could soothe any man who laid eyes upon them. The lavenders and pinks of the nascent sunset bounced off the sands and made them shine like mother-of-pearl.

The path broke into three directions on the beach. To the right was a villa, made of treated beech wood, with a lush courtyard and a pool filled with water that was cleaner than an operating room. There was even a parking spot outlined in the sand for the red truck. To the left, the path stretched down the coastline as the beach curled around a small bay.

Directly in front of them, leading to the water, was a small round cocktail table, covered in a white tablecloth, with a single place setting and a bottle of champagne (always champagne) chilling in a silver bucket. The setting had no flatware, only a large turquoise charger plate with a corked glass vial sitting in the center. Past the table, the path opened wide to greet the water.

There was a place card behind the plate. Someone with elegant penmanship had written the name:

Ben

He got out of the truck and picked up the card, feeling the fibers of the thick paper stock. Cisco unsheathed his sword and scanned the beach for potential predators, but there was nothing. Ben wasn't as paranoid as the Spaniard. This was a place where they could remain undisturbed. Voris was gone. This was their reward. They would be safe here.

Cisco peered over Ben's shoulder and looked at the place card. "What does it mean?" he asked.

"It means I have to go into the sea," Ben said.

"But I go the other way."

"That's right. The path wants us to split."

"I do not want to do this."

Ben clapped a hand on the explorer's shoulder. "I don't either, old friend."

"You must drink from that vial?"

"At some point, yes."

"Do you know what it will do to you?"

"Yeah. It's gonna turn me into a fucking crab."

"That cannot be possible."

"You've seen the things I've seen. Why doubt this?"

"Is that what you want? To be a crab?"

"Cisco, what I want hasn't mattered for a long time now." Ben walked over to the steps leading up to the villa and beckoned the explorer to follow. "Come on. There's no rush. We may as well enjoy ourselves."

The villa was an open-air, three-bedroom suite. In the center of the courtyard was a large table that featured a buffet of fresh offerings: mangoes, pineapples, olives, rows of sliced mozzarella cheese and beefsteak tomatoes, chilled lobster tails, huge slabs of carved roast beef, whole filets of smoked salmon longer than park benches, carafes of every last possible squeezed citrus.

Also, there was beer. Cold, cold beer. Cans and bottles. Ben didn't bother with the food. He wanted the beer. He grabbed two bottles, knocked off the caps, stripped down to his boxers, ran out of the villa, and plunged into the bay. A little bit of salt water got into the beer, but that made it taste even better as he stared at the sunset reflecting off the ocean's glittering skin. A shirtless, awkward Cisco came running to the surf behind him, staying upright in the water because he couldn't swim. Ben stood up and the men clinked bottles.

"Merry Christmas," Ben said.

"How do you know if it's Christmas?"

"I don't. But Merry Christmas anyway."

"And to you as well."

They chugged their beers. Cisco pointed to the branch of the path winding around the bay.

"Tomorrow morning, I will go," he said.

"So soon? You should stay here a while and rest up. You look like shit."

"No. My God and my queen are calling me. I will not rest here a second longer than I have to." He turned to Ben. "But you know, there's something to be said for never seeing you again."

"Well, I love you, too, Cisco."

"No, I mean this. I do not want this friendship to linger. I do not want it to wither and die. It will end here, as strong as it's ever been. And this is a good thing. I don't want to be around long enough to disappoint you."

"I think it would be more likely to be the other way around."

"It's not possible. You have brought your family honor."

"Cisco, honor doesn't mean jack shit to me." He sat down in the surf again, letting his toes poke out of the water. Then he wiggled them as a way of saying hello to himself. "You know I can't even remember what my kids look like anymore? I remember my drawings of them better than their actual faces. I try to picture them now and I know I've gotten it wrong. And it's been years. Even if I get back to them, they won't be the kids I knew, and I won't be the dad they knew. They probably won't even have the same hair color anymore. We'll all be perfect fucking strangers. I've wanted to go home for so long, Cisco. But now I know home isn't gonna be anything I recognize. I don't even know what I would say to my wife if I saw her now."

"You don't have to say anything. It's love. Love doesn't require an explanation."

"I don't know, man. I'm scared to death. I bet I'm more comfortable walking along this goddamn path than I would be back home. It's ruined me. Do you know how fucked up that is? I don't know what to do with myself anymore. The only reason I'm still alive is out of sheer habit."

"It is honorable."

"There's no honor in surviving. It's what you're supposed to fucking do. Half the people who survive stuff don't even know why or how they did it. I know *I* don't. 'Honor' is some bullshit word men made up to jerk themselves off. You can get away with anything if you just say you did it with honor."

The Spaniard didn't respond. Instead, he went back to the villa, opened up two more beers, and brought them to the bay. They drank a dozen between them as the sun finally tagged in the two moons, and a far less predatory brand of night took shape over them: cool and open and inviting, macaws jabbering from the jungle behind them.

There were clean towels and razors and clippers in the villa bathrooms, so the men washed and shaved (Cisco retained a lengthy goatee) and retired to bed. When Ben closed his eyes, the sleep walled him off from everything. No dreams. No visions. No part of his past came back to make amends. There was only rest.

In the morning, Cisco insisted on leaving. The explorer was still skinny and fatigued from their escape out of the desert, but this was all still a grand adventure to him: a new and mystical continent that he would soon divulge to the rest of Europe. No matter how hard Ben tried to convince him otherwise, Cisco remained adamant about seeking his fortune.

They stood at the three-pronged split in the path and said goodbye. Ben handed him the keys to the pickup truck.

"Are you sure?" Cisco asked.

"Yeah. Everyone drives where I come from. No reason you can't figure it out, too. You're probably already better than most Maryland drivers."

Cisco hopped up in the cab and gripped the steering wheel, closing his eyes and savoring the power.

"Remember," said Ben, "the pedal on the left makes you stop. The pedal on the right makes you go."

"I wish I had a gift to leave you with," said the explorer. "But I know you won't be able to take anything with you."

"I don't need it," Ben said. "Like you said, no reason for this to linger. We end our friendship here today with it as strong as it's ever been. And when I get back, I'll look you up in a history book."

"Maybe your 'America' will be named after me, and the FILTHY GARBAGE PERSON Vespucci will rot in the depths of . . ."

"That's altogether possible, yes."

Cisco gazed at him.

"What are you doing?" Ben asked.

"Getting a good look. The last time you see a person is the thing you remember best about them. God be with you, Ben."

"You too, old friend."

Cisco stomped on the gas and nothing happened.

"Cisco, you have to turn the key first."

"Oh."

The Spaniard turned the key and jerked the gearshift. The truck moved forward in jerks and spasms at first, eventually smoothing out and rounding the bay beach, finally turning out of view around the cape. And Ben found himself alone once more, but he knew he wouldn't be that way for long. There was someone he had to meet, presumably on the opposite side of that sea.

But that could wait. For now, he feasted. He drank all the beer and ate all the lobster and showered three times a day, gaining pounds on his frame at a visible pace. Every night, he sat in the bay with his beer and said howdy to his toes and looked up at the freakishly assembled stars and the two moons and then retired to a night of rest that felt like a bath in amniotic fluid. Maybe he could stay at this villa forever. Would that be so bad? He had gotten good at being alone again. There was nothing to confront here at this beach: no monsters, no past, no future. Everyone left him alone, the ultimate desire of any middle-aged man. The safety of it all wooed him. Coddled him.

A week later, he had another night vision. Only he wasn't in his past this time. No, this time he woke up exactly where he had fallen asleep: in the villa, in the smooth white queen bed. He saw someone come out from behind the bedroom door, and there, standing in the moonlight, was Teresa, clad only in a sheer white robe that just barely reached past her hips. She let the robe hang open, her body like a cello. Ben got out of bed and came to her. He put his finger on her chin and traced it all the way down, never touching fabric. Then he reached under her robe and hoisted her up, wrapping her tan legs around him, kissing her so hard that their faces went perpendicular.

Ben turned and laid her on the bed. He wanted to be inside every last part of her. She cupped his face in her hands and asked, "Now do you remember?"

"Yes. Oh, God, yes."

"Then come for me."

"I will."

"Come for me now."

All his joints cracked in unison.

He woke up alone, between the white sheets. The sun was rising over the jungle canopy back east. In the courtyard, the buffet had been thoroughly scavenged. All the beer was gone. Despite the temptation to retire permanently in this oasis, it was time. A week of any vacation is plenty. He walked out of the villa and to the round table overlooking the surf. Then he uncorked the vial at his place setting and held it up for a lonesome toast.

"Bottoms up, Mr. Producer."

He felt a burning in his throat, and not a liquor sort of burn, more like a shot of pure acid. He flopped down onto his belly and began to convulse. His head retracted into his neck. His muscles drew so tight that it felt like his entire body was cramping. His field of vision split into eight thousand separate parts and then coalesced back together into a single, myopic blur. Everything smelled: the ocean, the sand, the air. Every odor amplified and rushed into his brain like it was a subway car. His limbs grew stiff and immobile. His fingers froze and began to conjoin.

He could feel other, small limbs growing from his rib cage. Two, then four, then six: each one stiff and sharp, each leg perfectly engineered for sand skipping. A pair of paddle fins grew out of his butt and started waving around. Two hairy antennae sprouted out over him and hung in front of his eyes, like fishing lines. His skin turned to armored plates, all fitting snugly together. Within moments, he felt the nerves from every new limb connect to his brain and he gained control over his body, able to move everything and have it all feel totally natural.

"Hello?" His voice sounded deeper. Packed down.

He skittered over to the sea and let the water flood his gills and fill his lungs. He could still breathe. He felt light and dexterous, able to move in any direction with equal speed.

Then he peeked out of the water and looked back at the table where his place setting was. It looked huge. Everything looked huge. A crushing wave came and now Ben found himself pulled away from the villa, the beach, the split in the road. It whisked him out into the sapphire waters and tossed him around like a beer can. After a few moments, he figured out his paddle fins and righted himself, barely able to discern the difference between right-side up and upside down. He could only see three feet in front of him, and what he saw was little more than murk. The water felt so hot. Boiling. He could feel the sun behind him, and he knew it was time for him to move away from the shore, out of the warm shallows and deep into the wide, cold ocean.

He swam. He could swim like a master now.

III.

CHAPTER TWENTY-EIGHT

# CRAB

F ish parts. He discovered that fish parts were the best. They usually settled down on the ocean floor after the sharks were done with them. Other fish would scavenge the bits on the way down, but there was always just enough left for Ben to gobble up. That's the way the ocean worked: plenty of dead stuff for everyone to share.

There were more parts to snack on at night, when the sun didn't sell him out by illuminating every last piece of food (including himself) floating around in the water for all takers to see. When it was particularly bright, he would sink deep and bury himself in the sand for hours at a time, burrowing forward and occasionally bumping into stonefish, or isopods, or other ghastly sea creatures. Here, under the whitecaps, he couldn't speak, and no one else spoke to him. But he was too concerned about predators to make any kind of noise anyway. They could hear everything. They didn't even have to *see*, they were so good at sensing everything around them.

He lived in a nearsighted fog, scrambling and swimming around in the current until random things popped into his limited field of vision. In a single day, he might encounter food (good), monster-jawed anglerfish (bad), whales (terrifying yet astonishing), coral (annoying), and any number of random, squishy invertebrates crowding the ocean floor (whatever). Anything that could kill him out here could do it quickly. He felt bad he'd eaten crab so many times himself. *But it's what everyone in Maryland does!*

Swimming was the best part. When Ben was a kid, his mom would take him to the community pool—a hot, swarming place for all the families that weren't rich enough to join one of the proper country clubs—and he would try to stay underwater forever, floating spread-eagle just above the bottom of the pool, pretending he was drifting off into outer space. But of course, he couldn't hold his breath for very long, and soon he would rise to the surface and be surrounded by all the other kids operating at peak obnoxiousness. Then he would drape his arms over the soaked concrete lip of the pool and rest his head on it, taking in the sun and feeling the water in the concrete pores grow as hot and thick as human sweat.

But now he was a crab, and oxygen intake wasn't an issue at all. He could dance and shimmy underwater all day long if he felt like it. In fact, that was pretty much all he *could* do. Entertainment options were limited down here. There was swimming, and there was eating, and there was not being eaten. He planned his days accordingly, knowing that the path would deliver him to the beaches of Courtshire at some point. Right? *Right?*

It was taking a little bit longer than Ben would have liked. He spent weeks tunneling through muck and dodging sharks. On those rare occasions when he would venture up to the ocean surface, he never spotted dry land. He grew antsy, his confidence in the path wavering as he became, day by day, a prisoner of the endless sea. *This is all some big fucking joke. Fight off a bunch of monsters and survive being imprisoned twice (twice!), and all you get for your trouble are these lousy crab claws.*

And then, one night, he was trudging across the sand when he found himself tripped up. He tried swimming up to the surface but bounced against a mesh barrier. It was a trawling net, sweeping the floor clean of everything: lobsters, clams, eels, shrimp, tuna, scrod, boots—you name it. Ben tried to snip the rubberized nylon with his pincers but it was no use. The net drew tight, pulling him up with his seaborne colleagues and lifting them up out of the water. Then the net swung over and dumped them all on a rolling conveyor belt. He saw a gauntlet of hands in chain-mail gloves sorting through the fish, discarding pieces of driftwood and tossing inedibles overboard.

Ben was not an inedible. A mighty hand plucked him off the belt and held him against a measuring caliper. He was big enough to keep. Into a barrel he went with a bunch of other crabs.

"Psst!" Ben whispered. "Any of you shitheads talk? Anyone? Anyone?"

They did not. He was the only magically transformed human forced to serve an existential tour of duty there among them.

"Just my luck."

He tried scrambling up the side of the barrel but it was hard to find sure footing among the teeming crustaceans. A man in a yellow slicker picked up the barrel and carried it into the galley of what appeared to be a massive freighter: all iron, belching exhaust out of every possible opening. The galley had plain white walls and black rubber mats all over the floor. Ben could only see out of the top of the barrel, but what he saw wasn't comforting: a range top, and a pot of boiling water the size of a trash can. The steam was racing out of the pot, coating the white walls and making them sweat. These kitchen walls probably hadn't been dry in years. He could hear one man shouting instructions at the rest.

"Remember: If you are caught smuggling any extra food for yourself, you *will* be tossed overboard. Failure to adhere to rationing is punishable by DEATH."

A chorus of voices responded in unison. "SIR, YES, SIR."

"Freezer number one is now stocked full. All rations are to be vacuum sealed and packed into freezer number two. Load back to front, side to center. Do not block the front of the freezer or I will personally put my foot in your ass. Is that clear?"

"SIR, YES, SIR."

"Yo!" Ben cried out from the bucket. "Can anyone get me out of here?"

No one replied. Instead, another chain-mail hand reached into the barrel and started grabbing crabs by the handful, dumping them in the pot. Ben dodged the hand again and again, wishing he was in the company of friendlier giants. The barrel was growing empty now. The hand dug deep and swept around the bottom, finally plucking up Ben and a few other stragglers. But before it could lower Ben into the steaming pot, he wriggled free and dropped down to the black mat on the floor. There was just enough room under the range for him to fit, so he bolted across the mat and tucked himself under the enormous appliance.

"God dammit," he heard a voice say. Now he saw a broom handle come sweeping across the floor under the range. Ben skittered, dancing under a steel shelf and then an industrial fridge, spotting a pair of double doors with black flaps only five feet away. There were two lines of white tape running out from the bottom of the fridge and under the door. Ben looked down and saw that he was sitting in between them. *The path.*

He made a break for it, walking across the open galley floor and dodging a good number of angry footfalls. He was faster than all of them. Smarter, too.

Outside the galley, he emerged into a bustling hallway lined with screaming cooks, janitors, stewards, and passengers. Everyone looked haggard and disheveled. Whatever clothes they had on appeared to be the only clothing any of them possessed. Ben bobbed and weaved around everyone, staying within the white tape lines. An excited toddler knelt down for a closer look and Ben whispered, "Hey kid, can you get me out of here?"

The kid screamed bloody murder. Ben just barely dodged the little boy's mother trying to stomp him to death.

There was a single swinging door at the end of the hall with a little porthole window. The passengers were streaming in and out of it without any rhyme or reason. Many people were crying and consoling one another. All of them looked freezing, desperately covering their faces with their sleeves or with heavy scarves. They all had multicolored armbands and on those armbands they could project a display in front of them that showed them anything they liked: games and text messages and photos. Mothers kept children occupied by screening movies for them in midair. They all seemed so destitute, and yet clad in the most wondrous technological wear.

He scrambled out of the door and found himself outside on the main deck. Men in camo garb patrolled the outside area with big, powerful rifles. Again, he was far too conspicuous.

"Mommy, a crab!"

Another kiddie hand went for him and this time, he gave the kid a firm pinch. The kid whined and mewled like he was dying. *Jeez kid, get your shit together.*

He looked up at the bridge of the freighter and saw that there was no captain. The ship was steering itself. The LED fog lights scanning out from the conning tower were brighter and more concentrated than any lights he had ever seen.

There was a steel lip that curled around the freighter deck, and

Ben couldn't see past it. The two taped lines ran up and over the side, off the ship. He made his way to the railing as people randomly gave chase and eventually he was able to climb over the lip and hang off the side of the freighter. The two white lines extended down the hull into the water below.

The wind caught him. He had no clue they were going so fast—40 knots—until that moment. He was barely hanging on, about to drop back into the sea, when he looked out and saw land. The ship was cruising across a bay, at the mouth of a wide river. It was the Hudson, lower Manhattan on the right and New Jersey on the left.

Even from this distance, and with his crippled eyesight, Ben could see that the entire city was dead. The buildings were submerged up to twenty stories up, some of them halfway coated in fresh volcanic rock. Whole spires had come dislodged and were floating in the water. Anything that wasn't wet was burning. Ben grabbed the hull and stretched out farther to try to see more, but the sky was still so dark and cloudy. Or were those even clouds? They were so black and menacing that they should have been dumping rain all over them.

No, they were plumes of ash, hanging over the water and blotting out the sun entirely, even as the morning came. It was as if one of Voris's Smokes had imprisoned the world. On board, Ben could hear people crying and begging each other for food among the bloops and blorps coming from whatever technological wonders they had strapped to their forearms. The freighter cruised past the ghost of New York City with no thought of stopping. The land was dead and fallow. This freighter was all that was left of the world: all the people and food and fuel. All of it was here on a single ship that was just holding out a little bit longer, delaying the inevitable.

*No. This is not . . .*

Suddenly the sun grew bright, alarmingly so. Ben looked up and saw it burn through the ash cover and turn an angry shade of red, spewing out flares and intensifying until seconds later, it was extinguished, turning eclipse black. A chorus of screams came from the deck as a Kelvin-scale wind swept over the freighter and froze everyone in place. Below Ben, the sea was quickly crystallizing into permanent ice. A whirlpool formed right beneath him, tight and fast, with a cone in the center that seemed to go down into the Earth's core. The air was growing so cold that he felt it through his thick shell, so he dropped off the side of the freighter and fell into the great sucking vortex, spinning around in the black iciness until he passed out. *Can crabs pass out?* They could now.

When he awoke, he was floating in the shallows, the sun sitting safely up in the sky, the way it was supposed to. He could feel sand now, soft and movable. He buried himself back down in the ocean floor and shuddered at the vision of the entombed skyline and all the screaming passengers witnessing the sun's last gasps. *It's not real. I didn't go through all this just for that to be the ending, just for everything to be so black and meaningless.* Why would anyone show him that? What did he need to see of the absolute end of humanity that he couldn't already guess on his own? *Fuck that.* There was a little space of history that he was trying to crawl back into, and whatever came before it or after it didn't matter. That boat? That was a part of the future that he would never have to participate in.

The waters grew shallow and Ben skittered up onto a sandy spit of beach lined with summer vacation homes on stilts and two parallel lines in the sand that led to a house that was a story taller than the rest. Ben didn't have to crawl up those steps to know what was in the attic. Sure enough, along came a thirty-eight-year-old man with a scar that looked like a running tear and a backpack slung over his shoulder. Crab buried himself as the man walked by and went into the house with the extra story. He could hear the Younger Ben trashing the inside of the place in a blind fury. And then, for twenty minutes, there was silence. After that came a struggle up in the attic, and then the Younger Ben flying out of that house bleeding and screaming like a fucking horse on fire.

"Hey. Hey, you."

"Hello?" the Younger Ben asked.

"Here. I'm over here, Shithead."

# CHAPTER TWENTY-NINE

# THE TWO BENS

I t was amazing how much the Younger Ben annoyed Crab. He was an embarrassing yearbook photo come to life. Crab wanted to poke him in the eye. He had learned so much about maritime exploration from Cisco, and yet he could barely apply any of that knowledge to his travels with his past self, because the thirty-eight-year-old Ben was such a comical dolt: gunning the hovercraft before unmooring it, trying to unmoor it *without* cutting the engine, going to fucking *sleep* and leaving a tiny crab in the cockpit to keep them on course. (Try as Crab might, he eventually had to wake up the Younger Ben because he couldn't turn the steering wheel enough to keep them from veering off the path.)

Everything that Crab said to Ben was a word-for-word recital of everything Crab had said to *him* years ago. It was as if he were reading off a script he had memorized: every warning, every insult, every clue he gave to the Younger, oblivious Ben. Every time he tried to think of something new and different to say, he found himself saying Crab's exact words anyway. It was automatic. They were the correct words. And fucking with Younger Ben was half the fun. When they came to Fermona's mountain, Crab magically stuck to the side of it, and so he had a marvelous time skittering up the peak while the Younger Ben clung desperately to his ice axes. He could laugh at him because he knew how things would turn out.

Soon they reached Fermona's cave, and the Older Ben discovered a new appreciation for all the things Crab had done for him when *he* was trapped in the hole. Crab left Ben alone in that hole for a full week, but only because he was scavenging Fermona's pile for hours at a time as the giant slept, looking for the seed bag despite his limited eyesight.

"Where is it?" he whispered to himself, scouring through the pile one agonizing piece at a time, the cans of food as massive as boulders to him. One time the giant stirred, and Crab settled down and became part of the enormous pile, impossible to detect. The giant went back to snoring loudly, and Crab resumed his tedious work. Once he unearthed the seed bag, he dragged it over to a corner of Fermona's chamber and buried it out of sight, where he could easily get to it during the surprise dwarf fight. He had to retrace the layout of the cave virtually from memory because his eyes were getting so bad. He explored the other dungeon cells as well, each one housing a naked prisoner who was hairless and deranged, babbling nonsense.

"Hey, you!" Crab whispered to one of them. "Do you need help?"

"Gdsfkjhsadasdlkfasdfdsjlk!"

They were barely human. He couldn't bear to look at them for very long.

The day of the fight, the Younger Ben commanded him, "Go into that pile and find me a weapon." But the Older Ben had already found something. He had it in place and ready to deploy, like a good soldier. When he saw the Younger Ben fight the dogface and win, he beamed like a proud older brother.

The hardest part of mentoring his younger self—aside from letting the hovercraft smash into that iceberg because the path led directly into it—came after they defeated Fermona and were walking along the open prairie, when they saw the mirage of Ben's old house. With his lousy crab vision, he could barely make out the blurry sight of little Peter out on the stoop in his jammies, smiling broadly. From that unreachable distance, he may as well have been looking at a small pet rock. But Crab knew what he was looking at.

*That's your home, but it's not really your home anymore.*

*Don't say that.*

*You know it's true. It's your* former *home now. The path is home.*

*Shut up.*

He watched the Younger Ben howl in grief and envied him for being so determined, so frenzied in his mission to get back home. He wasn't like that anymore. *There comes a point in life when you've seen so much that hardly anything surprises you or bothers you, and that's a shitty moment. Wisdom is so terribly overrated.*

They came to the split in the road and now it was time for Crab to find out what was down the left-hand side of that path. He waved a pincer at the younger, more annoying version of himself, just as Crab had to him all those years ago.

"Do you want to take anything?" the Younger Ben asked him.

"I don't need anything," the Older Ben said. "One day, you won't need anything either."

Right on cue, he abandoned his younger self in search of the end, passing through the invisible barrier to the path without hindrance. He had served his time. He should have been close to the end by now. That's what would have been *fair*.

He should have known better.

# CHAPTER THIRTY

# THE TRAIN

Across the prairie Ben skittered, eyeing the split-rail fence for a sign of whatever might come for him next. But all he saw in his limited scope of vision were tiny yellow buttercup flowers and the shores of ponds that, thankfully, were filled with plain water instead of blood. A colossal thunderstorm swept across the fields and Ben had to dig into the side of the path to prevent getting swept away.

For weeks and weeks he crawled along the road, only "sleeping" in a crab's way of resting while alert. He scoured murky puddles for fresh worms and other food, but it was hardly enough in the way of sustenance. His claws, once so nimble, were starting to feel stiff and brittle. His already lousy eyesight was getting lousier. Soon, he was moving mere feet per day, like he was stuck in clay.

Back before the hike, he and Teresa would take the kids to the beaches in Delaware every summer, and they'd occasionally stumble upon a crab shell sitting perfectly still on the beach. It would look like a living crab at first, but then the kids would get closer and give it a poke, and their stick would go right through the shell. Then they'd turn it over and it would be hollow. Here now, dragging himself along the interminable path, he felt like his insides were ready to fall out of him, leaving only a petrified exoskeleton around for passersby to grind under their boots. *Maybe I'll turn into a rock. Maybe they'll turn me into a fossil and I'll be trapped in layer after layer of sediment for billions of years, and dinosaurs will come and go again, and asteroids will pummel the planet, and humans will re-evolve out of microbes before they set me free.*

The storms became less frequent and the sun pounded down on the prairie, sapping the grass and leaving it dull brown. He stopped for hours at a time, growing delirious in the stultifying heat, not even remembering why he was on the path or why he was still bothering to follow it.

And then, one day, he walked into a wooden leg.

"Ow."

It was a varnished pine table, sitting right in the center of the path. Ben looked up but could barely see two inches in front of him. He crawled under the table, into a patch of gratifying shade, and saw a pair of feet. Old-lady feet. Black Mary Janes. Nude panty hose. Then he heard a voice call to him.

"Would you like to be human again?"

*I know that voice.*

"Mrs. Blackwell?" he asked.

"Yes, I am Mrs. Blackwell. Would you like to be human again?"

"Yes?"

"'Yes?' You don't sound terribly convinced."

"I'm sorry. I have a fuckin' headache, and I don't even know what day it is."

"It is any day, Benjamin. There are no days or dates to keep track of here. You're losing time. You'll be dead of dehydration and starvation in just a few moments if you don't answer my question."

"Yes," he said softly. "Please . . . make me human again."

He heard a cork pop and felt a shower of clear liquid rain down on him.

"Drink up," she said.

He sucked the liquid out of the dirt. It took a moment, but once the potion began to circulate, Ben could feel the transformation. His insides became swollen and bloated. His field of vision exploded and coalesced into a clear panorama as his head grew out of the little crab shell, pushing through it like a newborn through its mother's birth canal. His hands—real, human hands—pressed against the inside of his shell and broke the claws to pieces. He was wearing his father's ring again. The tiny crab lungs that were drying out in the heat expanded and now he was purging the last of the water trapped inside those lungs out of a *human* mouth—coughing, hacking, on the verge of vomiting. His vestigial limbs fell off. Thick, sturdy legs grew out of his paddle fins. Long bones. Elastic skin. Scraggly, mannish leg hairs. Feet! Yes, he had feet now. He could float in the sea and wiggle his toes with a bottle of beer in his hand again.

He was lying on the ground now, under Mrs. Blackwell's table. Still emaciated. Still starving. There were tiny bits of crab shell lying all around him. He could barely move.

"Do get up," she told him. "We have business to tend to."

"I'm dying of thirst here."

A bottle of chilled water landed on his head.

"Drink," she said.

He did as instructed.

"Now get up."

He fumed. *Always following orders from this path and the people running it. So sick of this bullshit.* So he didn't get up. Instead, he reached from under the table and grabbed Mrs. Blackwell's stupid leg.

Immediately, a hungry Rottweiler with a killing face poked under the table and growled at Ben.

"Let go of me," Mrs. Blackwell ordered.

That cowed Ben quickly enough. He drew his hand back and rolled away from the dog in a fright, gathering dust all over his naked body. Mrs. Blackwell threw a pair of black workout shorts and an orange T-shirt at him, along with a pair of socks and sneakers.

"Get dressed."

"WHY DO YOU KEEP FUCKING WITH ME?!"

"Do you want me to sic the dog on you, or do you want to find out what's next?"

"Fine. You *complete* assholes."

He slid the shorts and T-shirt on and finally got on his feet. She was sitting behind the table, hands folded neatly in front of her. The table was covered in food: deli meats and cheeses and platters of charred roasted vegetables, the stuff of a starving man's daydreams. There was also a fully loaded handgun lying among the spread.

Behind Mrs. Blackwell was a train. This was the beginning of the line. There was a red caboose at the back, with a fenced-in porch for viewing. The caboose was coupled to a series of six rail coaches: a sleeper car, a café car, a quiet car, a first-class car, and two standard passenger cars. At the front was a single diesel locomotive.

Ben didn't bother asking permission to eat. All the food was in his hands and mouth within seconds. He spied the Rottweiler at Mrs. Blackwell's feet. It was sedate now, gentle as a puppy. He wanted to kick the thing into another dimension.

"Had enough?" Mrs. Blackwell asked.

"Jufft uh thecond." His mouth was full.

She was growing impatient and tapping her foot. "Let's be on with it."

"Jufft talk while I eat."

"You should be paying full attention."

"Fine." No more eating. Mrs. Blackwell gestured to the train with her thumb.

"The train leaves in two minutes. It will take you to the Producer. Despite your conduct here, you've proven a good, strong lad. The Producer thinks you're ready for him now. Alternatively, you can pick up that gun, step off the path, and shoot yourself."

"Why would I do that?"

She leaned in. "I can't tell you how long you will be on that train."

"Why not?"

"It's entirely at the discretion of the Producer. Could be fifteen minutes. Could be years. You'll survive, of course. By now you've learned that nothing on the path will ever kill you, not even old age. As long as the path goes on, *you* go on."

"What's on the train?"

"Nothing is on it."

"Well, is there *food*?"

She rolled her eyes. "Yes, there's food. But now there's no time. So your choice: the train or the gun."

Ben swiped the gun off the table and felt it in his hands. Just the right weight. He aimed it at Mrs. Blackwell. The dog turned feral immediately. He lowered it back down.

"Tell you what," he said to her, "Death lasts millions and billions of years, too. So I'm not gonna shoot myself today, Mrs. Blackwell. I'm gonna keep little mister gun here, and I'm gonna get on that train, and when I get to your Producer, I'm gonna shoot him in the fucking face."

She gave Ben a sarcastic grin. He ambled past her and climbed up the steps at the back of the caboose. Out on the porch, he extended a single middle finger at her.

She shook her head as the train pulled away from the buffer, rattling and swaying until it picked up enough speed to run smoothly. Ben walked toward the front, through the empty caboose and into the passenger cars. He had ridden on a train like this countless times through the Northeast Corridor, and he recognized all the familiar accoutrements: the cheap fabric seats, the bathrooms with the heavy sliding doors, the little pull-curtains, the overhead bins with floppy doors that always hung down just low enough to bash him in the head, the white cord that could make the whole train grind to a halt. *Rudy would like this train.* His older son loved trains. The boy even *sounded* like a train. He made WOO-WOO! sounds whenever he was playing in the basement.

The train was devoid of passengers. The coach cars and the first-class car and the cute sleeper car were all empty. He could sit anywhere, sleep anywhere. The train belonged to him.

Except for the café car. It was the last car he entered, located at the front, right behind the diesel locomotive. When Ben slipped through the door and walked around to the open café, he saw a creepy old man with pancake makeup standing behind the counter. It was Voris's clerk. The Regenerator. Ben took one look at the ghoulish old man and stepped back.

"Can I help you, sir?" the clerk asked. Behind him was a standard selection of chips and drinks and crummy frozen pizzas. And a tip jar.

"You can talk now?"

"I could always speak."

"I thought we killed you," Ben said.

The clerk gave him a crooked, leering smile. "The Producer wanted me back."

"Who's driving this train? Is it Voris?" It shouldn't have been possible. But of course, it was highly possible. It was the *most* possible thing now.

"No one is driving the train," the clerk said. "May I get you anything?"

Ben sprinted out of the café car and through all the seated areas to the dingy caboose at the back. Out on the porch, he scanned around for a good place to jump off, but the train was hurtling down the track too fast, maybe over 150 miles an hour. They weren't on the prairie anymore. The dry grasses had given way to a barren salt flat, the sun lingering over the bleak whiteness. He turned back toward the sliding door of the caboose, accidentally bashed his head on the steel threshold above, and passed out.

———

When he woke up, he was in a bed with truck sheets. In a house. Football posters on the white walls. What happened to the train? *Train, what train? There's no train. You're home. With Mom and Dad. Remember? It's Saturday. You get sugary cereals today.*

Ben felt around his body. He was small and pale. Seven years old. His father ambled in, smelling like a portable toilet.

"Mom's doing a weekend shift," he told Ben. "You're coming with me."

"Where?"

"It's a surprise."

They piled into his old man's speck of a sedan and got on the road to nearby Shakopee. Ben could see the Ferris wheel from the highway.

"That's right," his dad said, reaching into the glove box for a warm Schmidt beer. "Valleyfair. You're riding the Corkscrew today."

"Dad, I don't want to."

"Nonsense. Your mom's not around. This is the best time for you to finally ride a roller coaster."

"I don't like roller coasters."

"Yes, you do. Every time we've come here with your mother, you walk right up to that line and then puss out at the last second. Time to sack up."

Ben started clawing at the door. "NO."

"Relax."

The Corkscrew was a twisting black contraption that ran loops and took passengers upside down over and over again—an understandably frightening prospect for a young boy with a limited understanding of centrifugal forces. They parked in the hinterlands of the Valleyfair lot, the coaster a scorching one-mile walk away. The old man was already drunk. They got to the line and when Ben tried to escape, his father grabbed him by the shoulder and held him close. Ben twisted and squirmed and begged his dad not to force him into the machine. Other people started to notice.

"You'll be glad I made you," his dad said, a cloud of stale-beer air all around him.

"I don't wanna go," said Ben, shaking.

"Don't be a coward."

"I'm not ready."

His father knelt down and leaned into him, more for structural support than affection. "Listen to me," he said. "Just pretend you're driving it."

"What?"

"Pretend you're in control of it. It's a set track. You have no real control over where it goes. But if you *pretend* you do, it won't seem so bad. Does that make sense?"

"No."

"Just trust me."

He nudged Ben forward and the boy whimpered. He was clinging to his drunk old man now. More people stared, wondering whether or not to say something. (They didn't.) The old man dragged Ben into the shiny black car and lowered the shoulder harness over him.

"No going back now," he told Ben. Ben began to sob as the operator pushed the button and the car began its long, terrifying journey up to the top of the track along the thick black girders. Ben could hear the chains rattle as they grabbed the cars and dragged them forward. He could hear all the clinks and clunks. His old man whispered in his ear again, "Remember: Drive the thing."

They were eighty-five feet in the air now. The chains stopped their rattling and the ambient sounds of the park below faded away. All that remained in that empty patch of sky was pure, horrible silence. The cars crested at the top of the coaster and then, with the utmost cruelty, the ride paused at the edge of the drop, so Ben could see how far down he was going to fall. Now he was crying his eyes out, and his father did the exact wrong thing by laughing and giggling and shouting, "Isn't this fun?" It was not fun. Ben was about to die. The cars released and he let out the primal wail of an infant. The Corkscrew threw him back in his seat and then lifted him back up and then ripped his stomach out again.

But somewhere along the ride, while praying for it to end without killing him, Ben began to lean into the curves. The track would twist and he would angle his body, like a motorcycle racer speeding around a turn. When the time came to go upside down, he reared way back and pretended to push an afterburner button, like a jet pilot evading incoming fire. He stopped crying. He was focused. He was driving. When the ride came to a stop, his tears were gone. He dashed out the exit and circled back to get in line again.

He rode the coaster ten more times that day. In the car ride back, before his old man got pegged for yet another DUI and the cops had to drive Ben the rest of the way home, he burped and told the boy:

"I'm sorry I made you cry, kid. I'm fucked up."

"I know you've been drinking, Dad."

"No, I mean I'm *fucked up.* But I got my reasons. I know I never did anything good for you, Ben. But just remember that everything bad can be made good if you know how to use it."

———

He woke up. Something had turned inside him. All those years of res-ignation and hardening and evolved indifference—they fell off him. There was that urgency again. That frenzy.

He stood up on the porch of the caboose, looking at the growing line of track behind the barreling train. He had no control over the path. It had dictated everything to him. But that was over now. *Drive the thing.* Yes, he would drive it. He would drive it right back to Teresa. He would come for her. *I put the path here. This is where I wanted it to go.*

The clerk, who had walked to the caboose all the way from the café car, tapped Ben on the shoulder.

"You need to come inside before dark," the clerk said.

Ben turned and smashed the clerk's face in. Then he pounced on the old man and began choking him, bashing his head with the butt of his gun.

"Stop!" the clerk cried. "You need to come inside."

"How do I get into the locomotive?" Ben demanded to know.

"It's very dangerous!"

"I DON'T FUCKING CARE."

"Through the café car," the old man wheezed. "There's a ladder you can climb to get into the cab."

"Who's driving it?"

"I told you: No one is. It drives itself."

"Not anymore, it doesn't."

"The Producer won't let you. . . ."

"*I* am the Producer."

The clerk smiled at him. "Now you're catching on."

Ben let the old man go and marched through four of the passenger cars before encountering a dogface in the first-class cabin.

"I've been waiting for this since . . ."

"Fuck you." Ben punched the dogface square on the chin and knocked him into the seats.

He ran to the café car, slid the front door open and stood on the coupler attaching the locomotive to the rest of the train. It was topping off at 200 miles an hour now, the outside air a vicious beast roaring between the locomotive and the café car. On the back of the locomotive was a ladder reaching up to the roof. Ben grabbed the rungs and pulled himself up, adrenalized like a boy thirty years younger. On top of the locomotive, he saw the track bending to the right along the great salt flat, heading into a darkened mountain range.

There was a tunnel at the base of the mountains. At this speed, it wouldn't take long for the locomotive to go sailing into it, sweeping Ben off the top of the train. No matter to him. He was a bull now. In the darkening sky, he saw a red triangle forming up high between two luminous moons that were now hanging up and to the left of the mountain tunnel. The triangle looked as if it had been drawn by lasers. He crouched down and slid along the top of the locomotive as the wind did everything it could to peel him off. But Ben had hands again. It felt good to have hands. Hands were useful.

The tunnel grew closer and the great triangle in the sky widened as Ben made it to the front of the raging locomotive and found a ladder running down the side to the door of the cab. Just as he climbed down and looked through the window to see an empty engineer's seat, a great black Smoke with white fire eyes flew beside Ben and gave him a silent, angry stare.

Ben didn't hesitate. He furrowed his brow, leaned into the Smoke's body, and began inhaling deeply, sucking the ghost up like a bong hit. He could see the Smoke panic, its eyes growing wild with fright. Ben didn't stop. He sucked every last bit of ash out of the sky, including the Smoke's pathetic, glowing eyes. Then, he turned to the window and spat the Smoke back out of his mouth as hot fire, using the flame to melt down the glass and form an opening. The wind cooled the melted glass in place right away, and Ben slipped into the engineer's seat and saw the red triangle still expanding up in the jumbled night sky.

The train was half a mile from the tunnel, but Ben had no interest in entering a mountain ever again. He strapped himself into the seat and grabbed the black throttle, jerking it backward. The train shrieked as a holiday's worth of sparks lit up under the wheels. The locomotive tipped to the left, balancing along one rail. Ben pressed the SAND button, dousing the rails in hot friction, and then rammed the throttle forward again.

He leaned in and to the left. The train began to lift off the ground. Ben could feel it separating from the rails and veering away from the mountain, the other cars trailing behind the locomotive as the train began to take flight. It was speeding upward, into the red triangle in the sky. Through the windshield, Ben could see the sides of the triangle expanding and pulsing. Two parallel lines of glowing purple swans flew in front of the train and formed a path directly into it.

But then the train began to slow down. After taking off from the ground like a rocket, gravity suddenly came back into play and Ben could feel the locomotive losing its buoyancy, poised to fall rapidly back down to the ground. There was a fire extinguisher in the cab next to the engineer's seat. He unbuckled his seat belt and grabbed the extinguisher, bashing it into the windshield and clearing every last shard of glass. Just as the train was about to fall, Ben walked to the back of the cab and ran toward the open windshield, leaping out headfirst, diving toward the swans.

He blasted into the air as the locomotive went limp and the train plunged back down to the salt flat, splitting open on impact and forming a long line of fire in the salt that looked like a freshly opened tectonic plate. Ben didn't look down. He was flying now, in complete control, leaning into the atmosphere and picking up speed—a living comet. The moons, bright and silver above him, converged on the triangle, closing in and spinning like buffers at a car wash. He shot into the red triangle as the moons kissed and now Ben was out of the stratosphere and in the open black of space, surpassing the speed of light, moving so fast that he left his own body in the dust. His hands in front of him turned to white lightning as the swirling nebular clouds billowed up and fell behind him. The deep space was transforming before his eyes now, compacting into a single flashing tube that was changing color so quickly that he couldn't keep up with what he was seeing. *New* colors. Colors beyond anything that he had seen before.

His lightning hands merged with the white at the end of the tube and now he was moving so fast that every atom in his body sloughed off and reduced him to a single, precious particle, moving faster than anything has ever moved, compacting and picking up heat until every quark within it was ready to break apart and blow out into its own universe. He had become a photon. He *was* light. He took a deep breath (was it a breath?) and the white became everything.

A moment later, he was sitting in a white room with no doors or windows. Two parallel black lines stretched out from his chair, turned left, and ran into the bare wall. Sitting at a white desk across from him was Mrs. Blackwell. She seemed surprised to see him.

CHAPTER THIRTY-ONE

# THE PRODUCER

He was human again. Landbound. Affected by gravity. No gun. But he wasn't forty-eight anymore. No, now he was ten years younger, or at least looked it. His hands were pristine: no scar on his palm from the knife fight with the giant cricket. His body was healthy and vigorous. He probed his mouth with his tongue; the tooth Cisco had pulled out was rooted back in place. Anchored. All of that extra mileage, gone. He felt something in his pocket. He reached into his black mesh shorts and found a hotel room key. The inn. Room 19.

"You're here earlier than I expected," Mrs. Blackwell said to Ben.

"I'm a late bloomer. But once I bloom, I bloom fast."

"Well, wait right there and we'll be with you shortly."

"Where am I?"

"The Executive Producer's office."

"*I* am the Producer."

"You are, but this is the *Executive* Producer's office, and he's a very busy man. So he'll see you in just a moment."

"No."

"No?"

"No, I won't wait."

She sat back in her chair. "All right. You can see him, if you can find him."

There was nothing else in the room except for a black Sharpie sitting on top of the white desk. No door. No stairs. No way out. Ben got up and walked over to the bare wall. It was clean, with no cracks or hidden levers. He got down on his hands and knees and looked under the desk.

"He's not there," she said.

"I can see that."

He got back up. It took a moment, but then he saw the Sharpie and knew what he had to do. He swiped it off the desk and walked back to the wall. He hadn't forgotten all that drawing he had taught himself in the desert. Perspective. Contours. He drew a frame, then two hinges, and then a thin black void inside the frame. Then he made the door, rectangular and thick, with four brickmold panels and a black handle. For an added flourish, he wrote "PUSH" across the top of the handle. Then he looked back at Mrs. Blackwell and threw the Sharpie onto her desk. It rolled right off.

"Good-bye, Mrs. Blackwell."

"Good luck, Ben."

He pushed the door open and found himself in a wood-lined office, with tasteful paintings hanging from the walls and two shiny leather chairs facing each other in front of a large, hand-carved oaken desk. On top of the desk there was a silver letter opener and a bottle of—what else?—fine champagne. Behind the desk were two more doors. The globe of an unknown planet—all misshapen continents and strange oceans—sat spinning off to the side. One of the leather chairs was empty. In the other chair sat an elderly man, perhaps in his seventies, wearing a white linen suit and white slippers with no socks. He was frighteningly tan all over. Even his lips were tan. From his neck hung a thick gold chain with no pendant. His face was stretched back, like he'd had work done on more than one occasion. His hair was perfect silver and he was rocking sunglasses indoors. He stood up and opened his arms wide when Ben came into the office.

"Ben, baby! You made it. I'm so proud of you."

"Who the hell are you?"

"I'm Bobby. I'm the Executive Producer. Love your work. Have a seat."

"I'm not gonna have a seat. I'm gonna fucking kill you."

The Executive Producer grinned. "Ben, I'm sorry, but that's not going to happen. See, I'm the one obstacle you *don't* get by. Now sit down, and I'll tell you everything. You must have questions."

"When do I go home?"

"I think we should talk a bit before circling back to that." He sat back down and gestured for Ben to do likewise. "Come on. Relax. Would you like anything to drink? Eat? Caviar? Champagne? I *do* love champagne."

"No."

"You're very focused. It shows up in your work."

"Where am I?"

"My office, of course."

"Are you God?"

"No, but that would be a better title for it. No one ever knows what a producer does. It's a shame, really."

"Why did you do this to me?"

"Oh, it wasn't me. I'm a consultant, Ben. A fixer. The path *chose* you, don't you know that by now? Since the beginning of time, the path has been here, ready to claim worthy subjects. Once it chose you, I consulted. I *studied*. I learned about your hopes and fears and dreams, and all of that informed the path as it shaped itself just for you. Your hike was on the longer end. We had another fellow go for a full million years. Helluva sight. I've never seen such perseverance. Anyway, I help sculpt the path, like a landscaper. And your subconscious generously helps to fill in the gaps. Hence the dog theme for you. It's like a birthday party."

"Voris?"

"From your journals. Great character. Says so much with those eyes of his."

"Fermona?"

"Standard path obstacle. Good chemistry between you two."

"Cisco?"

"Ah, Cisco. No, Cisco was a man, like you. Little overlap there. Again, *great* chemistry."

"Why?"

"What do you mean, why?"

"Why does the path pick people?"

"We're past *why* here, Ben. This is just how it is."

"How do I get home?"

"Ah. Now, this is where it gets interesting."

"I have to kill you, don't I?"

"No. Like I said, baby, you don't get to kill me. You and I, we hang. We just hang. No rancor." He reached behind his chair and poured himself a glass of champagne. "You can go home simply by walking out the door."

"Which one?"

"Either one. You go through the door on the left, and you return to your life as it was the day you ventured onto the path. Everything the same. That familiar, boring world that you know and occasionally love."

"What about the other door?"

"Oh, that?" the Executive Producer said with one eyebrow arched. "That's heaven. You walk through that door, and you get to be a Producer eternally. You remain on the path, and you can make it go anywhere you like, one endless red carpet rolling out for you. You can make a billion dollars. You can invent the flying car. You and your wife can have sex five times a day. *Good* sex, too. Like you had at the villa. You have complete control to shape your life any way you like. There are no limits. And you can live forever, Ben. You and your kids. Your loyal, perfectly well-behaved children. Go nuts. You can fly to Mars and build a resort colony there. You know those wonderful dreams you had? Sexy Annie Derrickson? No dogs ripping your face in half? That's all waiting for you. One endless, fabulous fantasy. The life you deserve, Ben."

Ben sat stone silent, processing the offer.

"You're full of shit. This is a trick."

"Not a trick. My word is bond."

"I know who you are," Ben told him.

"Kid, I am so far beyond what you think I am, it would make you sick."

"Why are you selling me on this so hard? What's in it for you?"

"I told you: I'm a consultant. This is what I do. I *consult*."

"What door did Cisco take?"

"Oh, I'll never tell."

Ben stood up. "I want what I had."

"Why?" the Executive Producer asked. "Why would you want that? I'm green-lighting the ultimate prize for you. Monks sit in dark rooms their whole lives hoping for a chance to walk through *that* door. And not all of them get the chance, I promise you."

"It's not real."

"Oh, please. You know it's real. You saw it yourself, didn't you? You could see it, touch it, taste it. It was as real as anything else you've ever known."

"It's not the same." Ben was grasping now, desperate. "Not real."

"Who said *your* life was real, Ben?"

"Don't say that."

"Who's to say you haven't been on the path this whole time, Ben? Huh? Don't you find it remarkable that you were born into such a wondrous time in history? The most advanced technological civilization in the history of the universe. The richest country *in* that civilization. The most advanced species on that lucky little planet of yours. You could have been a microbe, Ben: a tiny, insignificant, single-cell animal that lives for a day and no longer. Or you could have been a *crab,* hmm? But no: You were a person, with a cute wife and three lovely kids. Born a *man*, and a white man at that. Never killed off randomly. Never homeless. Never raped. Doesn't that strike you as unfathomably lucky?"

"Given that you kept me prisoner for ten years and change, I don't feel lucky at all."

"You should. Who's to say we didn't produce *you*? That *you* are the only man who has ever lived, ever? All the world's history—everyone you've ever met or heard of—all background for you, the greatest story ever told. Your parents weren't real."

"Stop it."

"Your wife and children were props."

"STOP IT."

"Who's to say this wasn't just one big test run for a model universe? Who's to say that you, lucky Ben, are not the *first* man . . . the prototype of humanity? And who's to say that the path isn't God Himself, welcoming you in His arms, asking you to build the universe with Him? You can't go back."

"I will."

"You know too much now. You now know that everything that once seemed so definitive to you, up until the day you set foot in *my* woods, is just a series of arbitrary limits. Gravity. The sunrise. Time itself. The rest of the universe doesn't play by any of Earth's rules. Why should you? Why be bound by orbits or revolutions? That world you want back into is *ordinary*, kid. And dying. Remember the freighter? Remember that freighter you saw sailing through the end of humanity? That's not far away, baby. That's *close*. Your family might be on that boat, and that's if they're *lucky*."

"I won't listen to you."

"Oh, I'm about to make it even harder. Because, you see, if you choose the left-hand exit, you cannot ever, under any circumstances, tell anyone about your time on the path. Not even your wife. You'll be struck dead before the words reach your mouth from your brain. Same fate if you try to write it down, or use sign language, or tap out Morse code to tell the world your story. Your heart will explode that instant. And you won't end up back in this office. Do you understand? This is your only chance to walk through that other door, to be the master of the path and live forever in ecstasy. Maybe you should think before acting so certain, baby. Don't throw away the mother lode. This is your life and the afterlife merged together in one perfect, endless existence."

Ben felt his knees buckle.

"Sit," said the Executive Producer. "That's what the chair is for."

But he didn't sit. He walked up to the door on the right—the door to heaven—and gripped the round, brushed satin knob, letting it slip around inside his palm. Then he turned to the Executive Producer.

"What happens if I leave them?" he asked.

"You still don't understand. You're *not* leaving them if you go through that door."

"What happens to the world behind the door on the left if I don't go through it?"

"It doesn't exist. But what difference does it make? Everything is the same, but better."

"Will I be dead?"

"There is no dead. Think bigger than just life and death."

"It's not a trick."

"Of course not."

"Then it's a test."

"No, it is not a test. It's as real and binding as life on Earth."

But his life on Earth . . . that was *realer*, right? Ben backed away from the door and sat down, rubbing his temples and groaning loudly. The Executive Producer stood and poured him a glass of water, then gave him a kind pat on the back.

"It isn't easy," he said. "I know. It's a lot to take in, baby. Fortunately, you're in the right spot. You're free to deliberate for as long as you like. I'll stay here forever with you, if that's how much time you need to decide."

Ben buried his head in his hands. He had flown between two moons only to end up forced into this spot. Another goddamn puzzle to solve. The path had taken him and plunged him into this awful, horrible, fantastic world. And yet it had been protecting him the entire time, keeping him alive, wooing him with food and drink and things he had never seen before. *The path was good, wasn't it? If you just walk through that door back onto the path, you'll see them again and you'll live forever and it will be so terribly wonderful and easy . . .*

And yet, "It doesn't exist." That was what the Executive Producer told him would happen to the world he once knew. It would be gone forever: everything he'd ever seen, everyone he knew, everything that he had ever been through thanks to a scary world that was far beyond his control. All of it would disappear.

Ben glowered at the tan playboy across from him. *I could stab him. That letter opener on the old man's desk. That would do the trick. Just stab the fucker right in the eye.* Over on the wall, Ben noticed one of the paintings included a nighttime beach landscape, with a little blue crab propped up on the dunes and two full moons in the background.

*Two moons. Two goddamn moons. Why are there always two moons?*

And then Ben had an idea: a marvelous, insane idea. Oh, what a brilliant idea he had. He stood back up.

"I want what I had," he repeated to the Executive Producer.

"More faith in life than God Himself, huh?"

"Yeah. More faith in life than God Himself. But it's more than that. You said I can do whatever I want on the path, right?"

"That's right," said Bobby.

"Soon as I walk through that door on the left, the power's gone, yes?"

"You got it, kid."

"But I still have it *now*, don't I? I'm still on the path."

He walked over to the desk and picked up the letter opener. It was sharp. Heavy at the handle. The Executive Producer eyed him curiously.

"What are you going to . . ."

Ben jammed the letter opener directly into his own forehead. A trickle of blood slid down his face as he drew the blade all the way down to his groin, then between his legs and up his spine, over his head and back to the puncture wound in his forehead. Then he dropped the bloodied knife on the rug and dug his fingers inside the rift in his abdomen, pulling himself apart.

But no wound opened. Instead, as Ben pulled, more of him emerged. From his left side came more of his right side. From his right side came more of his left side. He pulled and pulled until a second pair of legs came flopping out of the slit he had made. And now a pair of arms as well: a right arm on the left and a left arm on the right, like one man standing in front of two angled mirrors. He was a zygote splitting in two. His head came apart: three eyes, then four. One nose, then two. Two sets of ears. Two mouths. By the time he was finished pulling, there were two Bens standing in front of the desk: one thirty-eight years old, the other forty-eight years old. Both men weary, but strong and full. The Older Ben had a little crab tattoo on his upper arm.

The Younger Ben turned to the Executive Producer.

"I'll be taking both doors," he said.

"My God," said Bobby. "I do love your work."

The Younger Ben turned to his old doppelgänger.

"I'll take the left door. You take the right."

"You sure?" the Older Ben asked.

"Yeah. Look out for me over there, all right?"

"I will."

"Go. Go before he changes it up on us."

The two Bens shook hands and the Younger Ben watched his older, crabbier self walk through the right-hand door into the bright white light at the entrance of Shangri-la.

And then the door closed. It was just the Younger Ben now. Singular. He turned to the old leather-skinned executive and pointed to the left-hand door.

"I'm going through there now."

"You certainly are." The Executive Producer shook Ben's hand. "You did great work here. You've got a future in this business, kid."

"Go fuck yourself."

"'Atta boy. Never lose that fighting spirit."

Ben went for the left-hand door.

"Remember," said the Executive Producer. "Not a word."

"Yeah, yeah." And Ben turned the knob and walked out.

# CHAPTER THIRTY-TWO

# CROCUS DRIVE

The door closed behind Ben and he found himself inside an aluminum shed. He heard a whirring sound coming from outside. The double doors on the other side of the shed were unlocked and hanging loose. He pushed them open and walked out onto a path at the base of a small mountain in the Poconos. There was a white pickup truck parked out front. Two burly men were laboring off to the side, ripping a chain saw through a fallen poplar. When Ben came out of the loose doors, they turned and stared at him. They had human faces. Nonthreatening. A friendly Rottweiler came running out from behind the shed and licked Ben's hand. He froze in place.

One of the guys took off his construction earmuffs.

"Hey man," he said. "You lost?"

Ben said nothing.

"You staying at the hotel? We can give you a ride."

"No. No, thank you, sir. I'm fine."

He walked carefully away from the shed and the truck, past a wide swinging iron-bar gate, and then he broke into a run. Delirious. Buoyant. Soon, he came to a junction marked by two trees with split trunks.

*I know those trees!*

He followed the path back up the mountain, to a clearing with a circular fire pit and sawed-off log benches.

*I know those benches!*

He sprinted along the top of an esker and saw markers every tenth of a mile. And birdhouses: elaborate little birdhouses with stepped gabled roofs.

*I know those birdhouses!*

He looked down the mountain and saw a bunch of fancy Pennsylvania McMansions, each house large enough to accommodate a giant or two.

"Hello, you big fucking mansions!"

He saw the hotel. The same dumpy, unpopulated country inn he had come from. He sped to the front door and saw his car parked exactly where he had left it. In the lobby, there was a young girl in a cupcake nightgown dancing around in her bare feet in front of a table of souvenirs and maple-leaf cookies and overpriced tchotchkes. She bumped right into Ben. The girl's mother came up and chastised her.

"Will you *please* go back to the room and get dressed? We'll never be able to see Stroud Mansion if you don't hurry up!" The mother turned to Ben. "I'm so sorry."

"It's okay," he said, smiling warmly. "I have three of my own."

"Oh, God. Three?"

"Yeah, that about sums it up."

Ben sprinted up the stairs, through the narrow hallway, to his creepy old room. He took out the key and opened the door. Everything in the room was exactly as he'd left it . . . except now his phone was sitting on the nightstand. Screen intact. Fully charged. He grabbed the phone and called Teresa.

"Hello?" she asked. Her voice knocked him dead silent. "Hello?"

"It's you."

"Ben?"

"It's really you."

"Are you okay, Ben?"

*Not one word.* "I'm fine. In fact, my dinner was canceled. I'm gonna come home. Right now."

"Ugh, they sent you all the way up there for nothing?"

"Well, I did get to check out some of the scenery."

"The kids'll love to see you. You think you'll be home in time for dinner? I'm making crab cakes."

". . ."

"Ben?"

"You know, I think I'll get dinner on the road. Don't worry about making extra for me."

"You sure you don't wanna stay there? Have the night to yourself?"

"No. No, I'm coming."

"Okay. Then we'll see you soon. Love you!"

"Love you, too."

He hung up. He hadn't said a word about the path. *It'll only get easier from here, amigo. Everyone needs to have something inside them that no one else can have.* He texted his vendor to tell him he had come down with something and that he wouldn't be able to make it. Then he packed his rollerboard without bothering to shower or change clothes.

The front desk was unmanned. Ben came trudging down the steps with his suitcase and rapped on the counter. The clueless old lady walked out from the back.

"I need to check out," he told her. He laid his key on the counter.

"But you just checked in."

"Strange, isn't it? But I have to check out now."

She appeared remarkably inconvenienced for someone with so

little to do. God bless her moronic soul. "Well, I still have to charge you for the room."

"That's fine. I don't care. You can e-mail me the bill."

"E-mail?"

"Never mind."

He walked past the little girl, still dancing in her nightgown, and out to the parking lot. He jumped into his car and gunned it like it was a pickup truck.

There was traffic on the way home. Of course there was. The Executive Producer probably wanted to hammer home the fact that the Younger Ben had chosen to go back to the real world in all of its annoying glory. But Ben wasn't rattled. He didn't speed. He didn't honk. He didn't cut anyone off, like a dick. He didn't futz around with his phone. It was all fine. He was the only serene driver in America.

*I'm coming, Teresa.*

Halfway down Route 15 he saw an exit for CISCO. He slowed down for just a moment to make sure he hadn't read it wrong. Another twenty miles later, he saw an exit for FERMONA.

"HA!"

The roads were clean. No deer this time. He hit a patch of thickly grooved pavement and it thumped in lockstep with his bursting heart.

It was close to 8 P.M. when Ben finally made the turn onto Crocus Drive and into his old neighborhood: the creek running along the street, the little playground up on a hill that was routinely infested with bees, the signs stapled to the telephone poles noting the final day of leaf pickup for the season. He made his way up the hill and pulled in front of the distressed white brick house, with its crumbling driveway and retaining wall. In the dark, he saw the plastic castle slide laying sideways in the yard. The kids loved knocking it over more than they liked sliding down it. Teresa's white minivan was parked by the steps. Everyone was home.

Ben parked on the street and the red front door opened wide, his three kids running to him and screaming at the top of their lungs. Flora was cuddling a stuffed fox. Rudy was holding a train. Peter was wearing his pajamas, as always.

"Hi, Daddy!"

"Did you get us anything?"

"Did you bring us candy?"

They swarmed his legs and he bent over to cry and smell their hair and kiss them. He could see that Peter's jammies were wet.

"Were you messing around in the sink?" he asked the little boy.

"I was, Dad."

"That's all right. We can get you new jammie pants."

And then he looked up and saw his wife come out of the storm door in her jeans and long-sleeved T-shirt. She gave him a little wave.

"Hey."

"Hey."

His heart grew giant. She smiled and came closer, and he finally burst into tears. He couldn't help it. He held his hand over his mouth. The whites of his eyes were beet red.

As Teresa got closer, she saw his tired eyes in the glow of the outdoor lamppost. Something was different about Ben. Off. She stopped a few feet away from him as the kids mobbed him.

"Ben, are you okay?"

"I'm fine. Everything is great."

But she could tell he was lying. He was always such a terrible liar. He looked adrenalized, but exhausted. Older. Wiser. Why, he looked as if he'd been away for . . .

And then she gasped. Ben saw her reaction and couldn't understand what she had seen in his eyes, until . . .

*Hey, how old is Teresa? She's thirty-nine, right? Remember that one night a few years ago? When she came home from the hospital and wouldn't stop crying? And then stayed silent for a couple of days afterward? You thought she had just lost some patients that night she went catatonic, right? She never really did explain. She never told you why she liked painting horses, or why she took up fighting, or why she would rub her wedding ring with her thumb in the occasional still photograph. Remember what she said to you, Ben? She said she killed people. She said . . . she said . . .*

"I can't tell you or it'll kill me."

He gazed deep into her pupils and saw the soul of a woman who wasn't thirty-nine at all, but far older.

Maybe ten years older. Or twenty.

"Oh my God," he said.

For a long time, they stood there and stared at one another, dumbstruck. They didn't say a word. They couldn't.

THE END

# ACKNOWLEDGMENTS

Special thanks to my family, Byrd Leavell, Tim Marchman, Jesse Johnston, Howard Spector, Allison Lorentzen, Devin Gordon, and Spencer Hall. And to East Stroudsburg University, thanks for the little stroll.

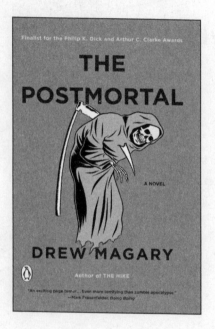